THE CEMETERY GAME

BY JOSEPH J. CHRISTIANO

David kept his eyes on the spirit – he could no longer think of it as just a groupie – as he moved beside his sister. Diane remained a statue, her eyes wide, her mouth agape. (Di, let's go. We've been in here long enough.)

Her lips trembled. She gave no sign that she heard him.

David grabbed her shoulders and spun her to face him. Her eyes remained glued to the old spirit in the robes but at last she focused on her brother.

(C'mon, Di, let's get back.)

He turned her back the way they had come.

Something hard and made of ice landed on David's shoulder. He gasped, spun quickly. The old spirit stood directly behind him. Its hand held David, and its skeletal fingers drove themselves into his skin. Its mouth parted, and it was close enough that David heard the hinges in the thing's jaws creak. "She is mine!" it said.

Diane screamed. David, unprepared for the assault on his senses, reeled. The thing's fingers carved grooves into the flesh of his shoulder. He had the presence of mind to throw an arm around his sister and they bolted away. Tendrils of ice wormed their way beneath his skin. David gasped and gritted his teeth to keep from screaming.

(Time to go, Di. Time to go right now!)

They stopped and Diane looked at him. Her eyes were wide and wet with fear. She looked back the way they had come, stiffened, and closed her eyes. She faded from his view, leaving only the swirling fog in her place.

David didn't look back. If the old spirit was there, he didn't trust himself to be able to concentrate enough to get back to the real world. Instead, he closed his eyes and willed himself out of the fog. The last sensation of which he was aware was of something bitterly cold grabbing for him.

First Edition

This one is for Gary.

All you that in the condemned hold do lie
Prepare you, for tomorrow you shall die
Watch all and pray, the hour is drawing near
That you before the Almighty must appear
Examine well yourselves, in time repent
That you may not to eternal flames be sent
And when St. Sepulchre's bell tomorrow tolls
The Lord above have mercy on your souls

—*Author Unknown,*
Bellman's chant for the condemned,
Newgate Prison, London

I.

THE TWINS

CHAPTER ONE

LIKE RIDING A BIKE

David Walsh became aware of a distant pounding, as if a giant were making its way ponderously in his direction. Ridiculous, of course. There were no giants on St. Thomas, even in his dreams. There were plenty of beautiful women, super models, really, and they laughed at his jokes and sipped wine and champagne while the mid-afternoon sunlight turned the beach into the tropical paradise he remembered from his one and only visit.

The pounding continued, getting louder. The girls around him became translucent, although they seemed not to notice. David's eyes whipped in all directions. He was horrified to see the beach becoming less distinct, the ocean receding farther into the distance. "No, no, no," he murmured. He dug in, tried to hold his ground, to will the women back into existence. They continued their fadeout until he found himself alone. The women were gone, the ocean was gone. Even the sands were slipping away. He doubled his effort, willed himself away from the large sofa upon which he lay, but the attempt served only to awaken him further.

The pounding again. No giant, of course, just someone at his front door. David groaned his annoyance into the cavernous living room. The dream was gone, replaced by his home in the Hollywood Hills. He became aware of the dull throbbing that seemed to have taken up permanent residence behind his eyes. He groaned again and massaged his temples. *Someone better be dead*. The irony of that thought would not occur to him until later.

The knock repeated itself, and he recognized the pattern. He rolled off the sofa and steadied himself with one outstretched arm. His bare feet found several empty beer cans lying crushed on the Oriental rug. They clattered across the hardwood in various directions. David swore, teetered, but managed to keep his balance.

The dull throbbing behind his eyes graduated to a pounding. He shook his head to clear it and grimaced when the movement brought only more pain. The open bottle of aspirin was in its customary place on the end table. He shook out three tablets and downed them dry.

Sunlight poured through the big windows behind him and to his left. Unlike the pleasant light on the beach, this seemed harsh, judgmental. Mornings always seemed like that, at least lately. David might have felt a twinge of melancholy about his activities of the previous night, had mornings like this not become so frequent. He squinted a bit and lurched in the direction of his front door. He could see the silhouette of a rather large woman raise her hand to the frosted glass and knock again. David stumbled the last few feet to the door and opened it.

Joyce Clark was his manager, his friend (in some way that David could not codify) and a shockingly poor substitute for the supermodels whom he had just left on the beach on St. Thomas. She was short, squat, and morbidly overweight. Her white hair was pulled back so tightly she appeared bald from a distance. Her features were stern even when she smiled. She was smiling broadly now.

"David!" She clapped him on the shoulder and moved past him across the threshold.

David remained at the door for a moment before he closed it. "Come on in."

Joyce crossed the living room and tossed her enormous pocketbook onto the sofa. She plopped herself down next to it, and the springs squealed their protest. She crossed her feet and draped her arms along the top of the sofa and beamed a giant smile his way. "I love what you've done with the place. Early American Alcoholic, isn't it?"

David reached the recliner and lowered himself quite slowly onto the cushion. He held his head in his hands. "It's a little early in the morning for recriminations, isn't it, Joyce?"

"It's 12:47," she replied after a glance at her watch. "In the afternoon. I'm going to give you enough credit to assume you knew that part."

David grumbled. His fingers massaged his temples again. He closed his eyes and tried to sink into the recliner. "What's up?"

"I got a call last night from a woman in Michigan. She would like us to come out there and see what we can do. She said she used to watch the show, and she thinks we can help her."

David continued to work his temples while he waited for the aspirin to kick in. "We're retired, aren't we?"

"And retirement is treating you *so* well."

She kicked an empty beer can across the floor. The noise echoed off the walls and made him wince. "Can we lower the volume a little? It was a rough night."

"My keen powers of observation told me as much."

Joyce rattled around in her purse. After a few moments the noise ceased, and she started to read from something.

"Emily Andrews, aged ninety-five. Resides in Lansing, Michigan. Wife of George, recently deceased." Her tone changed, became a bit more stern. "She's convinced her husband had a lot of money stashed away, but he passed suddenly and didn't tell her where it was." A pause for dramatic effect. "So, she called us."

David remained unmoving and silent.

"This could be good for us, David." Joyce's tone changed again. It was soft, almost tender. "After that disaster in Nebraska our image took a pretty big hit. People out there think you're only in this for the money."

He still did not move. The throbbing behind his eyes had finally begun to let up a bit. "I thought we didn't take clients like that. Doesn't play well for the camera, right? Even the recreation is boring. Who's gonna want to watch that?"

"Spooky murder-solving isn't the goal this time. We need something that hits the heart strings. This could be the one that gets us back in the public's good graces."

David sighed and opened his eyes. "Joyce, look at this house. Go down to the garage and look at the four cars I have in there. While you're at it go out to the rear deck by the pool and gaze out at the Hills. Then fly out to the Hamptons and see what Di has. Does it look like we give a shit about the public's good graces?" He sounded harsh, even to himself, and he regretted it immediately. It wasn't Joyce's fault he was hungover. He nearly apologized, but he'd learned long ago not to show any weakness in front of her. He shut his eyes again.

"David, look at me."

"My eyes hurt."

"It wasn't a request."

David turned his head, slowly, so as not to bring back the throbbing. He opened his eyes a sliver. Joyce was sitting forward with her hands in her lap. Her demeanor had changed drastically since her arrival. Her smile was gone, her jovial tone vanished. Her faded blue eyes were serious and pleading. He didn't need Di to sense Joyce's desperation.

"We need this. My office receives calls every day about the two of you and what happened in Nebraska. Most are people looking for an interview but a good number of them end with death threats. Against you and Diane, against me. I'm not living my life this way, David. And I'm not acting as a buffer for you and your sister anymore."

She took a breath and visibly calmed herself. "Something like this can show people we're not a bunch of greedy assholes who don't care about anyone or anything but our bank accounts. We fly out there, you and Di do your thing. I have our old camera crew on standby, and they're ready to shoot the whole thing. I doubt it'll lead to a series reboot or anything like that, but the Discovery Channel might be willing to air a special episode. Hell, the cable networks might want in, too."

David looked away. "I didn't know about the death threats."

Joyce's voice was even. "Of course you didn't. I was keeping that part to myself until you levelled out. But now you should know. And we should go out there and help this poor woman and get on someone's good side for a change." She swallowed loudly. "What do you say?"

"I don't know, Joyce." He shook his head slowly. "I meant what I said about being retired. You, me, and Di all agreed we needed to go underground after that bullshit. It was only, what—a year and a half ago? That's not a very long time."

"It's long enough. I have a good idea how much you and your sister are worth, but I also know you're bored out of your skull, and this is the result." She picked up one of the empties from the floor and held it for him to see, as if she were a prosecutor displaying evidence to a guilty man. "After everything that happened, how the show was cancelled, one would think you'd have learned your lesson and cleaned up your life."

David turned on her quickly. The throbbing threatened to turn up a notch, but he closed his eyes and took a long, steadying breath. He even managed to stifle the moan that almost made it past his lips. "I'd get mad at you, but I'm too frigging tired."

"You know I'm right." Joyce placed the empty beer can on the end table. She rooted through her purse again until she found her leather cigarette case. She took out a cigarette and rummaged for her lighter. "This is going to solve a lot of problems for us, David. So you're going to do this. And so will Di. For all of us." She lit her cigarette and flicked the ashes into the empty can. "Besides, Michigan is quite nice this time of year. The colleges in Lansing are mostly out of session except for a few summer students so we'll have a lot of room to work and plenty of time for you two to do what you do."

"Sounds wonderful." He meant it to sound sarcastic, but his tone held a measure of sincerity.

"Just one more time, that's all I'm asking here."

"What's it pay?" He didn't care about the money, not much, anyway, but she would be expecting the question.

Joyce puffed on her cigarette and didn't answer.

David removed his head from his hands and looked at her. Her reluctance to speak told him everything he wanted to know.

"Okay," she said finally, "it's not much. In fact, our fee is predicated entirely on you two confirming the old guy did indeed have a secret stash hidden somewhere. You find it, we get a cut." She held up her hands when he rolled his eyes. "Let me finish. Doing this for her, with no guarantee of payment, will be a good thing. She's exactly the little old lady everybody pictures when they hear the term. If we turn her down, we'll look like insensitive assholes who don't give a shit for anyone other than ourselves. And I'm telling you, our image doesn't need another hit like that. So what do you say?"

David leaned back slowly. "You know Di will say no. I seriously doubt she'll want to see me. I'm not even sure I want to see her." He held up a hand when Joyce began to protest. "But okay. Count me in. And good luck talking Di into this. If you can somehow get her to agree, I'll do it."

"Is she clean now? I mean, is she *really* clean, or is she faking it?"

"How do I know? I haven't seen her."

"You can't find out?"

David cast a sideways glance in her direction. "At this distance? No. And that was the whole point, wasn't it? It's why she moved out there in the first place. We had to get away from each other." He shook his head again. "At this range the only thing I can tell you is she's alive. Beyond that, *nada*."

"I'll be able to tell as soon as I see her," Joyce gave him her trademark smile. "I'll get her onboard with this." She smiled again. "You know how persuasive I can be."

David shrugged; he did, indeed. "Let me know what she says."

After Joyce departed, David sat on his sofa, face in his hands. He felt a powerful urge to call Joyce and tell her he changed his mind. It had little to do with going back into the field or any reluctance to help the old woman in Michigan. It was Di, plain and simple.

Their parting was under less-than-ideal conditions. (*You fucking bitch!*) He found he had no desire to find out if their time apart had eased some of that hostility. *What the hell are you doing? Call Joyce right now. It's perfect because she's driving so you won't even have to talk to her. Leave a message, tell her to forget it, and don't answer the phone when she calls back.*

He very nearly reached for his phone. His hand stopped a few inches short. "For fuck's sake," he whispered. *She's your sister, not some demonic force in human skin. You grew up together, went to school together, got rich and famous together.* And it had been nineteen months since they last saw each other. Maybe it was time to try to work out the problems between them.

David did not call Joyce to cancel the plan. Three days later a messenger arrived with his plane ticket.

Diane Walsh poured two cups of coffee and took them to the kitchen table. She placed one in front of Joyce and took the chair across from her.

"Thank you, dear," Joyce said with a smile.

Diane returned her smile, hoped she appeared sincere. "Anytime."

She was surprised to see Joyce at her front door but, in retrospect, she should have known it was coming. It had been at least nine months since she last called, and she had never crossed the country to visit. But back then Joyce was still trying to salvage the show. Her absence led Diane to believe she had finally accepted it was over. And yet here she was. Joyce's visit could mean only one thing.

"Where's the job?" she asked before Joyce could begin her sales pitch.

Joyce looked surprised, but her act did not fool Diane. Her manager was far too clever to think the reason for her visit would not be obvious immediately.

"Oh, please. You didn't fly across the country just to say hello."

To Joyce's credit she did not carry her feint too far. "Michigan. Lansing, to be precise."

"Never been there."

"It's nice, especially this time of year." Joyce sipped her tea and lit a cigarette. "You'll love it."

"Uh huh." Diane swirled the dark liquid in her cup.

Joyce regarded the tray of goodies Diane had placed on the table and helped herself to a single chocolate chip cookie. She turned it over in her hand, looked at it longingly, and put it back. "Goddamned diet. It'll be the death of me."

"No, *that* will," Diane replied, and pointed at Joyce's cigarette.

"You know, my doctor is a perfectly dreadful little man. He's given up getting me to stop smoking. But I'm afraid he's drawn the line quite boldly when it comes to what I can and cannot eat. If it tastes good, it's off-limits."

"That's a shame." Diane sipped her coffee.

Joyce placed her cigarette in the ashtray Diane had provided, and folded her fingers together. "Di, can I ask a frank question?"

Diane knew what was coming. She had expected the question before Joyce even made it into the kitchen. Diane was impressed the older woman had managed to hold off this long. "Of course."

"Are you still on that shit?"

Diane leaned back in her chair. "Well, that is pretty frank." A long, loud sigh escaped her. At last she shook her head. "No. I've been clean for almost five months."

"Really."

Diane held up her first three fingers. "Scout's honor." She smiled her practiced smile before she could stop herself. It had indeed been five months since her last experience with the white powder, but the learned behavior of a drug addict stayed with her. She blushed. "I mean, I smoke an occasional joint, but that's the only substance I've touched lately. Promise."

Joyce nodded and returned her attention to her coffee. She sipped for a few moments. "And you're sure about that?"

"One hundred percent."

Joyce nodded again. "Okay, I'll take you at your word. Don't make me regret it, honey."

"So what's the deal?" Diane didn't bother to wait for a segue; she wanted off the topic quickly.

Joyce told her the same story she laid on David. Diane listened to the end and asked, "So what's the takedown?"

Joyce clearly dreaded the answer. She took a deep breath before she put it all on the table.

Diane pursed her lips. "I'm not gonna lie, Joyce. I could use a decent payday. But flying fifteen hundred miles with no guarantees doesn't really appeal to me."

"I understand completely," Joyce replied with her most understanding tone. She finished her cigarette and put it out in the ashtray. "But we do this job for the publicity. More jobs will come, and we'll be back to making the kind of money we were making before."

"Before Nebraska."

"Yes, before Nebraska. Trust me on this, Di. The requests will start coming in again. All we have to do is help out this little old lady who goes to church every Sunday and pays her taxes every year." Her smile returned.

"I assume you already talked with my brother." Diane took a cookie from the tray.

"He's in if you are."

Diane nibbled on the cookie. "Let me think about it, okay? Give me a day or two. I'll call you."

Joyce seemed less than ecstatic with the answer, but she also seemed to realize it was all she was going to get for the moment. "Very well. Call me when you make up your mind."

She pushed her chair away from the table and stood. She leaned for a moment on the back of the chair. Her eyes went to the cabinet above the sink. They lingered there for only a moment before she retrieved her pocketbook.

Diane caught her glance and forced herself not to smile. *No coke in there, Joyce. Not anymore. And how'd you know about that in the first place?* "I'll walk you out."

They reached the front door in silence. Joyce opened it and stepped out. "I'll be waiting for that call, dear."

"Two days, max," Diane replied. "Maybe sooner."

Joyce hugged her and walked slowly to her rental car.

Diane waved again as the Caddy pulled out of her driveway. When it vanished from view, her smile faded, and she closed the door.

Was she really going to do this again? It had been just nineteen months since their last time out and that had not ended well. And to top it off, David would be there. She hadn't seen her twin since *then*. That was intentional on both their parts. She came close to calling him only once, last Christmas Eve. She'd been entirely too high to even attempt a civil conversation. She got as close as calling up his number in her contacts, but her finger froze inches above the call button, and she never pressed it.

And now she was about to agree to see him again. No phone call to break the ice first, and there was too much distance between them for a simple hello using their Inside Voices. That, at least, would give her an impression of his attitude toward her. No, their first contact in nearly nineteen months would be face to face. That thought alone was enough to make her get her stash and roll a fat one.

Diane stood by her back screen door and smoked. Maybe Joyce was right. Maybe they did need something like this. If nothing else it might kick-start a conversation, a real conversation, with her brother. For the first time in more than a year and a half, Diane found she missed him. She wondered if he missed her, as well. She might have attempted to contact him right then if they weren't three thousand miles apart. At this distance she would be able to sense nothing other than his existence.

Yes, she would take Joyce's offer. Even if they were unable to do anything for the old lady, it was possible Diane would leave Lansing with her and David back on speaking terms.

She was less than enamored with the idea of playing another round of the Game. Diane wondered how it would feel to reenter the fog after so long. *It'll be like riding a bike,* she thought. "Yeah, I don't know about that," she answered herself. "But we'll give it a go."

She nearly picked up the phone to call Joyce but in the end she waited the two days. The last thing she wanted to appear was enthusiastic.

CHAPTER TWO

INFAMOUS

The flight started out all right for Diane, but became progressively worse. She had never been a good flyer to begin with. The cocaine, back when she was using, had helped her somewhat, but those days were over. She had been unable even to smoke a joint before she left the house. She was one of the unlucky few who absolutely could not drive while high. With nothing to calm her nerves, she boarded the plane at JFK. Her hands maintained a death grip on the armrests and came off only when the flight attendant offered her a drink. She was fortunate the flight was not much longer than ninety minutes. Her nerves wouldn't last far beyond that.

A few moments after she was seated, she scanned the plane. She saw no one and nothing out of the ordinary. It was a typical first-class group in every respect. More importantly, no one took much notice of her. Even the flight attendant who checked her in and read her name on the boarding pass did not so much as raise an eyebrow. That suited Diane just fine. *Welcome back to anonymity, dear,* a voice that sounded like Joyce's whispered in her ear. *Enjoy it while you can because our comeback starts when this plane lands.* Diane rolled her eyes. It might at that.

She was served a vodka tonic after the plane reached altitude. Diane sipped her drink and gazed out the window. Without her twin next to her, she would have the flight all to herself. She smiled and did her best to appear calm.

The flight was uneventful in every way and the wheels touched down at Capital Region International without incident.

Diane disembarked and retrieved her luggage from the conveyor. A quick glance at the giant board above the information desk informed her David's flight had touched down twenty minutes before. Diane headed for the main entrance.

She caught sight of David right away. He stood beside a late-'90s Cadillac with Joyce and another man she did not know. The stranger wore a dour expression, and his body language bespoke his impatience and general unpleasantness.

Diane's breath caught in her throat. She ducked behind a thick concrete pillar and took several deep breaths. *Get out of here*, she thought. *Go back inside and get on the first flight back to New York before they see you.* She had dreaded seeing David again, but the fear had been abstract. With her twin no more than fifty feet away, it had become real. Her heart raced, and the blood pounded in her ears. Diane closed her eyes, willed her heart to slow.

You're being ridiculous. You're a grown woman, for Christ's sake. Start acting like it. He's your brother, not the goddamned boogey man. Grow the fuck up.

The voice was right, of course. It took several more moments, but she at last regained control of her body. Several deep breaths finished the job. Diane took a moment to generate her fake smile and approached the trio.

Joyce and the driver ceased to exist for her. She centered her eyes on her twin. There was nothing in David's expression or body language to suggest hostility toward her. If anything he seemed pleased to see her. She even caught a quick impression of his mood and nothing about it put her on edge. So why was she so nervous? *Get your shit together. For the first time in a long time you're both sober simultaneously. Imagine that!* Diane smirked. The voice was right. She quickened her pace.

"Di! So happy to see you!" Joyce exclaimed. She threw her arms wide and hugged the air from Diane's lungs. Diane hugged her back and pulled away so she could breathe once more.

"Hello, dear sister," David said to her.

"And hello to you, dear brother," she replied and hugged him and kissed his cheek. "You look good."

"And you."

That was it? After all this time. With the way things ended the last time they had seen each other. A hug and a kiss and all was right with the world? *See? Nothing to worry about. It's like North Platte never happened.* Diane felt her brother's arms around her, and she had to admit, it felt good.

"Is that your only bag?"

Diane turned toward their driver. Up close he appeared even more unpleasant. His expression was that of a man who would rather be anywhere than there, and with anyone but his present company. She cast a glance at her brother. David shrugged.

"Yes, this is it."

As the large and unpleasant fellow dragged the suitcase toward the trunk Diane caught Joyce's eyes following them. The older woman looked away when she noticed Diane watching her.

"See, Joyce? Nothing illegal. The old me wouldn't have let that bag out of my sight if there was anything in it."

Joyce smiled politely. "I believe you, dear." She watched the driver, a fiftyish oaf with thinning hair and a sizeable beer gut hanging over his belt, slam the trunk lid closed. "I'll need a minute, son. I just went five hours without a cigarette, and the one I had a minute ago didn't do it for me."

"Take your time, ma'am," the driver said.

"Good man." Joyce rummaged through her purse.

David and Diane stood by the car with the driver and waited for Joyce. "Where are we off to?" David asked the driver. "The hotel first or the old woman's house?"

The driver scowled. "The old woman is my mother."

The old David, drunk David, would have laughed. Diane would have joined him. She was thankful they were both sober.

"Sorry."

"We'll worry about the hotel later," the driver replied with a scowl. "My mother wants to see you people as soon as possible."

"That'll be fine."

They waited a few more minutes for Joyce, then they were in the car and heading for what Diane hoped would be a decent payday.

The city of Lansing soon gave way to a quiet, wooded area. The sounds of car horns and street construction diminished gradually until they could hear only the tires on the uneven pavement and an occasional bird squawking somewhere among the trees.

David sat in front with the old woman's son. The portly man responded to most inquiries with "My mother will tell you whatever she wants to tell you" so eventually David stopped asking questions. They rode in silence the rest of the way.

Mr. Andrews turned onto a narrow, gravel-covered road, and it took David a moment to realize it was a driveway. The woods were still thick on both sides of the old Caddy, but he could see a clearing taking shape ahead of them. After another moment the woods parted, and a mid-size Colonial sat in the middle of a large field at the bottom of a steep hill.

"Nice house," Joyce remarked from the backseat.

"That's the guest house," Andrews replied. "My mother's house is around the next corner."

David glanced over his shoulder at Di. She mirrored his expression. *(Old lady must be loaded,)* he told her.

Di started at the contact. David wondered why until he realized it had been a very long time since the twins had communicated in this way. *Too much too soon?* he wondered.

Di surprised him by making a fast recovery from his question. *(And we're still doing this for free?)*

Their Inside Voices were just as sharp as ever, David noted. Their time away from each other had done nothing to diminish their link. And with both of them sober at the same time—for the first time in years—the Voices were clear and in Dolby Surround, as they were when the Walshes were just discovering their ability.

David returned his attention out the window. A moment later the Andrews residence came into view. It was a large Victorian, larger even than David's own home. It was also old. David was hardly a student of architecture, but he pegged the house's construction to the 1930s or maybe the 1940s. There were three floors above ground, and he could see windows at basement level. Spires dotted the corners and there looked to be a walkway between them. *Must be a hell of a view from up there.* A deck wrapped itself around the front of the structure and disappeared around both sides. The front door was enormous and arched at the top. Ancient windows looked out at them and observed their approach.

As the car drew closer, David started to see the flaws in the structure. The paint flaked and some of the exposed wood was clearly rotted. At least two of the windows sported hairline cracks although no glass appeared missing. The deck around the front door sagged a bit in the middle. The lawn was mowed but there were numerous bare patches that dotted the area. The perimeter of the yard was full of trees, most towered above the house. They blotted out the sun and added to the impression that they were nowhere near a major city.

(Okay, so maybe she isn't loaded.)

(Yeah, you might be right,) Di replied. *(But let's see what happens.)*

Andrews brought the Caddy to a stop around the side of the house, in front of a detached three-car garage that had seen better days. He killed the engine and stepped out.

David followed him out and opened Di's door from the outside. "Beautiful home," he said to Andrews.

"Mm hmm."

When Joyce joined them, he led the way to the front door. It creaked as he opened it. He stepped aside and motioned for them to enter.

The inside of the home was much warmer than the outside, although it echoed the decay evidenced on the exterior. The ancient hardwood creaked a bit under their combined weight as Andrews led them into the living room.

The fireplace took up nearly an entire wall; it was stone and large enough for a few men to stand abreast within its confines. The furniture looked to have been new around the time the Dodgers played their home games in Brooklyn, although it was in nice shape. A modern widescreen HD, completely out of place inside the living room, stood on an oak cabinet against the wall opposite the fireplace.

The old woman sat in a thick recliner upholstered in a coarse, green fabric. A wheelchair, folded for now, stood propped against the closest wall. She smiled at the new arrivals.

"Mom, these are them," Andrews said by way of introduction.

Joyce pushed past David and Di and thrust a meaty hand at the woman. "Joyce Clark, Mrs. Andrews . Nice to finally meet you face to face."

"And you, dear." Mrs. Andrews took the offered hand and shook it weakly. "And these are the famous Walsh twins," she added with a nod and a smile at her other two guests.

"Infamous, maybe," her son muttered.

"Brian, you hush," the old woman scolded her son. "They're our guests. They're *my* guests. Why don't you go make us some coffee? Everything is in the kitchen."

Brian Andrews muttered again and exited the room.

Mrs. Andrews leaned forward a bit in her chair. "I watched all your shows. Never missed one, not even when George started to get sick. We'd watch you together!"

David took the old woman's hand in his. "Very nice to meet you, ma'am."

"Hello, Mrs. Andrews," Di added.

Mrs. Andrews smiled amicably at both of them. "If my George were here, he'd be excited to meet you, too. Please, please, sit down. I'll strain my neck if I have to keep looking up at you. My, you're both so tall."

"You have a lovely home," Di offered as she sat on an old sofa. Joyce took the spot next to her and David the other end.

Emily's eyes swept the living room, and she smiled again. "My George built it as a wedding present. Construction started the day after we married. That was in March of forty-seven. Been here ever since. Only took about a month and a half from start to finish. They used to work fast in those days. Now you see houses going up, and it takes them six months to build a ranch." She shook her head. "The garage was added later, and the guest house, too. I'm afraid that only gets used now when the grandchildren come to visit. But there were times when there wasn't an empty bed on the property." Her voice warmed a bit on that last statement.

"Do you have a big family, Mrs. Andrews?" Di asked.

The old woman's smile widened. "Six children—Brian is the youngest—seventeen grandchildren, and, let me see, eight great-grandchildren. And me and my George, of course." Her smile vanished, and she lowered her eyes. "Until this January."

"We're very sorry, Emily," Joyce replied with compassion in her voice.

It was not a lie, not exactly, but David knew Joyce's condolences were merely a formality for his manager. She appeared jovial and sympathetic, but he knew she was champing at the bit to get down to business. He was, as well. The sooner they talked to the old woman's husband the sooner he would be back on a plane to Los Angeles.

Mrs. Andrews made the "pooh-pooh" gesture that seemed to exist solely in the realm of little old ladies. "Thank you, dear, thank you."

David heard Brian Andrews rummaging about in the kitchen. A few moments later he emerged from there with an elegant silver tray with a coffee pot and four cups riding atop it. He placed it on the coffee table and said, "I'll be back with the milk and sugar," and he vanished back into the kitchen.

"I like it black," Joyce said and reached for one of the cups. "How about you, Emily?"

"Lots of cream and lots of sugar for me," the old woman replied. "But you go ahead, dear. We don't stand on ceremony around here."

Joyce smiled and nodded and filled her cup with the steaming black liquid.

A moment later Brian returned and placed a bowl of sugar cubes and a small ceramic container of milk on the tray. He fixed a cup for his mother and went to stand behind her chair and looked at the floor.

Emily took a tentative sip, smiled, and took another. "I suppose we should get to it. I don't want to take up any more of your time than I have to."

"When you're ready," Joyce replied.

"I'm ready now, dear." And she began.

"My husband, George, was a wonderful man. He worked as a construction contractor, and he bought this lot and kept it a secret from everyone until our wedding day. Our closest neighbors back then were the Coopers, about a mile and a half that way." She hooked her thumb over her shoulder. "This whole area was nothing but trees and open fields back then.

"Anyway, when he retired, in the fall of '89 our savings were pretty substantial. Since our children and grandchildren were doing well for themselves—" She raised an eyebrow at Brian, who failed to notice. "—we decided to do a little travelling, see the world, that sort of thing. Rome, Venice, London, most of Western Europe. George hated the Commies, so we didn't go east of Austria."

Diane bit her lip to stop from laughing. It was something their own mother might have said had she lived to be as old as Emily Andrews.

"Last year he started losing weight. Had no appetite, no energy. We knew something was wrong, so we went to see our doctor." Emily's breath hitched in her throat. "He quit smoking thirty years ago, but it was already too late." She regarded the twins. "You don't smoke, do you?"

Diane shook her head. "Not since high school, no. David doesn't smoke, either."

Emily smiled. "That's good. Filthy, filthy habit. Anyway, the doctors gave him a year at most. I took it harder than he did. He went about putting everything in order. You should have seen him. He was all business, and yet he still took the time to mow the lawn and keep up with the yard work. Our oldest boy, Henry, even bought him one of those riding mowers. George hated it, but I guess he had to admit he didn't have the strength to do the whole thing with the push mower, anymore. I think that was when he really accepted it, that he wasn't going to be around much longer."

Brian squeezed his mother's hand. She smiled at him and squeezed back.

"Take your time, Emily," Joyce told her.

"Oh, it's okay, dear. It's been six months, now. I can talk about it."

"Okay." Joyce refilled her cup.

"After George was gone Brian moved back in to help me around the house. He's been quite wonderful about it." She smiled at her son. He smiled back and patted her shoulder gently. "We had some savings. George's life insurance was paid up and for once the greedy bastards didn't put up a fuss when the claim rolled in. But George always hinted that he had a lot of money hidden somewhere. He never came out and actually said it, but I knew my George, and I knew his mannerisms. Trust me, he had money hidden somewhere around here. But he passed before he could tell me where. That's why I need the two of you." She placed her coffee cup on the table and folded her hands. "I knew from your TV shows you do this kind of thing. I just knew you could help me."

Diane glanced sideways at David and saw her twin looking back at her. Diane licked her lips before she spoke again. "Mrs. Andrews, maybe you don't know all the particulars of our operation." She glanced at David again and Joyce for confirmation before continuing. "There's no guarantee we can find out anything. Most of the time we do, but there have been times when we couldn't learn a thing. It's up to the individual, and sometimes they don't want to talk. I'm telling you this because I don't want you to get your hopes up."

Brian mumbled something but continued looking at the floor.

"My sister is right," David continued. "Chances are we'll get something, but understand we can't make any guarantees."

"I'm aware of your success rate, young man," Emily responded. "Your TV show was very enlightening. Although calling it *The Cemetery Game* makes it sound like you're not really serious about all this."

Joyce held up a hand. "That was the network's title. We tried to get them to change it, but they liked it too much. They said it had zing, if you can believe that. We understand it's not a game to our clients, and we take this very seriously."

The old woman held on to Joyce's gaze for a few moments before returning her attention to the Walsh twins. "All I ask is that you see what you can do. If nothing else, it'll help me sleep better at night, knowing one way or the other."

"We'll do everything in our power to get answers for you, Mrs. Andrews." Joyce beamed her most confident smile at the old woman. "That I can guarantee."

Emily returned the smile. After a moment her eyes returned to David and Diane. "Just help me. Please."

Brian placed a reassuring hand on his mother's frail shoulder. She clasped his hand in hers.

"We'll do everything we can, Mrs. Andrews," David said. He placed his half-empty coffee cup on the table. "We'll need the location of your husband's grave and your written consent to allow us access to it."

Emily nodded and dabbed at her eyes with the kerchief her son produced for her. "Brian will handle that."

"Then we have a deal," David replied. "We'll go tomorrow, if that's okay. First we have to find a decent hotel."

Emily waved him off. "Nonsense. My son prepared the guest house. It has plenty of room for the three of you. I wouldn't think of making you stay in a hotel, while I have a perfectly good roof and no one under it."

"Oh, we couldn't impose," Joyce said. "Besides, we have two more showing up soon. They're our camera crew. A hotel will work for us."

"It's quite all right, my dear. Five will fit just as well as three. It's no trouble, and the work has already been done. The fridge is even stocked with the essentials. Brian will show you to it. And you can use my old Concorde to go into town if you need anything for tonight. It hasn't seen much use since George passed but Brian starts it every week and makes sure it has enough oil in it. It's in the garage all the way on the left. Please, I insist."

Diane looked at both David and Joyce, saw they were satisfied with the old woman's offer. She smiled pleasantly at Emily Andrews. "We'll be happy to stay here. Thank you, Mrs. Andrews."

"Anytime, my dear. Brian?"

Emily's youngest son stood and made for the door. "This way. And Mom, I'll clean up when I get back. No need for you to do anything."

"He's so sweet," she said to Joyce. "Always taking care of me."

Brian planted a kiss on his mother's forehead and made for the front door.

"It was nice meeting you," Diane said before following him. She heard David and Joyce say their good-byes and they, too, entered the foyer. A moment later they were back at the Caddy, and Brian Andrews was removing their bags from the trunk.

"This way," he said, and headed down the gravel driveway to the guest house. Diane hefted her small carryon and brought up the rear as they made their way to their temporary residence.

The guest house was not quite as large or well-appointed as David's home, but it was close. The cornerstone outside was inscribed with the date 1959, and, like the main house, it had seen better days. It was not rundown but a new coat of paint and some updating of the living areas would not have been out of order. Andrews gave them a brief tour which ended in the kitchen where he showed them the fully stocked fridge. He told them he would have the appropriate paperwork ready by morning. He made his way up the hill toward the main house.

David plopped his bag on the floor of his room and plopped himself on the bed. He had noted the lack of anything alcoholic in the fridge and had seen no evidence of a liquor cabinet on their tour. He could use a drink, especially after the flight and the long ride that brought him to Emily Andrews's guest house. He might be taking the old woman up on her offer to use her Chrysler. Lansing was a college town, and he had no doubt he could find a bar nearby.

He took out a pair of sweatpants and an old Godsmack concert shirt that served as his pajamas and laid them on the bed. He glanced at the old TV on the dresser and the equally old remote on the nightstand. No. He didn't want to watch TV, he wanted a drink. And he was willing to bet both Joyce and Di would want one, as well.

He found them in the living room. "Anyone wanna go into town for a drink?"

The younger woman exchanged a quick look with the older woman. "No thanks," Di answered.

"Oh, I suppose one round wouldn't hurt," Joyce said. When Di looked at her again she held up her hand. "One drink. It's been a long day. And tonight's the last night it's just us. The camera crew should be here by morning, so if we're gonna have any downtime it'll have to be tonight."

Di glanced at her brother. "Guess we're in."

"I'll go see about the old lady lending us her car. Be right back."

A few moments later Brian handed David the keys to his mother's Chrysler Concorde. A few moments after that he was back at the guest house rounding up his companions. Twenty minutes later they bought their first round.

CHAPTER THREE

THE FOG

David came downstairs at 10:35 the following morning. He was not hungover, although he probably looked it. The one drink Joyce agreed to had turned into five rounds. Di made it only to the third before she bowed out. David and Joyce ordered two more before they started back for the Andrews guest house. He had felt a little buzzed, but he was far from drunk. Still, Di had insisted on driving, and he found he had no energy for an argument. *Don't start a fight six hours after seeing her for the first time in nineteen months,* he had told himself. So he hadn't.

Joyce lay across the backseat humming drunkenly along with the radio. It had been tuned to a Christian talk program, but David had managed to find a college rock station. Joyce warbled her own off-key version of old REM and Sarah McLachlan tunes. David and Di had shared a few bemused glances during the ride home.

Di was at the kitchen table with a cup of coffee in front of her. An empty plate covered with crumbs sat on the table next to her cellphone. "Morning," she said by way of greeting.

"Morning," David replied. He opened the fridge and extracted a carton of orange juice. A cartoon sun with large eyes and an even larger smile beamed onto some very happy oranges wearing sunglasses. David found a tall glass in the cupboard and filled it almost to the top. He took the seat next to his sister and sipped his orange juice.

"Reception is for shit around here," Di said after a few moments. "I alternate between one bar and none."

"What do you expect? Look outside. You'd never know we were close to a city. Can't see anything, can't hear anything. It's like fucking Mayberry around here."

Diane snorted. "Good one."

"I try."

They sat in silence for several moments. David probed gently and tentatively, reaching out to Di, trying to get a sense of her. He could feel nothing, and he blamed that on the passive connection—*the window,* they sometimes called it—he was forced to use. If he went in stronger, and he was certainly capable of that, Di would know instantly. She wouldn't simply shut down the link between them, she might be angry enough to pack her bags and go back to Long Island—the old woman and her dead husband be damned. So he didn't probe with anything approximating his full strength. The *haze,* as they had labeled it when they were children, was too thick, and he began to pull back after another moment.

Di turned in his direction, peeked at him over the rim of her cup. "Why don't you just ask me, David? Why try to sneak around like that? Like I wasn't going to know the second you opened the window." She seemed offended, not that he had made the attempt, but that he thought she would be unaware.

David might have blushed, but this was not the first time his sister had caught him slinking around her subconscious. He looked sheepish and shot her a half-smile. "Okay, you're right. Sorry." He took a breath, and his fingers drummed a jazz beat on the tabletop. "You're clean, right?" He winced as soon as the words escaped his lips. She was going to go nuclear. There would be yet more negative publicity about the Walsh twins plastered online. They would be cast as uncaring assholes who left a little old lady crying in her home, while they scurried back to their mansions. But that would be after Di ripped him for nagging her about her addiction, while he had indulged his the night before. He looked away, ready to hear Di push her chair away from the table and storm upstairs to collect her things.

Instead, she said, "I'm clean. No coke, no anything in quite some time now. Well, some weed on occasion, but that's it." When he looked at her again, she smiled and said, "Yes, really."

"Glad to hear it," he replied, content that she was still at the table.

"It was tough, David," she continued. "I tried rehab but that didn't last long. Too many sad sacks and way too much fake sympathy for me. So I went through it on my own. Just locked myself in my house, disconnected the internet, and just went through hell for about two weeks. You remember I told you about Bridget Gomez?"

"Vaguely. She's the little old lady next door to you, right?"

Di nodded. "That's the one. I handed her my car keys and my phone and told her not to give them back to me under any circumstances for one month. She did, too. Tough old gal. Used to be a teacher, I think, or maybe a drill sergeant." Diane paused, took a deep breath. "I hit rock bottom so fucking hard I almost died. But it was worth it, all of it. Haven't touched that shit since."

David saw her smile again. He placed his hand over hers and squeezed. He could not remember the last time either of them had made that gesture. It was certainly not something the old Di, cokehead Di, would ever have tolerated. And drunk David wouldn't have thought to reach out to her in the first place. Maybe she was clean, after all. Maybe it was something he could look into for himself when he got back to the Hills. "That's great, Di," he said at last.

They remained at the table, drinking their drinks, listening to the birdsong coming through the open screen windows, smelling the fresh air. They heard the heavy footsteps on the floor above and knew Joyce had finally awoken. They remained sitting in silence until their manager made her way down to the kitchen for her first cup of coffee.

Brian Andrews knocked at the door at 11:30 precisely. His expression was unchanged from the day before. He was still clearly annoyed by their presence. And would likely remain so until they found the dead man's buried treasure or were on their way back home, having failed the old woman. Once inside the kitchen he handed an envelope to Joyce and said, "Everything you need to access the gravesite. We'll be ready to go in about an hour."

Joyce took the envelope and handed it to Di. "We'll be waiting," she replied.

Di took the folded pages from the envelope and placed them on the table. Joyce put on her glasses and read through the signed documents. "We're good to go," she announced when she finished. "I'll call Jim and Ted and have them meet us at the cemetery."

David's eyes went immediately to his sister. He was never certain Jim LaMontagne was Di's dealer, but he knew the man was into some shady shit. If David turned out to be right and LaMontagne got Di back on the powder, well, he would most certainly not like David's reaction. But Di did not react at the mention of the man's name, and David sensed no unease in her. Perhaps he had been wrong about the cameraman. He would have to wait until they met at the cemetery, and he could observe their reaction to seeing each other.

The clock on the stove read 12:36 when Brian Andrews once again knocked on their door. David held it open for the women and followed them out of the guest house. They piled into the back seat of the idling Cadillac and greeted Emily Andrews. She sat up front with the heat blasting and all the vents turned in her direction, despite the temperature in the low-80s. On the way to the cemetery, she spoke more about her life with George Andrews. David listened politely, but his thoughts turned inward, as they used to when he and Di were about to get on the clock. *This is for a payday,* he and Di would think together. *Time to get our head in the game.*

David came back to the one lie Joyce had told the old woman. Well, the one lie of which David was aware, anyway. No network suit had come up with the idea of calling it *The Cemetery Game.* David and Diane Walsh had been using that name since they were fourteen or fifteen, since they stood in a cemetery in Shreveport for their grandfather's funeral. It was the first time they had communicated with the deceased, and it scared the hell out of them. Calling it a *game* was David's idea, false bravado from a stupid teen boy trying to show his sister he wasn't scared. The name, somehow, stuck.

David winced at the memory. Best not to dwell on it right

now. He regarded Joyce again, and the lie she told Mrs. Andrews. After the blowback they received in the wake of Nebraska, Joyce had suggested dumping the name, at least for the time being. That was when they thought they still had a show, before the online petitions started, before the network pulled the plug on them.

For the first time since they signed with Joyce Clark, David felt a pang of guilt for beginning their association with a client by lying to them. *Don't tell me you're developing a conscience,* he thought to himself, quietly enough that Diane would not pick up on it. *That'll never work in this business.*

Twenty-five minutes after they pulled out of the old Victorian's driveway, they entered Mount Olive Cemetery. David glanced out the window, saw it resembled just about every other cemetery in which he had ever found himself. The small administration building was on the left, and what looked to be a mausoleum sat high atop a hill.

Brian stopped at the small building, went inside with the paperwork, and returned to the car. "Your friends are already here," he said without looking at the people in his back seat. "They should be waiting for us at Dad's grave."

"Thank you, Mr. Andrews," Joyce replied in a somber tone. She turned her gaze on the twins next to her. "Punctual, for a change. Maybe the time off did them some good."

David didn't reply, nor did Di. They rode through the sprawling cemetery in silence. At the top of the hill, past the mausoleum and to the left, they saw a parked maroon van. Two men stood at the open back doors and fiddled with expensive-looking equipment. Brian Andrews pulled up behind them and brought the Cadillac to a stop.

Jim LaMontagne and Ted Jung waved as Joyce and her clients stepped out. Brian walked around to the trunk and retrieved his mother's wheelchair. He brought it around to her door and he and David helped her out of the car. The elderly woman quickly pulled her shawl a bit tighter to her withered frame.

As David assisted with Emily, he kept an eye on both his sister and the cameraman. If there was anything between them, they did a marvelous job hiding it. Nothing in their body language suggested any connection beyond the professional, and he caught no knowing looks between them. He sensed nothing unusual in Di. It seemed he was wrong about them, after all.

They greeted David when he extricated himself from the old woman and her son. They were pleasant enough, as was he. They shook hands and exchanged pleasantries. Joyce stood by the side of the van and smoked. Di stood next to her and took in their surroundings.

"We're ready," LaMontagne said after another few moments checking the camera and sound equipment. "Lead the way."

Brian and his mother made their way past several large headstones. The rest of the group followed at a discreet distance, forced to walk at the old woman's pace. They moved over one row to the right and, a few moments later, stopped in front of an unremarkable headstone.

David glanced at the name carved in marble: *George A. Andrews, Loving Father, Husband, and Grandfather,* and, beneath that, *1926-2023.* A footstone lay in the grass before the grave. The engraving read, *George A. Andrews, Staff Sergeant, U.S. Army 1944-1947.*

"My plot is on the other side," Emily said in a small voice.

"Not for a long time yet, Ma," Brian half-whispered to her. He patted her hands.

Di and Joyce smiled sadly. LaMontagne and Jung readied their equipment.

David walked around the headstone. Emily's name and birth year were already engraved on the side opposite her husband's. He paid it little mind. This was a habit of his, one he would have stopped long ago but for Joyce. She had thought it played to the camera and added an element of mysticism to the show. It was nonsense, of course, but back then he was new to the business and naïve, so he went along with every suggestion his manager made. In the years since it had become so much a habit it was nearly subconscious. He almost started humming, too, but he drew the line there. That was another of Joyce's suggestions and easily the most ridiculous. *Not the humming, Joyce. Not anymore.*

Joyce was whispering to LaMontagne, and David saw the

cameraman following his every move. Joyce made eyes at him, held her hand outstretched as if reaching for something. David frowned but mimicked the move. This gesture was Joyce's invention, as well, another bit of nonsense for the camera that made his ability seem supernatural. He was starting to remember why he embraced retirement.

His orbit of the headstone complete, David stood in front of it. Di walked to him and took her usual spot on his left.

Joyce gave last-minute instructions to the crew. Mrs. Andrews looked anxiously from one twin to the other. Her son looked both hopeful and skeptical at the same time. David took a deep breath, closed his eyes.

(You ready?) he asked Diane.

(As I'll ever be.)

The twins clasped hands. Diane opened the door to the Waiting Room, as she always did. David followed her inside.

The Waiting Room with its black, featureless expanse, seemed familiar even after nineteen months. Diane didn't know if she should be comforted or disturbed by the implication. It was like walking into her childhood bedroom at her parents' house in New Jersey a decade after she'd last seen it. Everything was where she left it—the posters, the knickknacks, the small containers of makeup and nail polish on her dresser. *Except you won't find any of that stuff in here.* That was true. The Waiting Room tolerated no objects, no landmarks or features of any kind. Not for the first time, she felt it would be a peaceful place to stay, even as she immediately wanted to leave it behind.

The first indication they had left the Waiting Room was the fog. It rolled across the ground and wafted about them as they walked. Next came the headstones. Mount Olive Cemetery materialized slowly, although only its headstones and general geography were represented. The trees, the grass, the living, none of that was in evidence within the fog.

Diane was always nervous in the moments before first contact. Finding her way from the Waiting Room to the fog was not difficult, but she always felt as if she was being watched.

Having her brother next to her helped, but she knew that back in the real world she was holding her breath and goosebumps were rising on her arms. She was usually okay after they made contact with their target. Even if the deceased was belligerent and wanted nothing to do with them, she still felt safer after the conversation—however brief—was initiated. She was less thrilled, as usual, with the presence of the groupies.

David coined the term when they were still in their teens. As they moved through the fog toward their target, others would become aware of them. These spirits seemed to sense David's and Diane's ability to speak with them. The groupies approached them, although they never drew close enough to be anything more than vague shadows in the fog. Sometimes they tried to communicate but without David's or Diane's willingness to converse, the dead were powerless to speak. After their first experience with these spirits, David told her they reminded him of the groupies that tried to get close to rock stars as they left the venue for their tour bus. She disliked the term but found she could come up with nothing better. They flitted about the edges of her vision like wild animals moving in for the kill.

(*Sure are a lot of groupies this time around,*) David remarked from somewhere to her right.

(*I was just thinking the same thing,*) Diane replied.

(*Eyes on the prize, dear sister.*)

Diane chastised herself. Was she so obvious? Or had David felt her unease? Their connection to each other was strongest while in the fog. She was unsurprised he was able to sense her unease and even fear of the groupies. In the fog they were closer than at any other time or place.

(*He's up ahead somewhere. I think I got him,*) David told her.

They pressed through the fog, walking—if this could be called walking—side by side. The groupies became less numerous the closer they drew to George Andrews. Some still flitted about, but most had cleared away. It was not unusual, and Diane was always appreciative of their absence. *Go back to whatever you were doing before,* she would think, but not loudly enough for them to hear her. No, that was the last thing she wanted. *Nothing and no one to see here.*

The fog thinned a little ahead of them. Diane made for it and felt her brother keeping pace. A shadow stood to their left, arms at its sides, head back, as if looking at the sky. It seemed to take no notice of them at all. Diane slowed her pace, the old instincts coming back to her. More than once a target had refused to speak with them because their arrival was too aggressive. The last thing she wanted to do was frighten away the old woman's husband. Not when they were this close.

"George Andrews," she called.

The shadow in front of them did not react.

It wasn't unusual for the target to ignore them at first. The spirits were unused to this kind of communication. Sometimes it took them a few moments to realize what was happening. Diane called his name again.

This time the shadow turned in their direction. It flowed toward them; the twins took a step forward.

George Andrews separated himself from the fog. He looked young, as most spirits did. Their appearance was pure self-image, and the twins had learned long ago that most people considered their younger years to be their best. It was how they chose to spend eternity, young and vibrant and at their peak. George Andrews was no different.

His expression was neutral as he looked over the two living souls in front of him. His eyes wandered slowly, as if he were half-asleep. His arms remained at his sides, his feet seemed to hover a few inches from the ground. "I'm having trouble seeing you," he said with no emotion.

"Your wife sent us," Diane told him. "Emily. Do you remember Emily?"

His eyes wandered for another moment before they fixed on Diane. "I can see through you," he said. His voice was soft, tentative, as if he were afraid to speak aloud.

"We know," Diane replied. "We're here for your wife, Mr. Andrews. We're here for Emily."

"Emily." He spoke the name absently. His eyes began a slow right-to-left movement, as if he were watching an afterlife tennis match.

"She needs to know about the money," David said to him. "She needs to know where it is."

"Emily," he whispered.

Diane watched his eyes and waited. They had seen spirits do this before. Sometimes it took them a few moments to realize the conversation was real, that she and her brother were something different from them, and not simply a product of their surroundings. She had a feeling she was tapping her feet back in the real world.

"Yes, Emily," George said after a few more moments. He looked at Diane, really looked at her, for the first time. "She's my wife."

"She sent us here," David said.

"Where is she?"

"She's safe," Diane answered. "She's back in Lansing. She asked us to speak with you."

George looked from David to Diane. "I don't think you should be here," he said after a moment. He turned slowly, looked over his shoulder. "You should go."

Diane's brow furrowed. *(What's he on about? I don't think I've ever heard that one before.)*

(You haven't,) David confirmed. *(And neither have I. Something's wrong with this guy.)* "We'll leave as soon as we're done here, we promise," David said. "But first, we need to know where you kept the money. Emily needs it and she can't find it."

The fog undulated around them as if blown by a breeze. A sudden chill found its way into Diane's spine and worked its way up. Her eyes were drawn to something in the fog, something far away. It was difficult to make out; the distance was simply too great, and the fog was too thick in that direction to see anything clearly. It was at that moment she realized she and David were about to experience something altogether new to them.

Joyce stepped away from Jim and Ted and retreated in the direction of the van. She gave the elderly woman and her son a reassuring smile as she passed them. Emily appeared anxious, Brian, annoyed. The Walsh twins stood in front of George

Andrews's grave, as silent and unmoving as the statues of angels and cherubs that dotted some of the more elaborate headstones in their vicinity. They could come out of it in seconds or be in their "fog" for a few hours; there was no way to tell before going in. Joyce suddenly remembered how much she hated this part. In the editing room a game that lasted hours could be condensed into minutes, but until they reached that stage there was little for her to do.

Joyce reached the van and sat on the rear bumper. She lit a cigarette and blew thick smoke into the overcast sky. The clouds had rolled in five minutes after her clients had gone zombie. The clouds were darkest to the south and they seemed headed in her direction. The last thing she wanted was to be stuck out here in a downpour. She fidgeted, smoked, and hoped David and Diane would finish up their game before nature took a giant piss on them.

"Come on, come on," she muttered after another glance at the approaching storm clouds. She caught Emily Andrews peeking at her and Joyce smiled and waved. *It's all fine, this is perfectly normal*, that wave said. Joyce eyed the dark clouds nervously.

David's eyes were drawn to the distant figure in the fog. Unlike the other groupies, who had long since vanished from his sight, this one did not flit about. It did not move at all. Something about its lack of movement unsettled him.

(David?)

The groupie seemed suddenly more distinct than it had a moment before. No, not more distinct. It was closer than before.

(David?)

Pretty slick, my friend, David thought, his eyes never leaving the distant groupie. *Moving closer without actually moving. How do you do that, I wonder.* He peeled his eyes from the figure and returned his attention to George Andrews. Maybe it was best they get what they came for and leave. "Mr. Andrews—"

(David!)

His sister's unspoken shout ripped through his head

and buckled his knees. David nearly went down in front of George Andrews, but he willed his feet to stay under him. He lurched back, away from both the spirit and his sister. He felt the fog begin to lift, the familiar sensation of returning to the real world. For a single moment, he was back in Mount Olive Cemetery. Joyce was shouting above the wind and rough hands were trying to lift him from the ground. Something cold and wet dripped from his hair and thousands of tiny needles drove themselves into the exposed skin of his arms and face.

David kept his eyes closed and searched for his sister. She was still there, still in the fog. He could sense her, although she was now too far away to hear him. He willed himself away from the real world.

The cemetery and all those in it vanished. Once again thick tendrils of fog and mist wafted about him. He was so intent on finding his sister that he nearly failed to notice the absence of any groupies. He stopped, looked about. They were still present, and in very large numbers, but they were distant. They formed a distant semi-circle around him, as if they were spectators at a gladiatorial match, unwilling to get too close to the combatants. "What the hell ..."

(David!)

The groupies forgotten, David threw himself forward. He could sense Diane ahead of him, getting closer. She sounded not just frightened but panicked. He could not remember the last time anything in the fog frightened his sister. The thought that she might be in trouble had him moving faster through the fog than he had ever moved before. *(Di! I'm here! Where are you?)*

He stopped, although he did not want to, and closed his eyes. He got a sense of her immediately and took off in that direction. He found her a moment later, standing in the same spot in which he had last seen her, before her panicked shout had momentarily bounced him back to the real world.

George Andrews was gone, vanished as if he had never existed. Diane stood paralyzed, her eyes wide and her lips trembling. *(Di, I'm here,)* he thought to her. *(I'm right here. What's the matter? What is it?)*

He could hear nothing from her, nor was he sure she even heard him. Her eyes remained wide, and she stared into the fog in front of them. David followed her gaze.

The groupie he had seen before was very close, close enough that David could make out some details. It was male or had been when it was alive. It was also old; long wisps of white hair whipped about the man's head as if tossed by a cold wind. David could not see the groupie's eyes, but deep creases lined the skin around its mouth. At first David thought the old man was overweight, but after a moment he realized it was a robe. It furled about the body, in the grip of the same cold wind that whipped its remaining hair about. It seemed to be grinning.

David kept his eyes on the spirit—he could no longer think of it as just a groupie—as he moved beside his sister. Diane remained a statue, her eyes wide, her mouth agape. *(Di, let's go. We've been in here long enough.)*

Her lips trembled. She gave no sign that she heard him.

David grabbed her shoulders and spun her to face him. Her eyes remained glued to the old spirit in the robes but at last she focused on her brother.

(C'mon, Di, let's get back.)

He turned her back the way they had come.

Something hard and made of ice landed on David's shoulder. He gasped, spun quickly. The old spirit stood directly behind him. Its hand held David, and its skeletal fingers drove themselves into his skin. Its mouth parted, and it was close enough that David heard the hinges in the thing's jaws creak. "She is mine!" it said.

Diane screamed. David, unprepared for the assault on his senses, reeled. The thing's fingers carved grooves into the flesh of his shoulder. He had the presence of mind to throw an arm around his sister and they bolted away. Tendrils of ice wormed their way beneath his skin. David gasped and gritted his teeth to keep from screaming.

(Time to go, Di. Time to go right now!)

They stopped and Diane looked at him. Her eyes were wide and wet with fear. She looked back the way they had come, stiffened, and closed her eyes. She faded from his view, leaving only the swirling fog in her place.

David didn't look back. If the old spirit was there, he didn't trust himself to be able to concentrate enough to get back to the real world. Instead, he closed his eyes and willed himself out of the fog. The last sensation of which he was aware was of something bitterly cold grabbing for him.

David collapsed to the cold, wet ground. Voices nearby. He picked out LaMontagne's a few feet away, but it was Ted Jung who had his hands on David's arms and was trying to lift him from the ground. David opened his eyes. The rain was coming down in buckets and the three men and one woman still in front of George Andrews's grave were soaked. David staggered in Diane's direction but LaMontagne had her on her feet and moving in the direction of the van. David allowed Jung to help him after them.

Once they were inside Jung tossed two towels at the Walsh twins and fired up the van. LaMontagne was on his phone, and he must have been speaking with Joyce because David heard him make arrangements to meet back at the Andrews residence.

David ran the towel over his face and head. He looked at his sister, who sat opposite him, her eyes wide and her lips trembling. When at last she looked at him, David thought, *(You okay?)*

It took her a moment, but she finally said, "Yeah, I think so." The towel was in her lap; she squeezed it with both hands. Her breathing was short and fast. "What … What the hell was that?"

David licked his lips. He looked out the back window as the van pulled away from the curb. The rain was driving down, and small horizontal rivers flowed over the window glass. He looked at Diane again and shook his head.

"I don't know."

THEN

David fidgeted with his tie. He always hated the damned things. Aside from his eighth-grade graduation ceremony, he couldn't recall a single positive event that required him to wear one. He could never get it right on the first try, nor the second or the third. This time when he was finally satisfied with its appearance, his mother had approached him and tightened it around his neck. Since that moment in his dead grandfather's living room David had stuck his finger between his shirt collar and his neck every time his mother wasn't looking and tried to buy himself an extra half-inch of space between flesh and fabric.

The rest of his outfit was likewise uncomfortable. He hated dressing up, hated it with every atom in his body. It was too warm when he was forced to wear it on Easter Sunday at home in Jersey City. On this July morning in Shreveport he thought he may actually pass out. He might even wish it to happen, if not for two things.

The first was his twin standing beside him. If anything, Di looked even more miserable. Her dress was long and covered every inch of her body save her hands … and she sported white lace gloves on those. Her heels, hidden by the length of her dress, were awkward and made her walk funny. David had almost laughed when he saw her, but their mother had been present, and she was in no mood for anything resembling levity.

The second was their mother's state of mind. The family had flown down there for her father's funeral. She stood behind David, her hands on his shoulders. Every so often one hand would disappear as she dabbed at her eyes with a kerchief. Her tears brought on tears for David, as well. They were not for his grandfather, not really. He barely knew the man. He had come to visit them only twice that David could remember. But seeing his mother so upset had upset him, too.

David cast a sideways glance at his sister. Di sniffled and wiped away tears with her gloved hands. He knew her grief was for their mother and not for the body in the casket. How could it be? She no more knew the deceased than did he.

There were many people standing about the gravesite as the reverend recited prayers from his bible. Other than his parents and sister, David did not know any of them. *At least the old guy had some friends*, David thought. Mom would be happy about that.

Di began to openly weep. David expected their father to offer a comforting hug or at least a squeeze on the arm. The man did neither. If anything, Di's sudden expression of grief made their mother cry harder. Their father wrapped one arm around his wife's shoulder. David reached for Di's hand and took it in his.

The bright skies of the early Louisiana afternoon darkened to black in an instant, as if someone had thrown an invisible switch. The mourners, including his parents, had vanished. Only Diane remained at the gravesite. The ground had disappeared along with the people; a thick fog blanketed the area, high enough to obscure many of the headstones.

Di screamed.

The sudden sound made David jump. He squeezed his sister's hand harder. "Di! What happened? Where'd everybody go?"

"Mom!" she shouted. "Dad!" Her eyes were wide, wild. Her head whipped about so fast she was almost a blur. Di was scared, maybe terrified.

David was in the same boat. His eyes scanned the midnight cemetery. He saw no one, heard nothing. (*Jesus, did we die?*) The thought sent a fresh bolt of panic through his body.

"Don't say that!" Di screamed at him. "We're not dead! Mom, Dad! Help!"

It wouldn't occur to David until later that he hadn't spoken at all, yet his sister had heard him loud and clear. For the moment, his mind was a whirlwind. If they weren't dead, what happened?

Where were their parents? Where were the priest and all the mourners? What happened to the sun? He continued to scan the cemetery, but it seemed they had the place to themselves.

David looked at Di. The tough tomboy who slept in the room next to his and stole his Guns N' Roses albums and played them at full blast, the girl who would fight any boy or girl in school if they got in her face (or his), was gone. His sister, who had once stolen a bag of candy from a store on a dare and jumped a narrow stream with her bike, was nowhere to be seen. The frightened girl next to him had banished his sister from the face of the Earth. The realization sent a fresh chill down David's spine.

"Di, we're not dead, okay? I swear we're not. I don't know why I said that. I'm sorry." He tried to sound calm, in command. He doubted his success at either.

"Where are we?" she asked. "I don't see nobody. What happened to Mom and Dad? Where's all the other people?"

David started to reply, stopped. He had no answers.

His eyes caught movement to their left. David turned, saw someone walking through the fog. His breath caught in his throat. He dove for the ground he could not see, his weight dragging his twin after him. She gasped and screamed at the unexpected move.

David put one finger to his lips. Di sniffled but turned silent. He pointed in the direction of the thing he had seen in the fog. His sister's eyes, wet and wide, grew larger still. Her lips trembled but she uttered no sound.

David tried to appear brave. If he got out of this with only a urine stain on his underwear he'd consider himself ahead of the game. He blocked out everything and tried to listen for the thing's footsteps, for any sound that would tell him it was moving away. He heard nothing.

They waited in silence, neither daring to move or make a sound. David had no idea how long they lay there, feeling but not seeing the cold ground of the cemetery. At last, he felt they'd waited enough. He motioned for Diane to stay down and silent. He poked his head up through the fog.

His grandfather stood next to the headstone behind which the twins had sought safety.

David shouted something incoherent. Di leaped to her feet. She saw the man standing before them. She screamed, as well.

There was never a moment in his life when David wanted to run as much as at this moment. His feet had grown roots into the ground. Likewise, his arms felt as if they weighed a few tons each. Even his voice was gone. He stood in place and trembled before the man in the fog.

"You're my grandchildren, right? Diane and David. Why didn't I recognize you at first?" His voice was soft, nearly monotone. His eyes wandered from the twins to the darkened cemetery and back.

"You're ..." Di started, stopped. Her voice was an octave higher than normal. She swallowed, tried again. "You're our grandfather? No. No, he's dead. And he was a lot older than you." She said this last as if she were an attorney in a courtroom who had just nailed a key witness for lying under oath.

"My name is John MacDonald," he said. His tone remained flat, as if the man were talking in his sleep. "My daughter is Julia MacDonald. She married Donald Walsh." His eyes continued their trek about the cemetery.

David still wanted to run, but his feet had other ideas. He swallowed hard, regarded the man. He did look like their grandfather, from David's few memories of the man and the photos he'd seen. But ... how ?

"Tell my little Julia Child that her Pop loves her very much. Tell her it's okay. I'm not in pain anymore. And I'm going to see my Barbara."

"But—"

Di squeezed his hand so hard David yelped and pulled away.

The lights came on so suddenly and with so much force David threw up his hand to shield his eyes. He noticed several things all at once. His mother's hands were back on his shoulders. The reverend was still reading something from his bible. A warm July breeze swayed the branches of the trees and made a *whoosh*. He was sweating quite profusely.

David squinted through the bright sunlight at his sister. Di was in a similar state. He looked about. The mourners were still in place, as were he and his family. The casket sat perched atop the open grave. Within it lay the body of John MacDonald, who was no longer in pain and was going to see his Barbara.

No one seemed to have noticed the twins' disappearance. The funeral service continued as if nothing out of the ordinary had occurred. Even their parents were oblivious. He wanted to tell them, all of them, what had just happened. Somehow, for reasons he was never able to articulate, David kept it to himself. As did his sister.

When he noticed Di looking at him, David mouthed, *What the fuck?*

Diane shrugged her shoulders ever so slightly. *I don't know,* she mouthed back.

The funeral service did not seem the right place or time to tell their parents. Nor afterward when the mourners gathered at their grandfather's home for food and memories. The flight back to Jersey might have sufficed but the twins were separated by the aisle from both parents on the return trip. David could not imagine relating the story to his mother while having to pause every time someone walked past on the way to the restroom. It was not until they were back home that David and Di approached their mother.

They plowed through their story as quickly as they could speak, not pausing even long enough for their mother to get a word in. She did not believe them, of course, and became angry and upset that they would make up such a story. It wasn't until Di got to the part about Julia Child that their mother's anger faltered.

The twins spent the remainder of that afternoon retelling the story in detail. Their mother ultimately believed them. After that her grief, although still present, seemed less than it was before.

"Maybe that's why he did it," Di confided in David when they were alone in his bedroom later that evening. "Maybe Grandpa talked to us so Mom wouldn't be sad anymore."

"Maybe," David agreed. It made sense at the time.

And anyway it was in the past. David doubted they would ever find themselves in that position a second time. So when their mother made them promise to not speak of this again, David and Di did as she asked.

The twins kept that promise. They didn't bring it up, even among themselves, until two years later, when it happened again.

CHAPTER FOUR

PAYDAY

David instructed Jung to head to the guest house once they arrived at the Andrews residence. He knew the old woman would want to know if they discovered anything. But he was cold and wet, and he wanted dry clothes more than anything. And a drink, a big, fucking drink. LaMontagne texted Joyce that they would come up to the main house once they got squared away. David directed Jung down the path to the guest house. Once there they ran for the front door.

Di was shaking when they entered the kitchen. David doubted it was because she was soaked through. He was trembling, as well, but the simple act of being in familiar surroundings made him feel better. He made sure Di was okay before he headed upstairs to his room.

He whipped off his shirt and jeans and rummaged through his suitcase. He did not become aware of the dull pain in his shoulder until he was putting on a fresh shirt. He paused, examined the area. Four shallow, thin welts marred his skin. David's heart skipped a beat. They were in precisely the spot the old spirit had grabbed him as he fell away. He ran to the mirror above the dresser and examined them further.

They were barely visible, and if not for the unexpected pain, he might not have noticed them at all. But they were there just the same. "What the hell?" he whispered. He felt around the wounds, as if certain he had hallucinated them. His fingers could make out the damaged flesh, but just barely. The skin was unbroken, just swollen a bit.

David sat on the bed. "That never happened before," he said matter-of-factly.

Diane made sure the water was hot, almost scalding, before she stepped into the shower. The cold had not left her, even after she had sipped some brandy from LaMontagne's silver flask. The cameraman helpfully offered to go out and get a bottle of the good stuff and bring it back for her. As good as it sounded she waved him off. What she really wanted was a hot shower.

She held her head beneath the stream and felt the cold leave her. She closed her eyes and breathed the steam deep into her lungs. It helped to steady her, although her arms still trembled a bit. She stayed that way for perhaps ten minutes before she got around to the shampoo and shower gel.

(*You okay?*) David asked from his room.

(*I'll be out in a few,*) she replied. She felt him retreat and sensed his embarrassment. "Can't a girl take a shower in peace?" she asked aloud. *The psychic equivalent of walking in on your sister while she's naked, boys and girls. Don't be rude when your sister's nude!*

She smiled, but it lasted only a moment. Her thoughts returned to the fog, and to the groupie who had approached them. She had never seen one like him before, and she knew her brother had not, either. Most groupies wanted to initiate contact, but they were far too weak to force themselves on the twins. They were always there, trying to start the conversation, their attempts coming across like mild static on a radio: barely noticeable, not enough to spoil one's enjoyment of the song. After the twins' first few times in the fog they realized this, and the groupies were largely ignored. This one was different.

Diane forced the train of thought from her head. It was not the time, not when she was just starting to feel human again. There would be enough time to hash it out later.

After the shower she did feel better. She got dressed slowly and brushed the tangles from her hair. When she was presentable she went downstairs.

David sat at the table with LaMontagne and Jung. The

cameraman had decided to go out anyway; a half-empty bottle of whiskey sat in the center of the table. Each man had a glass in front of him. LaMontagne filled a glass and pushed it across the table in her direction.

"Thanks." Diane filled the glass halfway and sat. The first sip burned, as it always did, and if any of the cold remained it vanished then. She felt better, but it was more than that. She felt *safe*. She avoided eye contact with her brother, only because he might assume that meant she was ready to talk about what happened. For the moment Diane wanted to steer the conversation clear of the unusual groupie.

Jung and LaMontagne were talking about driving to Detroit to take in a Tigers game. "We're not in this neck of the woods often," Jung said, accentuating his point with a soft belch. "I ain't never been to Comerica and I wouldn't mind checking it out."

"Who they playin?" LaMontagne asked, his words already starting to slur a little.

Jung consulted his cell. "Colorado. Interleague game. First pitch at 7:05."

"Ooh, a clash of the titans," LaMontagne remarked and laughed.

"I don't care who they're playing, I just wanna see the stadium. C'mon, man, it's America's pastime. We're an hour and a half away, two, tops. C'mon, you lazy fuck, whaddaya say?"

LaMontagne looked at David before he burst into laughter. David smiled politely and looked away.

When his laughter subsided LaMontagne said, "Sure, whatever. But the beer's on you. Deal?"

Jung's face fell a little, but he nodded. "Sure, I guess."

"Aren't you guys supposed to film us for the debriefing?" Diane asked.

The three men at the table looked in her direction.

"We didn't find anything," David said. "What are they gonna shoot, the old lady's disappointment?"

Diane bit her lip and glanced out the window. The rain continued, but the storm had lost most of its strength. She could even see the sky brightening to the south and west. She finished her drink and stood. The glass went into the sink.

(You okay?) David asked.

(Yeah, I think so,) she replied.

"One more drink and we'll go up the hill to the main house," David said. "Maybe the rain will have stopped by then."

"Ready when you are," Di replied.

David poured himself another tall one.

Twenty minutes later the Walsh twins were on their way up the hill. The rain had turned to a light drizzle, and the sun was back in its customary place. David's head swam pleasantly, and the warmth of the whiskey permeated his muscles. He was not drunk, certainly not by David Walsh standards, but he was comfortable, to be sure. His shoulder was nearly pain-free, probably from the alcohol, and that was fine, too. Di was quiet but she seemed much better than she had been upon their return to the house. The single glass she accepted must have worked its intended magic on her, as well.

"What are we gonna tell Mrs. Andrews?" she asked once they crested the hill. They were only fifty feet from the old Victorian's front door. Joyce was standing on the porch smoking, and looking at them.

"What can we tell her? We didn't learn anything. She knew going in that it was possible we wouldn't have any answers for her. It happens."

(And when are we gonna talk about what happened in there?)

David stopped, looked at her. He spared a glance at Joyce, who now stood next to the front door waiting for them. "Later, okay? Let's just get through this first."

Di frowned but she seemed to accept his unexpected verbal answer.

Jung's van, tires skidding and machine-gunning mud behind it, came up the hill and crunched along the gravel. It stopped beside them. Jung rolled down his window and said, "We'll be back later tonight. Don't wait up for us."

David waved and the van continued on its way.

"About time, you two," Joyce admonished when they

reached the front steps. "I thought we were gonna be waiting all day."

"Not now, Joyce," David replied. He mounted the steps and waited for Joyce and his sister to enter the house. He closed the door behind him.

Emily Andrews was back in her chair. She looked at them expectantly, her eyes wide and focused on the two new arrivals. Her son sat on the sofa, hands folded together and his expression blank. Joyce took a seat next to Brian, leaving the loveseat for the twins. David and Di sat. They shared a look before acknowledging their host.

"We didn't find anything," Di began.

Emily's face fell.

Brain muttered, "There's a fucking shock."

Di ignored him. "We tried. It's not an exact science, what we do. We did see your husband, Mrs. Andrews. We tried to communicate with him, but ..." She glanced at her brother. "Sometimes they don't want to talk to us. I'm afraid this was one of those times."

(Well done, sis,) David told her. *(Make him out to be the asshole.)*

(You want me to tell her someone else scared him away? Because I'm pretty sure that's exactly what happened.)

"It's not unheard of," David told Mrs. Andrews. "It's lousy but it does happen. I'm sorry we couldn't be of any help to you."

Emily dabbed at her eyes. Her breath hitched in her throat, but she managed to get out, "It's okay, dear. Not your fault. Sometimes my George just didn't feel like talking."

Brian stood and walked to his mother's side. He put one arm around her shoulders. The old woman sniffled and patted his arm.

"We could try again," Joyce offered.

Four sets of eyes turned in her direction. Joyce glanced at the twins before continuing. "It's been known to happen. Sometimes someone won't talk to them at first, but they will if they see them again. Something about them being familiar. Right, David and Di?"

Di looked at Joyce as if she had two heads.

David held up both hands. "That's extremely rare," he offered.

(It's not rare at all,) Di told him. *(In fact, it's never happened even once. Joyce is flat-out full of shit.)*

(I know but back me up here.)

"In this case I really don't think it would do any good," David continued. "The sense I got from your husband is he won't talk to us no matter what. I'm sorry." He looked at Joyce. "That being said, I'll try to go in one more time. I have to stress that it's almost guaranteed we won't come out with anything, but I'm willing to give it a go."

"Yeah, we'll let you know," Brian said. His voice dripped sarcasm.

(David, we're not going back in there and that's a fact!)

Joyce stood. "We'll give you some time to discuss it amongst yourselves. We'll go back to the guest house and wait for your decision."

Emily continued to dab at her eyes. "Thank you, dear. Thank you all."

Joyce signaled to the twins with her eyes. David got up and headed for the door, Di at his heels. Joyce brought up the rear. She exchanged a few more pleasantries with Emily before she shut the door behind her. Her expression was less than happy. "What the hell was that? You're supposed to back me up. I am your manager, you know."

"I did back you up," David replied as he started down the hill after his sister. "We'll talk about it at the house."

Di was already pouring herself a glass of whiskey by the time David and Joyce entered the guest house. She downed it and promptly refilled the glass. She returned the bottle to its place in the center of the table "The rest is yours. This'll be it for me."

"What the hell is wrong with you two?" Joyce asked after she closed the door behind her. "I'm trying to get us a payday here. If that means you have to try again, I say do it."

Di drained half her glass in one gulp. She coughed, wiped whiskey from her lips. "Are you gonna tell her or am I?"

"Tell me what?" Joyce asked.

David locked eyes with his sister. He said nothing, thought nothing at her. Finally, he said, "Okay, go ahead. You tell her."

Di finished her glass and put it on the table. She pulled out a chair and sat and waited for David and Joyce to do the same. When they were seated, Di began. She described the behavior of the groupies, and of George Andrews. She told Joyce how she had become aware that the groupies pulled back and stopped their attempts to force a dialogue.

"That's not unusual, is it?" she asked, rummaging in her purse for her cigarette case.

"It's not only unusual. It's never happened before," David said. "Not like that, anyway."

"Really?" Joyce sounded skeptical.

"Mm hmm," David replied.

Joyce pulled a cigarette from her case and lit it. Di reached across the table and snatched it from between her fingers. "You don't smoke, Di." Joyce sounded both indignant and surprised.

"What I need is a joint the size of a baseball bat. Until then this will have to do." She puffed on it, coughed, grimaced. "Christ, that's terrible. No wonder it never took." She puffed some more.

Di continued, relating how George Andrews had pulled away at the approach of the robed groupie. She shuddered, fidgeted in her chair.

Joyce lit a fresh cigarette, glanced suspiciously at Diane, and put the case back in her pocketbook. "A robe? Like a monk?"

Di shook her head. "No, not like a monk. At least, I don't think so."

"It's kind of hard to describe," David added. "You have to remember perception is all kinds of fucked up in there. That's mostly because of the fog. The way it swirls around, it really screws with your eyes."

"And why did he look old?" Di asked her twin. "How many spirits have we talked to who appeared old?"

"None that I remember."

Joyce held up both hands. "Okay, now you're just fucking with me. What possible difference does that make?"

Di explained self-image, and how spirits always appear

young regardless of their age at the time of their passing. "No one wants to feel old, Joyce, not even the dead," Di explained. She looked at her brother. "Not in our experience, anyway."

"So? So what? This one didn't have any illusions he was a young buck. I still don't see why it's relevant."

"Maybe it isn't," David said after a moment's silence. "Or maybe it is. We don't know."

Di reached across the table and took Joyce's hands in hers.

"Joyce, David and I have been doing this since we were fourteen years old. When our grandfather died, and we were in the fog for the first time, I was scared. Even the second time threw me. After that I haven't had a reason to be scared." She took a breath. "Not until today."

"You're out of practice is all," Joyce said. "We probably should have seen that coming. It's like an athlete who gets hurt and spends a long time healing up. When they first get back in the game they have to deal with nerves, too. I think that's all this is. Nerves. You'll see." She smiled her patented everything-will-be-fine-trust-me smile.

"It's more than that," David said after a moment. He emptied the rest of the bottle into his glass. "It's way more than that." He pulled his shirt collar down and exposed his shoulder.

CHAPTER FIVE

1843

Diane lay in her bed. She watched the dark shape of the ceiling fan spinning above her head. She had come upstairs almost two hours before, and still she couldn't sleep. The image of the welts on her brother's shoulder remained with her even as the wound remained with him. The welts had gotten even Joyce's attention. She insisted on putting some ointment on them, and David did not argue. The balm seemed to help and eventually he went upstairs. Diane had remained in the kitchen with Joyce but only for a few minutes longer. The older woman wanted to talk about the next job, or past successes, anything but what happened at Mount Olive. Diane had no wish to reminisce about anything or speak about future jobs, so she'd gone upstairs, lay in her bed and stared at the ceiling.

She became aware her fingers were tracing the path of her brother's wounds on her own shoulder. She felt no pain, no discomfort, and there were no raised tracks of flesh. Had there been evidence of any of those, she would have packed her bags on the spot and walked to the airport if necessary. She was still freaked out about the old spirit in the fog. Anything else that ramped up the creepy factor, and she would be gone. Making things worse was the growing, familiar anxiety she had hoped was gone for good.

She thought of another night, not dissimilar to this one, barely three weeks before. Lying awake in her bed, she'd nearly picked up the phone three times to call her special friend. She had been uncomfortable then, squirming beneath the covers, trying and failing to find a comfortable position. The urge had come from nowhere. The day hadn't been particularly stressful, she hadn't witnessed anyone snorting their own supply—nothing out of the ordinary at all. Her counselor had warned her there could be days like this. Diane simply hadn't expected the urge to be so great. *Just a couple of lines*, she thought then. *Two, three at most, and I'll be fine.* Diane resisted the urge and ultimately made no calls that night. But she had come close. God, she had been able to *taste* it. She could not taste it now, but she thought she might if they did not leave this dark, unfamiliar house soon.

(You awake?) she asked.

She received no reply, did not even sense her brother picking up the phone at the other end. She almost tried again but stopped herself short. After what David had been through, he did not need to be awakened just to hear her complain about their present surroundings and her need to return to New York. In her current state he would have no problem discovering the real reason for her discomfort. Best not to give him a reason to worry. And was there a reason? No, she did not believe so. A moment of weakness, sure. After what happened who could blame her? But that was one particular nightmare she would never relive. Of that she was certain.

Diane was still awake when she heard Ted and Jim enter the guest house. They stumbled about, using the loud whisper employed by all drunks when they tried to be quiet. *At least someone's having fun around here.* The last time she checked her phone it read 3:17 a.m. Diane fell asleep sometime after that.

If she dreamed, she did not remember any details. She awoke at 9:30 a.m. A bit later than she had been sleeping recently, but early compared to her party days. She had to wait to use the upstairs bathroom until Joyce emerged wrapped in a towel and brushing her teeth. A few moments later with the hot water cascading down her body she started to feel better. The craving was gone, too, and even the old spirit in the fog had been relegated to the back of her mind. Diane enjoyed her shower and stayed in there until her fingers pruned.

She identified the room occupied by Ted and Jim by the

loud, uneven snoring which was clearly audible even with the heavy oak door closed. She smiled and thought, *Enjoy the hangover, boys.* She made her way downstairs to find Joyce and David at the kitchen table, a plate of pastries and burnt toast in the center. Diane sat down and picked a bagel for herself.

"Your brother and I talked, Di," Joyce began. "We want to try again." She held up both hands before Diane could protest. "Hear us out. We think it would be a good thing to leave here having done our good deed for Mrs. Andrews. That didn't happen yesterday, so we'd like to give it one more try. But of course, we need you."

Diane paused. She took a bite of her bagel and chased it quickly with a few sips of coffee. At last she shook her head. "I don't think that's a good idea. Do you, David?"

Her brother shrugged. "Joyce has a point."

"Mm hmm. So did whatever did that to your shoulder."

David tapped the area around the wound gently. "You can't even see it anymore. It doesn't hurt, just a little itchy." He puffed out his chest and placed his hands on his hips and said, in his best *I'll save you, Lois!* voice, "I can take it."

Diane shook her head. "This is so not a good idea. And it's so obviously so not a good idea."

"I'll tell you what's not a good idea," Joyce replied as she lit a cigarette. "Going home without doing what we came here to do. *That's* not a good idea. We're out here to try to patch our reputation. That's not gonna happen if we just go back home and leave this poor woman with no answers. You know it and I know it."

Diane chewed more of her bagel. "That's better than going home all cut up. I'm pretty sure you know that what happened yesterday has never happened before. If that spirit is still around—"

"Then we'll get out of there," David finished for her. "No ifs, ands, or buts. If it's still there, we hightail it out of the fog. We apologize to Mrs. Andrews, and we go the hell home." He switched his attention to Joyce. "That's the deal."

Joyce puffed on her cigarette, regarded Diane.

Diane shrugged. "I'd rather not, but I can see I'm outvoted.

Okay, one more try." She leaned across the table in Joyce's direction. "But that's it. *One*. Clear?"

"As a bell," Joyce replied. She smiled warmly at Diane.

Diane frowned and turned her attention to her breakfast.

It was nearly 5:00 p.m. when the small entourage of vehicles pulled up once again to the curb near George Andrews's final resting place. Joyce extricated her bulk from the back of Brian Andrews's car and felt the warm breeze on her skin. Despite the AC in the car she was still sweating. Her blouse was damp on her back and under her armpits. She withdrew a handkerchief from her pocketbook and dabbed at her forehead and neck.

Diane and David approached George Andrews's grave, walking in stride, heads down. LaMontagne and Jung followed at a discreet distance, camera and sound rolling. The two men appeared steady on their feet, but Joyce knew they were significantly less than one hundred percent. *As long as they do their job.* Mrs. Andrews sat in her wheelchair by the car, her son beside her. Her expression was hopeful, anxious. Joyce could relate; she felt a bit of both herself, if for different reasons.

Ten minutes after the twins went silent in front of George Andrews's grave Joyce retreated to the shade beneath a large oak by the fence that bordered the cemetery property. She leaned against the tree and lit a cigarette. She wished David and Diane would wrap this up quickly. There was a shower and a cold drink waiting for her back at the guest house, and she could not wait to get out of these clothes.

She glanced at the twins. Several headstones partially blocked her view. She could not see Diane at all, but David stood unmoving before the Andrews grave. Joyce puffed on her cigarette, ignored the sideways scowl she caught from Brian Andrews. He was growing impatient, as was she. It was not simply the temperature and humidity; she needed the twins to come through on this. A failure at the start of their comeback tour would almost certainly mean its swift end. And Joyce was not ready to give up, not yet.

She heard a half-whispered expletive from either

LaMontagne or Jung. Joyce straitened and craned her neck to get a better look at what was happening. She still could not see Diane, but David had staggered back several steps from the grave. Emily Andrews gasped and held her hands to her mouth. Brian Andrews hugged his mother a bit more tightly. Joyce dropped her cigarette and made for the Andrews.

Jung had abandoned the boom mic and was supporting David. The elder Walsh twin seemed unable to keep his feet beneath him. He staggered like a drunk man just tossed out of his favorite watering hole. His arms pin-wheeled weakly and it seemed Ted Jung had all he could do to keep the two of them upright.

Joyce asked, "What happened?"

Emily Andrews remained silent, her hands still pressed to her lips. Her son's look of bored contempt was gone. He looked nervous as he shook his head. "I don't know. He just started shaking and staggering."

"David?" Joyce called to him, but he seemed in no condition to reply. Worse, LaMontagne was moving as quickly as he could with the camera on his shoulder past the Andrews grave. It took Joyce a moment to realize he was following Di. She caught a glimpse of the junior twin strolling slowly and leisurely toward an impossibly large and ancient oak tree that shaded a corner of the cemetery. "Di?"

Joyce moved as quickly as she was able. She reached David and Jung, and regarded her client. His face was ashen; his hair, soaked with sweat, was plastered to his skull. He gurgled something incoherent. If Joyce didn't know better she would swear he was drunk. "Help him," she said uselessly to Jung. She paused only long enough to spot the dropped boom mic. She hefted the power supply off Jung's belt and picked up the boom. She started after LaMontagne and Diane.

LaMontagne was at the edge of the shadowed area, the camera still on his shoulder. Joyce could not see Diane at all. The darkness provided by the old oak might as well have been deep space after the brightness of the late-afternoon sun. She focused instead on LaMontagne and made for him as quickly as she was able.

He activated the light atop the camera just as she arrived. The light was bright; it had blinded her any number of times when they were shooting the TV series and the networks wanted them to film at night in order to "set the mood." During those times Joyce had tried to keep her distance or at least to look away. Most of the time she succeeded. This time she blinked spots from her vision and tried to locate Di in the zone of darkness in front of her.

Joyce could hear the younger woman's footsteps as she crunched the carpet of dead leaves on the ground. There was something unsettling about the steady rhythm of those footfalls. It reminded Joyce of the *thunk* of an industrial press. "Di? Di, where are you? We can't see you."

"I got her," LaMontagne whispered. "Kinda. I can barely see her, but I think she's about twenty, twenty-five feet in front of us, a little to the left. I think she's stopped."

"Diane?" Joyce stepped into the shadows. "C'mon," she added to LaMontagne.

Joyce could see little in front of her. She extended her arms and lowered the boom mic so she would not run into anything in the darkness. She stole sideways glances at the cameraman, hoping he would at least warn her before she bumped into the tree. "I still can't see anything."

"She's in front of me, about fifteen feet away. She's just standing there."

"Di? Di, where are you?" Joyce wanted to stop, to give her eyes even a moment to become more adjusted to the darkness. She could not. Whatever had happened to David might well happen to Di, as well, and then where would they be? Another failed comeback by pseudo-celebrities trying to extend their fifteen minutes. It might even be enough to run Joyce out of the agency. That thought alone galvanized her, and she managed to increase her pace. LaMontagne had to move quickly to keep up with her.

Joyce's eyes had adjusted enough that she was able to stop short of running straight into Di. She stood still as a statue, her back to them, silent. She seemed unaware of their presence.

Joyce placed her hand on Di's shoulder. "Di?" The younger

woman continued to ignore her. "Jim, the light."

LaMontagne fiddled with the camera until its light suddenly flooded the area beneath the tree. Joyce squawked a complaint about this second assault on her eyes. LaMontagne shrugged and refocused his attention and his camera on Di. Joyce did, as well.

The younger Walsh twin stood before an ancient headstone. Its surface was pitted and scarred. Joyce could see that even though most of it was obscured by Di's shadow. "Di? What are you doing?" Joyce's eyes moved from her client to the headstone and back. Di remained silent.

Joyce cast a sideways glance at LaMontagne. The cameraman was looking at her as well. He mouthed, *What's she doing?* Joyce shrugged.

Di dropped to her knees and began clawing at the old leaves and dirt at the foot of the grave. Joyce took an involuntary, surprised step back. LaMontagne stuttered but had the presence of mind to move forward and to his left. He worked the zoom from his new vantage point.

Joyce, over her initial surprise, moved quickly to Di's side. The younger woman's hands were a blur. Dirt and dead leaves flew and landed in her hair and on her clothes. Joyce caught some, as well. She shielded her eyes with one hand and grasped Di's arm with the other. "Diane, what the hell are you doing? Stop, stop!"

Di ignored her, continued clawing at the ground in front of the grave.

Joyce struggled with her, but she lost her grip on Di's arm. She nearly sprawled into the dirt. She threw out her hands and one of them found the headstone, and she used it to regain her balance. Joyce gasped and recoiled suddenly. The ancient stone was cold, even freezing. Joyce flexed her fingers and shook her hand. The skin on her palm was red and appeared swollen. Joyce backed away a few feet, her expression a mix of pain and surprise.

She heard rustling behind her. She half-turned, saw David and Jung rushing in her direction. David appeared unsteady, but he managed to keep his feet under him without assistance from Jung. He brushed past both Joyce and LaMontagne and dove for his sister.

He wrapped his arms around her midsection, and they rolled away from the grave. LaMontagne kept the camera light trained on them. Joyce could see Di struggle in her brother's grip. She was grunting with the effort, but it was obvious David, even in his weakened state, was stronger. Joyce and Jung rushed to them.

"It's okay," David gasped at them. "I got her. She's coming out of it." He brushed at her hair with his fingers while maintaining his hold on her. "Come on back, Di. It's okay, you're okay. Come on back."

Joyce watched the smaller of the Walsh twins slowly give up her struggle. Her eyes, wide and wild, at last focused on her brother. "David?" She turned in his arms and hugged him tightly. Tears spilled down her cheeks. She shivered in the hot July air.

Joyce watched the twins closely. "What the hell was that?" she asked no one in particular. She turned her attention to the old headstone. The camera light was powerful in the shade beneath the tree, but the single engraving in the stone was worn and indistinct. Joyce stepped closer, traced the path of the characters etched into the stone. It was four numbers, nothing more. *1843*. Joyce regarded the headstone for another moment before she returned her attention to the twins.

"That was a new one on me," Jim LaMontagne said as he opened his beer. He took a seat at the small kitchen table in the Andrews guest house and took a long, slow pull. "You ever see anything like that?"

Jung shook his head. "What the hell kind of life you think I lead?"

David ignored them, or tried to, anyway. After their retreat from Mount Olive Cemetery—and that is precisely what it was, a retreat—all but Joyce had piled into the van for the ride back to the Andrews home. Di had said nothing, simply rocked back and forth and hugged herself. Tears continued to stream down her cheeks and her breath hitched in her throat, but she remained quiet. David had alternated between speaking and thinking to her, but she responded to neither. He was able to feel her emotions, but even a total stranger could have pulled off that trick. He could go no deeper without her cooperation, so he gave up after they had put a few miles and about ten minutes between them and the grave beneath the tree.

She was little better when they arrived at the guest house. She rushed inside and upstairs and closed herself in her room. David stood at the bottom of the stairs and tried one more time to get to her, but her mind was closed off. He was still there when Jung and LaMontagne entered the kitchen.

He was polishing off his second beer and contemplating a third, when Joyce walked in.

"What the hell was that?" She stood in the doorway, hands on her hips, her heavy pocketbook dangling from one arm. Her face was flushed, and she was out of breath. She regarded the three men at the table in turn, but her attention settled on David Walsh. When he did not answer, she said, "Well?"

David sent another dead soldier into the recycle bin. He decided against a third. As much as he needed another beer, he needed even more to be clearheaded.

"I just spent the last forty minutes trying to put out the fire you two started. You know what's at stake here, David, and so does Di. This was supposed to be our chance to restart our careers, not add to the public perception that we're scam artists."

David wiped his mouth with the back of his hand, looked at Joyce.

Joyce's lips pressed into a thin line. "This is not how it was supposed to go."

"Joyce." David's tone was low, even. He kept eye contact even as LaMontagne and Jung looked at the floor, the ceiling, anything but at the two of them. "You have no idea what happened in there. This is really not a good time."

"Oh, please." She took the unoccupied seat and dropped her pocketbook onto the table. It landed with a thud that knocked over a few empties and vibrated the ashtray a few inches along the tabletop. "Enlighten me, Mr. Walsh, by all means. Because Mrs. Andrews is pretty upset, and her son is ready to throw us out of here on our asses. I don't know if that will be before or after he goes online and trashes us for all the world to see."

David slammed his fist on the tabletop. The ashtray moved several more inches and the few remaining upright empties tipped and rolled off the table. "I don't give a rat's ass what he does. And as far as throwing us out goes, I'm all for it. We should leave, anyway. I'd rather be back in the Hills than out here in the sticks." He gestured to the room, the house, the state of Michigan. "This place sucks."

Joyce sat back, folded her arms across her sizeable chest. "I don't believe this, I don't fucking believe this. And where's your sister?"

David inclined his head in the direction of the stairs. "Leave her alone. She went through even more in there than I did. Way more."

"What did you go through? What happened in there? I never saw either of you have that reaction before."

"Yeah, that was a new one, all right." He decided he would have another beer after all.

Joyce reached across the table and placed her hand over his before he could open the next can. "That's not gonna help." The anger was not gone from her tone, not completely, but it had perhaps exited the driver's seat. "What happened in there, David? And what was Di doing at that grave?"

David released his grip on the beer can. He stared at it longingly. He needed it, needed it badly. He was already two beers in and still he could feel his heart hammering away inside his chest. It took him three attempts to speak before he trusted his voice not to rise hysterically. "That was his grave, the groupie we told you about yesterday. I'm pretty sure, anyway."

"Well, who is he?"

David shook his head. "No idea. I don't really care, either. I think we should just go. As soon as Di feels better, I say we hightail it back to the airport and get on the next flight to LAX." He swallowed dryly. "This job is over." He opened the beer and upended it.

David drank two more before he headed upstairs. Joyce listened to his uneven gait on the steps and was pretty sure she heard him bump into the walls several times in the upstairs hallway. LaMontagne and Jung drank in silence, rarely meeting her eyes and never holding them for long. When the sound of drunken stumbling above their heads ceased, both men pushed back from the table and stood.

Joyce held up both hands. "Not so fast, you two."

They stopped, hands in their pockets and feet shuffling on the floor.

"I need you two to do some research. A Google search, the local library, old cemetery records, whatever. I want to know whose grave that is."

"I thought we were going back to LA." LaMontagne sounded hopeful and disappointed at the same time.

Joyce shook her head. "Not yet, we're not. We need to know what happened. I love those two, and they scared the shit out of me today. I want to know as much as I can."

The two men exchanged glances. "What if we can't find anything?"

"Then you're fired," Joyce answered quite matter-of-factly. She didn't know if she meant it or not. "Get me something on whoever is buried there. And do it quickly while we still have a roof over our heads."

They looked less than pleased. "Okay," Jung said at last. "We'll see what we can do."

"I'm sure the local libraries are closed by now," LaMontagne added. "Same with the cemetery office."

"Then check with one of the schools," Joyce commanded. "This is a college town. I'm sure some of the student libraries are still open. Try one of them. Try all of them."

LaMontagne looked as if he were about to protest, snapped a quick look at Joyce, and appeared to change his mind. "Okay." He and Jung exited the guest house without another word.

Joyce sat alone at the table. Her eyes went to the ceiling as if she could see through the old plaster and wood. David, most likely in bed with his head swimming, Diane probably in the same state. Joyce shook her head. She opened the last of the beers in the house and drank deeply.

CHAPTER SIX

CRYSTALS OF ICE

Neither Andrews asked them to leave that day. The sky darkened and turned black and still Joyce and her team occupied the guest house. LaMontagne and Jung had not yet returned from their excursion into town, and the twins had remained in their rooms upstairs. Joyce occupied herself returning emails and playing *Candy Crush* on her phone. She drank lots of coffee and smoked even more cigarettes. Her mind would return periodically to the old gravestone beneath the tree in Mount Olive, but she pushed the image away. She didn't wish to relive Di's frenzied scratching at the leaves and dirt. It had unsettled her at the time. Alone in the unfamiliar house, it raised gooseflesh on her arms and made her sweat.

She was in front of the television watching a rerun of *The Big Bang Theory* when she saw and heard the van pull up outside. She resisted the urge to leap from her chair—or as close to leaping as she could achieve—and instead remained in place. She lit another cigarette and tried to appear casual when the door opened.

"In here," she called. She lowered the volume on the television.

LaMontagne and Jung entered the small living room. They looked tired, even exhausted. *How much research did you do at the bottom of a glass?* Joyce wondered but did not ask. She regretted the thought instantly. She would be more than a little tipsy herself had there been more than that single beer left in the house. There was another bottle of wine, but she wanted something stronger. It was probably best she not become too judgmental; it had been a long day, after all.

Jung folded his arms across his chest. "We couldn't find a thing. Nothing's open at this hour."

LaMontagne yawned and asked, "Can we go to bed now?" He was unable or unwilling to hide his exhaustion.

"Not together," Jung was quick to add. "Same room, separate beds."

"You couldn't handle me on your best day," LaMontagne replied.

Joyce shook her head. Despite the long day, or perhaps because of it, she was utterly unable to hide her disappointment. "You found *nothing*?"

"Do you know what time we started? Everything was closed. We even tried a Google search but there are about three billion listings under those numbers. It's not enough to go on, Joyce." Jung confirmed. LaMontagne had already started for the stairs, and Jung leaned in that direction. "Maybe we can try tomorrow. Right now, I'm beat, and I'd like to go to bed."

Joyce nodded absently. The two men mounted the stairs with heavy feet and vanished from her sight. *The Big Bang Theory* gave way to a rerun of *Family Guy*. Joyce smoked two more cigarettes before she turned off the TV and walked upstairs.

Diane stared at the ceiling in her dark bedroom. The ceiling fan spun slowly, too slowly for her to feel any movement of the air from it. The windows were open, and the gossamer curtains undulated slightly but the breeze did not reach her. Her forehead, cheeks and neck were coated with a thin layer of sweat. Sometimes tears spilled down her cheeks, but she was not crying at that moment. She probably would be again before long.

She was, of course, thinking of the old spirit in the fog. The groupie who was no longer a groupie, if indeed that term would ever have applied to him. He had managed to catapult David out of the fog, not once, but *twice*. And what had he made her do? She could not remember, not exactly. The memory often became indistinct when one or the other of them was no longer in the fog. That only ever happened when they departed for the real world, and one was a little quicker than the other. This time had been different. To put it mildly.

She could remember little beyond a few vague impressions. The thin, bony fingers on her shoulder, guiding her deeper into the fog. The out-of-body sensation of standing perfectly still, the old spirit's robes flowing around the two of them like black wind, while in another world her fingers drove themselves into something hard and cold. Her brother, calling to her from somewhere far. Then she was back in the real world, lying atop the cold ground, her brother holding her tightly. What had she been doing? What had the old spirit done with her? She did not know. Still, she felt the skeletal fingers on her shoulder, even in her warm room in the Andrews guest house. The fingers seemed to press, release, press, release, as if their owner were anxious.

Diane shuddered. Despite the temperature in the room, she felt a wave of frigid air sweep across her body. In the weak moonlight filtering through the thin curtains, she thought she could see her breath frost the air. Ridiculous, of course. So why was she shivering?

All at once Diane needed a shower. She bolted from her bed and her room and a moment later she was stepping into the shower still fully clothed. The water cascaded down her body as she tore off her clothes. She angled the shower head higher and let the water wash the sweat and tears from her face.

She lost track of time as she stood beneath the showerhead with the warm water coursing down her body. She might have remained there even longer had the water not started to cool. Diane felt a shiver work its way up her spine. She started to turn the dial the rest of the way to the right, determined to get to the last drop of hot water. Something stopped her hand inches from the dial. It was cold, whatever it was, and strong. Something that felt like fingers wrapped themselves around her wrist and squeezed.

Diane gasped, tried to pull her arm back. There was a moment when she thought she would be unable to move, but after a pause the limb obeyed her commands. She pulled her arm back, looked at it. Crystals of ice wrapped around her forearm like a bracelet. The skin beneath the crystals was red, raw.

Diane screamed.

David was in the fog again. He was dreaming, and he knew it. It was nothing new; he often found himself back in the fog after a recent excursion. It was always more pleasant to dream of the ether than to actually be there. The spirits were always more cooperative, the experience more pleasant. And he was always alone in his dreams. Diane was never present. He was confident she also dreamed of the fog, and that he was absent from her dreams. They had never discussed it, but he thought it was so. Not for the first time he wished their infiltrations into the fog could be as pleasant as they were in his dreams.

He found himself in a cemetery, as he usually did when he dreamed of the fog. What was unusual was the realization he was in Mount Olive Cemetery. The cemeteries of his dreams were always generic, with gently sloping hills and vague outlines of headstones and perhaps a mausoleum. This was definitely Mount Olive. Worse, he found himself moving past George Andrews's grave and toward the large tree near the fence line. David could not see the headstone cloaked within the shadows at the base of the tree but there was little doubt it was his destination.

He passed beneath the outer branches and the light dimmed considerably. The fog was thicker here, thick enough to obscure the headstone. His eyes went to the spot, but he could see nothing. "Time to wake up," David whispered. He closed his eyes and began the countdown from ten. When he got to zero, he opened his eyes.

David found himself standing before the old, pitted headstone. His brow furrowed. That trick usually—no, *always*— worked. Why was he still asleep? David turned, or tried to. His feet refused to cooperate. His muscles strained but still he could not turn from the grave. To his horror, David felt himself advance forward.

He stopped directly in front of the ancient headstone. The engraving, *1843*, seemed more vibrant in his dream than it had in the real world. He watched himself kneel in the dirt and dead leaves. Cold radiated from the ground and numbed his knees. David squirmed but could not stand. The rest of his body had joined the rebellion begun by his feet. His hand reached for those engraved numbers.

He expected a skeletal hand to erupt from the dirt and snare his wrist. It didn't happen. His fingers brushed the numbers. The cold coming from the ground was a warm July breeze compared to the arctic blast he received when he touched the stone. He cried and tried to pull back his hand. Instead, his fingers traced the path of the numbers, pressing firmly, even painfully, against the cold stone. On the bottom of the 3 his fingers continued down the pitted surface. David thought he was tracing some arcane symbol on the headstone. It took him a moment to realize his mutinous fingers were scrawling letters onto the frigid stone. An *S*, elongated and looking more like a snake, followed by an *I*.

David closed his eyes tightly and gritted his teeth. With everything he had he pulled back on his arm. His fingers lost contact with the ancient stone, and David lost all semblance of balance. He tumbled backwards, arms pin-wheeling, looking like Charlie Chaplin teetering on a high wire. The instant before he went down, he pushed with both legs. The last-minute maneuver propelled him clear of the tree and its dark secret. David landed in the clear, among the other headstones of Mount Olive Cemetery.

A moment later he awoke to screaming.

Diane stumbled from the bathroom, water dripping from her naked body, clutching the wound on her forearm. She made it three steps into the hallway before her legs gave and she dropped to her knees. She knelt on the stretch of carpet that ran down the center of the hallway, shivering, gasping for breath.

She became aware of the sound of rapid footsteps. A moment later her brother was kneeling beside her, asking her what happened, placing one arm around her shoulders and using his free hand to brush the wet hair from her eyes.

"Di, what is it? What happened?"

She stuttered, clutched her arm more tightly.

Jung and LaMontagne stepped into the hallway from their room and stopped in their tracks. She did not look at them, but she knew they were staring at her. Subconsciously she covered up as best she could.

"Come on, let's get you to your room." David nudged her to move.

Diane got her feet under her again. She leaned heavily on her twin, allowed him to guide her toward the closed door of her room.

"It's okay, guys, I got this."

"Need any help, man?" Jung asked.

Diane could hear the genuine concern in his voice. Had she been capable of coherent speech at that moment, she might have thanked him for his kindness. As it was, she could not even make eye contact.

"We're good. But see if you can find a first aid kit. Check the bathroom cabinet."

She shrank against her brother when Jung ran past them. She was in her room a moment later. David guided her to the bed and sat her on the side of it. He knelt in front of her and brushed more hair from her eyes.

"What happened, Di?"

Her lips trembled. Her hand remained clamped over the wounded area on her forearm. It wasn't as cold as it had been in the shower, but the skin felt wrong, somehow. She was afraid to look at it. She presented her arm to her brother.

David reached out to touch it, drew his hand back instead. "What the fuck happened?" His voice was barely a whisper. If her room were not so silent, she might not have heard him. He did touch her arm, close to her elbow, and turned it over slowly. "Jesus. What did this?"

Jung knocked from the other side of the door and said, "Got the kit, man."

David stood and opened the door about eight inches.

"Thanks." He reached through the opening, took the kit, and closed the door again.

"She okay?" Jung called.

David was at his sister's side again. He opened the first aid kit, rummaged through its meager contents. "Shit. I don't think there's anything in here we can use." He looked into her eyes; Diane looked away.

(Di, what did this? Talk to me.)

She heard his plea. It cut through the fog that had wrapped itself around her head. It was not enough to dissipate that fog, but she felt she could see through a small, thinner section of it.

"I don't know," she whispered. "I was in the shower … Something was in there with me … I don't …"

"We need to get this looked at," he announced. "Let's get some clothes on and we'll go to the nearest hospital. Come on."

Nearly twenty minutes later Jung was pulling to the curb in front of Grady Memorial. He assisted David in supporting Diane through the emergency room doors. Diane still clutched the wound, although her brother had wrapped a bandage around it. She could no longer feel the skin beneath the bandage, and the pain and the cold had receded enough for her to concentrate. She could feel her twin's anxiety, although it was so obvious even the nurses and aides working the reception area could tell he was concerned.

"Need a little help here," Jung shouted as they approached the front counter.

Several of the aides and orderlies were already in motion. She heard David trying to explain the nature of the injury as they rushed her through a set of double doors. She was in an examination room a moment later. David remained with her even after the doctor arrived.

Two and a half hours later they were pulling into the Andrews driveway. Diane's arm was covered with a large bandage. Before applying it, the doctor, a middle-aged balding man whose badge declared him to be Dr. D. Petillo, soaked it in ointment. He assured her the frostbite would take time to heal but no permanent damage had been done. David had whipped up a story pretty quickly once he heard the prognosis. An accident with a can of Freon, he told the doctor, with just the correct amount of shame and regret. Stupid, how could he be so stupid? He knew better than to screw around with those things and yet, here was his twin sister, paying the price for his stupidity. Petillo appeared skeptical, but he let the matter drop. How else could he explain frostbite in July? He wrote her a script for some kind of super aloe vera and gave her a small bottle of Aspirin for the pain and sent them on their way. Diane complained about the itching, but she seemed able to resist the urge to tear off the bandage and scratch the shit out of her skin. She said she could make no promises she would be able to continue resisting that urge once she was alone in her room.

As they wended their way through the twists and turns of the Andrews driveway, David caught sight of red and blue strobes painting the trees in alternating colors. "What's that?" he asked, pointing toward the strobes.

"Cops?" Jung offered. He steered the van in the direction of the main house.

They rounded a corner and David saw the sound man had been correct. Two police cars sat parked near the front door with an ambulance between them. A police officer stood outside his car door speaking into his radio. He glanced in the direction of the van and gestured for them to stop. Jung did as indicated. The cop approached the van.

"What's going on, officer?" Jung asked.

"There's been some trouble here, sir," the officer replied. He trained his flashlight first on Jung, then at David and finally in Diane's direction. "You're the folks staying in the guest house, correct?"

Jung confirmed the officer's assumption. David looked out the side window and saw Joyce and LaMontagne crest the hill between the guest house and the main residence. Joyce appeared concerned as she approached the van.

"What's happening?" Joyce panted. She was in her pajamas and slippers. The walk up the hill had robbed her of breath. She gulped air and leaned on LaMontagne a little.

"I'll need to see everyone's ID," the officer said, ignoring the questions from both Joyce and Jung. "If you need to go to the guest house, I'll have one of the other officers accompany you."

David had his wallet out. He looked into the back of the van, saw Di weakly rummaging through her pocketbook. At last she produced her driver's license and passed it to her brother. David put his license atop hers and handed them both to Jung. The sound man found his own and handed all three to the officer.

"What's going on, officer?" Jung asked again.

The cop ignored him. He eyed both Joyce and LaMontagne as he returned to his unit. He was behind the seat, typing something into the car's computer, when several persons emerged from the Andrews front door.

The first appeared to be a paramedic. He carried one end of a stretcher and his partner followed him out. A body lay on the stretcher, covered by a sheet. The figure was small and frail. The two paramedics made for the ambulance.

Another police officer followed the paramedics. Behind him was Brian Andrews. A long coat hung from his shoulders and his hands were cuffed in front of him. A third officer completed the grim procession. Andrews's head was down, his feet shuffled. Someone had draped a blanket around his shoulders. He clutched it absently.

"Oh, no," David whispered.

His mind filled with images of a similar procession he had witnessed on a television screen nineteen months before. Back then he had been in his hotel room, lying on the bed and finishing off another bottle of Jack. The images on the screen meant little to him until he caught a glimpse of the house in the background. The house was located in North Platte, Nebraska. He was too drunk at the time for the implications to sink in. Standing outside the Andrews house with no alcohol to cloud his mind, David knew instantly what had occurred.

The last cop in line guided Brian Andrews toward his cruiser. Andrews almost made it. As the cop reached for the door handle, Andrews looked up. At first he appeared dazed. It took him only a moment to see Joyce and LaMontagne standing in front of the van. His eyes focused. In one motion he threw off the coat and the blanket and surged in their direction. The cop grabbed for him but in his surprise he missed. Andrews snarled and hurled himself at Joyce. LaMontagne, in his shock, stood rooted to the spot; Joyce gasped and shrank away, one thick arm thrown up to protect herself.

David was out of the van in an instant. He opened the door with such alarm he succeeded in knocking the officer off his feet. David lunged at Andrews. Both men sprawled onto the gravel. It cut at David's arms, but he managed to maintain his grip on Andrews's waist. Andrews was shouting incoherently at Joyce. David struggled to keep the larger man on the ground until the cops could reach them.

"You killed her," Andrews shouted. "You fucking killed her!"

It seemed like forever, but the cops finally reached them. David had trouble extricating himself from the pile. He succeeded only when both LaMontagne and Jung grabbed his legs and pulled him free.

Andrews continued to struggle but the uniformed officers were firmly in charge. David got to his feet and retreated. Diane had exited the van and stood next to Joyce. David joined them. Andrews managed to lift his head and glare at them. His eyes blazed hatred, but most of the fight had left him.

"You killed her," he rasped again.

Diane willed her trembling fingers to maintain their grip on the glass. She sat on the sofa in the guest house living room and sipped lightly at the wine. She resisted the urge to gulp it, but only just. Two quick sips and the glass was nearly empty. David gave her a refill without being asked and topped off his own glass. Diane took another sip before she replaced the glass on the coffee table.

She sat between David and Joyce. Jung and LaMontagne sat in the two recliners and kept their mouths shut. The disheveled man who introduced himself as Detective Ahmad stood in the center of the room, a small notepad in one hand and a pen in the other. He was a rather large man, thick in the middle but with arms and legs that hinted at a more athletic youth. His hair was still thick, and there were stray strands of dark brown among the gray. If he sported a fedora and chewed on a cigar he would have been the perfect image of a 1950s gumshoe.

From upstairs came the sounds of the Lansing PD searching through their belongings. Diane found she could track one of them. It was rare, being able to read the living. She could think of only three times in her life when this occurred without any effort on her part. David had to be near, and the individual in question had to possess a weak mind, someone easily given to suggestion and of somewhat ambiguous morality. This young officer, three months out of the academy, was both excited at the assignment and disappointed he had yet to come across anything incriminating. When he opened the top drawer of her dresser and sniffed a pair of her panties Diane wished she could do more than simply keep tabs on the little shit. But charging upstairs and slugging him would not aid their current situation. And she had no desire to explain to Ahmad just how she knew what the officer had done. Although Joyce had already told him about the show and their business with Mrs. Andrews, Diane was quite content to leave Ahmad believing it was all bullshit.

The detective's pen moved rapidly across the pages of his notepad as he interviewed everyone in the guest house. He volunteered no information regarding what had transpired with the elder Andrews, simply ignored any questions while he asked his own.

David asked his sister more than once if she was okay. Diane ignored him for the most part, nodded once while she kept her eyes on her wine glass. She answered the detective's direct questions and let the others in the room field the rest. The wine helped with the tremors in her hands but could not quell them completely.

The wound on her arm throbbed. She had put on her jacket after she entered the house and sat without drawing the detective's attention. She tried to keep her body language casual, or as casual as could be expected during a police inquiry. She sat with a throw pillow placed strategically over her arm just in case. Thus far, Ahmad seemed to take no special notice of her or her arm. That was fortunate, since Diane could no better explain her frostbite to him than she could to Dr. D. Petillo.

At last Ahmad closed his small notebook and regarded the people in the room. "Mrs. Andrews was found hanged earlier this evening." He paused as the people in the living room gasped. If he was looking for an incriminating reaction, he found none; the guests from out of town shared the same expression of surprise. "She used a ceiling fan. It couldn't support her weight but it lasted long enough to do the job. Given the position of the body and the woman's age and physical infirmity it's possible her son had something to do with it. While no one in this room is officially a suspect, I would strongly suggest no one leave the state until the initial investigation is complete."

Diane started to protest. David placed his hand on hers and said, "That'll be fine, detective. We want to cooperate in every way." A pause. "Any idea how long that'll take?"

Ahmad regarded David but offered no answer.

The cops came down the stairs and spoke quietly to the detective. Diane glared at the one who had searched her room. *I know what you did,* her eyes told him. The young officer glanced her way before returning his attention to Ahmad. A moment later the officers filed out of the guesthouse.

"You'll have to find a hotel in town," Ahmad told them. "This property is off-limits until we're finished with it. Given the late hour, I'm inclined to allow you to stay here tonight, but tomorrow find another place to stay. And let my office know where that is. If any of you think of something we should know, please contact me immediately. Here's my card." He placed it on the coffee table. Ahmad surveyed the people in front of him again. "I'll be in touch."

Joyce walked him to the door. Diane sat back and brought her arm out from beneath the pillow. She pulled the sleeve up and rubbed the wound through the bandage.

"That asshole hung his own mom?" Jung directed the question to the room. "That's pretty fucked up."

David finished the wine in his glass. He emptied the bottle with his next refill.

"Did he?" Diane whispered.

"You heard the detective, right?" Jung looked at her skeptically.

"That's not what she means." David stared at his sister, the wine glass halfway to his mouth.

Dianne dabbed at a tear taking up residence in one of her eyes before returning her hand to her bandaged arm. "I don't think we have a choice," Diane told him.

"Of course we do," David replied. "We wait till we get the all-clear from the Columbo-wannabe and then we go the hell home. Our job here is done, Di."

"What are you two talking about?"

Diane searched her brother's eyes. At the same time, she threw wide the roadblocks she erected around her mind anytime her brother was near. She felt David's presence as he gently probed her thoughts. Diane allowed him full access. When he found what he was looking for, she reinstated the roadblocks and gave him a curt nod.

Jung looked from brother to sister, clearly confused.

Diane said, quite matter-of-factly but with a measure of trepidation in her tone, "We're going to ask Emily Andrews what happened."

CHAPTER SEVEN

SHE IS MINE

David stared at the ceiling in the darkened bedroom of the guest house. He was unable to sleep despite the copious amounts of wine he consumed during and after the detective's line of questioning. The rest of the house may have been asleep—he could hear Joyce snoring from her room down the hall—but he was wide awake, and so was his sister. He could sense Di pacing slowly about her room, one hand massaging the ruined skin beneath the hospital bandage. Her thoughts were fast, almost manic. He could not make them out. She had resealed her mind after allowing him access to her plan. Distracted as she was by the wound, she had not closed the door completely. He tried to communicate strength and positive thoughts, but he doubted she would pick up on them. Her mind was moving quickly, a V8 muscle car at top speed, moving too fast for the driver to see the road signs. He hoped she could hold it together until Ahmad allowed them to leave.

He thought, too, of Joyce's outburst after Ahmad had gone. She had paced about the living room, chain-smoking, and chewing her fingernails. "This is going to finish us," she mumbled. "We're fucked now. Forget the Discovery Channel, forget basic cable. This is it."

Being finished with *The Cemetery Game* was just fine with David, and, he sensed, with his sister, as well. Joyce's reaction could have been a little more sympathetic. The agent in her had taken over a bit too quickly for David's taste.

They had agreed to remain in Michigan, but they had a

second reason beyond Ahmad's request. He knew Di wanted to talk to Mrs. Andrews. But it had nothing to do with clearing anyone's name from Ahmad's list of suspects, not that the detective was likely to believe them, anyway. If what Di— and David, to an extent—believed had happened with Emily Andrews turned out to be true, the no-nonsense big city detective would simply not believe them. It would look like the twins were so desperate to appear innocent they would say anything, even come up with a bullshit ghost story by way of explanation. Still, Di wanted to speak with the old woman, and David knew there was no arguing with her.

Besides, if it turns out Brian Andrews is indeed responsible for his mother's death, that might take some of the horror out of this. A case of matricide, as bad as that is, doesn't hold a candle to what Di suspects is the truth. That alone is a good enough reason to stay here a bit longer.

He had to admit, that was more motivation than Detective Ahmad was capable of generating. But how were they going to pull this off? They didn't know where the body was being kept, nor could they inquire without casting even more suspicion their way. Attending the old woman's wake or funeral was probably out of the question, considering Brian Andrews's feelings toward them. That meant sneaking into the cemetery after the casket was in the ground and the mourners had departed. That was a few days away, at best. David didn't want to bet either he or his sister could hold out that long.

As it turned out, they did not need to. David was mostly asleep when he heard Di in his head. *(David, I know how to find her. Get dressed and meet me outside.)* David thought back, *(Where?)* but his sister had already broken the connection. He groaned, wanting more than anything to be asleep, but he did as she asked. A few moments later, dressed and fully awake, David stepped outside the small guest house.

Diane stood a few feet from the door, arms folded against the cool night air. "All we have to do is stroll past the police station. If he's still in there, he'll know where she is."

"Assuming he's there and not in some lockup somewhere."

"Yes, assuming."

David stroked his chin. Diane seemed calm, but every few moments she would absently scratch at the bandages beneath her windbreaker. She was lucid, she was sober, but she was also nervous. David needed no psychic link to know that.

Finally, he said, "Okay. Let me go get the keys to the van."

Diane dangled them from her fingers.

David smirked. "Sneaky monkey."

From the moment the engine turned over until they had made it out of the Andrews driveway, David expected them to be caught. The van was louder than he would have liked, and he was certain the simple act of starting it had awakened everyone inside the guest house. The tires crunching gravel likewise did little to help their cause. Even as the van crested the hill and he lost sight of their temporary home, he thought he might see the front door swing open at the last moment and Joyce come flying out, shouting at them to stop. Joyce did not appear, nor did anyone else.

There was a police car parked directly in front of the main house. The officer behind the wheel looked at them as they drove past. David had an awful moment when he was certain the cop would light them up and stop them. He did not, however, and they were soon heading toward the center of Lansing.

Once they reached civilization Di took out Ahmad's card and found the address to the police department. The GPS on her phone directed David straight to the front of the building.

"He'll probably figure it out, you know," David said as he brought the van to a stop across the street. "Especially if he wakes up with a nosebleed and a splitting headache. He might remember what happened."

"It would be impossible for me to care less about that than I do right now," Diane retorted. "Besides, I'm not staying in this town any longer than I absolutely have to. Hopefully I'll be back home by the time they let him out."

David said nothing. Instead, he opened his mind to his sister, and the two of them entered the fog together. It was an altogether different experience, trying to communicate with the living. They had done it before, of course, but only a handful of times. Unlike the dead, the living never cooperated. The effort of prying loose the information they needed always left them exhausted, mentally and physically. David just hoped they wouldn't be so incapacitated they would be unable to talk to the old woman, assuming this worked at all.

The twins walked across the street. The fog was thick enough to blot out most of the stone building that served as the main headquarters for the Lansing PD. They mounted the steps together and glided through the front doors.

Details of the building's interior were few and far between. There was a zone of warmth at the front desk behind the glass. David could not see the man seated there; the world of the dead did not suffer the living to enter, other than the Walsh twins, it seemed. They could track a living person but seeing them was beyond their abilities. David got no sense of the man. Diane tugged at his arm, and David followed her past the desk sergeant. Perhaps the book of crossword puzzles in front of him occupied his attention.

They moved through indistinct corridors until they reached the holding cells. The twins entered the cells, sensing numerous zones of warmth that represented people, likely sound asleep, until they found the one they believed was Brian Andrews's. He lay on a small bench seat, his ample size a clue to his identity. Even in the fog David could hear the man's snores.

"Brian, it's Diane Walsh. We need to ask you something."

The zone of warmth began to coalesce into an indistinct image of Brian Andrews. It was as close as they could get to seeing a living person within the fog.

"Well, at least we have the right man," David remarked.

Andrews did not react. Di looked at her brother. David shrugged.

Some of the residents of the lockup stirred in their sleep and moaned.

"We have to be careful, here," David told her, although his warning was unnecessary. There were no dead bodies in close proximity, thus there were no groupies present, but neither twin knew fully what the effect would be on the people near their target. They could easily draw their attention, as well. The last thing they needed was a bunch of people waking with a start and drawing the attention of the officers on duty. If Andrews woke up, their job would be impossible. Even together they were not nearly strong enough to get this kind of information from a fully awake mind.

David felt his sister reach toward the sleeping man. Brian Andrews groaned and swatted sleepily at an imaginary fly buzzing about his head. Di pushed harder. David winced at the sudden, sharp pain blossoming in the back of his skull. Andrews groaned louder and his eyes fluttered.

"Di ..."

His sister's brow furrowed in concentration. David could feel the sleeping man's mind beginning to open. It was not much, but Di made the most of the opening. He felt her leave his side and for a moment David was alone with Andrews.

The headache suddenly upped the wattage. David yelped and dropped to one knee. The inside of his head felt as if it were on fire. He clawed at his scalp, felt himself collapse onto the holding cell floor. He became aware of someone screaming, and he hoped it did not turn out to be him. The pain increased and David came close to passing out. He shouted for his sister ...

David found himself back inside the van, half-slumped over the steering wheel. He shook his head, moaned at the throbbing that nearly blinded him. It took a minute, but he was able to steady himself and open his eyes.

Di remained in the passenger seat. Blood had run from her nostrils and down her cheeks where it mingled with the tears spilling from her eyes. Her breath frosted the air in short, hitched puffs.

"Di." He reached for her with an unsteady hand. "Di, are you all right?"

His twin came to all at once. With a start she sat bolt upright and shouted something. She cringed and held her head in both hands. "Son of a *bitch*, that hurts!"

"Are you okay?"

It took her a minute to steady herself. She finally opened her eyes again and massaged her temples. "Fuck the living. I am never fucking doing that again."

"I think we've said that before."

Di wiped at the blood on her cheeks before she looked at him. She surprised him by smiling. "I think I got it." She took a series of long, slow breaths and they seemed to calm her. There were napkins in the glove compartment; she used two of them to wipe the blood from her nose and jaw. "Let's go."

Diane's phone guided them to the Ingham County Coroner's Office. David parked in front. Several streetlights illuminated the building's façade, but the interior windows were dark. Diane looked past her brother at the large, white brick building until her eyes settled on one of the windows in the basement. "There," she said, and pointed.

David got out and Diane followed him to the indicated window. "She's in there. I think we're close enough."

"Well, we'll have to be. I'm not even going to attempt to break into this place."

"No argument here."

As she had in the lockup, Diane closed her eyes and reached for her brother's hand. She could feel him frown his disapproval before his fingers closed around hers.

David kept an eye on the edges of the fog. He saw only one groupie, a young man with dark hair who flitted about the periphery of his vision but seemed unwilling to come closer to the intruders. That was fine with David; it was most likely Di's agitated state of mind that kept the spirit away. The poor bastard was probably on a slab much like the one hosting Emily Andrews in the basement autopsy room of the Ingham County Coroner's Office. David hoped there would be no more groupies, no more poor slobs hanging around waiting for someone to declare a cause of death so they could be buried at last.

He saw Emily Andrews standing with her back to them. Her formerly white hair was dark and full, the self-image of a woman proud of her physical beauty. She wore what looked like a white robe. It undulated in the fog that swirled about her figure.

"Emily," Di called.

The old/young woman cocked her head.

"Emily, it's Diane and David Walsh. Do you remember us?" The twins moved closer to her.

Emily Andrews half-turned in their direction. "He's here," she said, her voice young and strong.

David led his sister around the spirit until they stood in front of her. She was beautiful, the woman from the old black and white photos she had on display in her living room, back when she was among the living. Her eyes were deep blue, almost black, her hair styled in a way that made David think of old time Hollywood starlets.

"Emily, we—" David stopped. His eyes and his mouth opened wide.

Di noticed it at the same time. She gasped and drew back. "David!"

There was a noose around the spirit's neck.

David overcame his initial surprise and forced himself to move closer to the old/young woman. He reached to move her hair away from the noose, but his hand stopped short. Even in the fog he didn't want to touch it. Instead, he leaned in for a closer look.

It clung tightly to her neck, tight enough that David could see the flesh around it was black and raw. The spirit did not appear to notice the hideous thing, nor did it seem to interfere with her breathing or speaking. It may have been a necklace for all the notice she afforded it. Her attention remained focused straight ahead.

"Emily, we have to know what happened," Di said after she, too, overcame her surprise. "Who did this to you?"

"Talk to us, Emily," David added. "We only want to help you."

The spirit smiled, the kind of smile reserved only for loved ones not seen in some time and spread her arms. "George," she said.

David turned in the direction the spirit faced.

There was another groupie in the fog. At first David thought it was indeed George Andrews. It made sense, at least in his experience. Sometimes the link between loved ones was strong enough that the distance between their physical bodies could be overcome for brief periods when they were both at last in the fog. He suspected George and Emily Andrews shared just such a link, even before she was to be interred next to him for all eternity. David started to relax.

The groupie moved closer, became more distinct. David caught sight of the familiar black robe and the wisps of white hair that clung stubbornly to the skull.

Di shrieked and pulled away from her brother. David was yanked off-balance by her sudden move and he found himself on the ground at Emily's feet. He scrambled to get up but went down again when he saw the old groupie loomed above him.

Emaciated lips pulled back from black, withered gums as the thing smiled. Emily Andrews turned slowly, her eyes clenched shut, her hands trembling. The old man's skeletal fingers wrapped themselves around the noose and he pulled violently. Emily Andrews moaned and staggered toward the thing.

David found himself back on his feet and inexplicably moving toward Emily Andrews. He reached for her, but his hand passed through her arm. He was not entirely surprised; sometimes the spirits went incorporeal—intentionally or not, he never knew. "Emily, come back."

The ancient thing continued to drag the woman back into the fog, a cruel master dragging a helpless hound to its doom. David took a hesitant step in their direction.

(David, we need to go, right now!)

David spun, saw the vague outline of his twin some distance away. "Di, we have to help her." But his twin was gone, swallowed by the fog. He could still sense her, knew she was still on this side of the divide, but he could no longer see her. He turned back toward the last location of Emily Andrews.

The old spirit rocketed out of the fog straight at him. David screamed and threw himself to the side. It passed over him and sped through the fog in Di's direction. The fog swirled violently in its wake.

(Di! Get out! NOW!)

He could feel her terror. It overwhelmed him and he stood frozen. Silently, his hands clenched into fists, he willed his feet to move. He staggered at first, his legs refusing to cooperate. He forced himself to run after the spirit.

(*Di, where are you?*) He waded through the thickening fog, felt its chill work its way into his skin. (*Diane?*) Someone stood a short distance in front of him. David could not make it out through the fog, which had grown nearly opaque. He approached cautiously, reached a hand toward the figure.

The ancient thing spun in his direction. David gasped and fell back. The fog was thickest close to the ground, and he found himself momentarily blinded by it. He held his hands out in a pathetic attempt to protect himself.

A skeletal hand shot from the fog and seized David's throat. Reflexively David's hands grasped the thin appendage and tried to pull it loose. Arctic ice coated his neck beneath the spirit's skeletal fingers. The fog parted for the thing, and it leaned in close to David. Its voice was cold, sepulchral, the vocal equivalent of worms and maggots dropping onto David's skin. "She is mine."

David tried to scream but no sound could force its way past the fingers wrapped around his throat. He saw the world around him start to blur. For the first time he wondered if it was possible to die within the fog. He managed a feeble, strangled grunt.

The thing released him. David collapsed back onto the ground and coughed violently. His hand massaged his throat, felt the thin layer of ice that began to flake and fall. After several minutes, he whipped his head about and scanned the fog. There was no sign of the thing, nor of his sister. He became aware he could no longer sense her within the fog. *She got out,* he thought with some relief. David staggered to his feet and rubbed his throat. The ice was gone, now, and he could feel some warmth reclaiming the skin. He closed his eyes and willed himself back to the real world.

He opened his eyes to find himself lying on the sidewalk outside the coroner's building. His muscles were weak and initially permitted no movement. Thoughts of his sister returned some strength to his limbs. He sat up too quickly and the world spun around him. He closed his eyes again, waited for the nausea to pass. As he did, he became aware of the dull throbbing in his throat. Eyes still closed David felt the crusted, ruined skin of his neck. His eyes flashed open.

Even as his fingers continued to probe the wound, he looked for his sister. He had the sidewalk to himself. Di was nowhere within his field of vision. "The van," he croaked and winced at the pain his voice brought to him. He staggered to his feet and walked like a drunk back to where he had parked.

The van remained in its spot and David opened the driver's door. "Di?" The passenger seat was empty. David looked in the back of the van, saw the sound and lighting equipment, but no sign of his twin. He reached for his phone before he noticed hers sitting on the dash. The edges of his vision began to blur, much as had happened when the thing in the fog grasped his throat.

(Di, where'd you go?) He heard no reply and he couldn't sense her at all. *(Diane?)*

The inside of the van began to spin. David closed his eyes against the assault, but it did no good. He felt weightless and breathless at the same time, an astronaut flying above the atmosphere without benefit of a space suit. Then he felt nothing.

II.

DAVID

CHAPTER EIGHT

A SLEEPY COLLEGE TOWN

"They'd better get back, soon," Jung remarked. He sat on the small bench to the right of the guesthouse front door, between Joyce and LaMontagne. "And that van better be in one piece. If those assholes went out and got drunk—"

"Settle down," Joyce said over the rim of her coffee cup. She watched the sun crest the treetops in the distance, felt its warmth on her skin. "After what they've been through the last day or two, if they needed to go out for a drink, so what? And that van was barely holding together, anyway. It's not like you'd notice a new dent in the fender. They'll be back. Don't worry."

LaMontagne sipped from his coffee cup. "We need to find a hotel, too. Barney Fife won't let us stay here much longer. I'm kinda surprised the cops haven't showed up to throw us out already."

Joyce frowned. "That's a little dramatic, don't you think?"

"How's this for dramatic? Cousin Jethro makes bail. His mother hung herself. He blames us. Or, at least, you. You think he's gonna go about his daily business with the people he thinks killed his mother—that would be us—staying in his guesthouse?" LaMontagne shook his head. "Not for a minute. He's gonna be looking for some payback. I suggest we be elsewhere when he does."

"Yeah, yeah, he's got a point," Jung agreed. "All these fucking hillbillies are armed to the teeth. Maybe we should get outta here."

"You two need to settle down," Joyce replied. She stifled a

laugh. Jung seemed to think anyone who didn't live on either coast was straight out of *Deliverance*. Joyce herself was guilty of that same way of thinking from time to time, so she could hardly scold him for it. She thought, however, *He might have a point.* The youngest of the Andrews offspring never wanted them here in the first place. With his mother's death their presence under his roof could only end badly. Joyce swallowed. "But maybe you're right. When David and Di get back we'll find a hotel like that detective said and we'll let him know where we are. No need to take chances with Mr. Andrews."

"Let's just hope those two get back soon," LaMontagne added.

Joyce took another sip of her coffee. The cool morning air chilled her for the first time since she sat down. Her eyes traveled up the gently sloping hill to the Victorian built by George Andrews in 1947. The house was still, quiet. Add in the bird song and the chatter of squirrels and chipmunks and Joyce should have found the entire scene relaxing, even for a city girl. Instead, her eyes lingered on the old house. She suppressed another chill.

David had to force himself to slow the van before the turn onto the Andrews driveway. He had been moving at a pretty good clip along the backroads, much too fast for the width of the road and his unfamiliarity with it. Fortunately, he encountered no one after leaving the center of Lansing, human, deer, or otherwise. It was the first thing that had gone his way since he got off the plane.

For the past thirty minutes he'd been calling his sister.

(Diane? Di, answer me, please.)

She had thus far refused to answer. He probed, gently at first, but with greater and greater urgency the longer his sister remained silent. He got nothing back, not even a sense of her. That was almost always a sign of distance between them, but he could not remember a time when the absence of her was so … absolute. Not when she went to D.C. as the guest of a science fiction convention, and he overslept and missed the plane. Even then he could still sense her anger at him for his drunken binge the night before. Too, when she moved to Long Island, placing three thousand miles between them, he could still feel her, if only peripherally. This, though, this was different. It was as if she had simply vanished off the face of the Earth. The gooseflesh on his arms had little to do with the chilly morning air.

What if she's still in the fog?

It was a ridiculous idea. Neither of them could remain in there for more than a minute or two without the other. They discovered that particular rule during a working vacation in Paris. Di had wanted to speak to Oscar Wilde, and so David went along with her just to shut her up. They stood in front of his grave at Père Lachaise and Di got her wish. The conversation bored David to tears. First, he conjured up a chair for himself to sit and then a futon when it appeared the conversation was getting deeper. The fog-furniture, at least, was more comfortable than standing there. Eventually he became so bored he simply left the fog for the real world. Di came back a minute after him, livid at her forced departure. She barely spoke to him the rest of their vacation.

So she couldn't still be inside the fog. *Then where the hell was she?*

The van crested the hill, and he could see the guesthouse below. It was at that moment a thought occurred to him for the first time since losing track of his sister. *What if she can't respond?* The idea hit him hard enough to make him slam on the brakes. The van skidded on the gravel and David nearly lost control. The woods that bordered the property grew very large in the windshield. He spun the wheel hard to the right and eased off the brake. The van corrected itself reluctantly. The officer watching the house regarded him and shook his head slowly. *Knock that shit off or I'll give you a field sobriety test right now, jerkoff,* his expression said. David waved at him and proceeded down the driveway at a much slower pace.

The idea nagged at him. Di could be hurt, she could be unconscious. That, at least, would explain the lack of response. *She could be asleep, too.* Possible but unlikely. He would still be able to sense her presence. Right now he sensed simply ... nothing.

He stopped in front of the guesthouse and killed the engine. It sputtered its protest for a moment before falling silent. He leaned back in the driver's seat and closed his eyes.

(Di? Di, honey, where are you? Talk to me, goddammit!) Her reply was the same as it had been since he lost her in the fog.

David swallowed hard and stepped out of the van. He stumbled and leaned back against it. His head still throbbed, he still felt off-balance and nauseated. He closed his eyes and breathed deeply the morning air. Never had it taken him this long to recover from the Game. Then again, never before had he experienced anything like he had the past few days. He took three more deep breaths and felt the nausea leave him. Tentatively he opened his eyes.

The first thing he saw was Joyce looming in the guesthouse doorway. The scowl she hurled his way was one usually reserved for uncooperative locals or network suits who tried to interfere with the show. Her arms were crossed, her brow was creased, and she tapped her foot like a teacher who has just caught her student with a cheat sheet.

"Well?" Her tone was as hard as her expression.

Her anger might be justified, from her own point of view, anyway, but David found he had little patience for it. "Joyce, we have a problem."

She craned her neck to look past him at the empty van. "Where's your sister?" Her tone was still hard, but it was now tinged with something akin to concern. "Christ, she's not in the hospital again, is she?"

David ran his hand through his hair. "I don't know. I don't think so. It's kind of a long story."

She grabbed his arm and pulled him toward the door. "Tell me while you get your bag."

"What?" David planted his feet and pulled his arm from Joyce's grip. "I'm not going anywhere. Did you hear what I just said? Di is gone, I don't know where. There's no way in hell I'm leaving here before she comes back."

Joyce's eyes softened, just a little. She stepped closer to him and placed her hands on his shoulders. "Honey, she'll be back. But I think we both know where she went. Come on, let's go inside. You can tell me about it while we collect our things." She paused, her eyes suddenly focused on his neck. "What the hell happened?" She reached for the withered skin, but her fingers stopped a few inches short.

David shrugged. "Forget about that. Joyce—"

She turned her eyes back on him quickly, so quickly David took a startled step back. She lowered her voice and hissed, "We can't stay here. You heard the detective. And what about Brian Andrews? He came at us last night, and that's when there were cops all over the place. If he gets out on bail and comes back, with no one here to stop him …" She shook her head. "It's safer for all of us, including Di, if we vacate the premises. We'll find a hotel in town and look for Diane from there."

"I'm not going anywhere."

"Sure you're not." She took his arm again and started for the door.

David allowed himself to be led inside. He saw Joyce's bags in the doorway between the kitchen and the living room. Noise from upstairs told him both Jung and LaMontagne were gathering their things, as well.

He tried his sister again. After several moments of silence, he slammed his hand down on the kitchen table. The pain was sharp and brief, and it cleared his head. He sat in one of the chairs and rubbed his eyes.

"No, no, no." Joyce was behind him, tugging on his arm. "We have to leave. What you're doing is the opposite of leaving. C'mon, David, get a move on. I already packed most of your stuff. Di's, too. We need to go."

"What if she comes back here?"

"She won't have to," Joyce replied. "Once we're out there you can do your thing and track her down."

David swallowed. "I can't feel her. Not at all."

"That doesn't mean anything." Joyce placed her hands beneath his arms and heaved him to his feet. "We'll find your sister. But first we need to leave this place." The soundman and the cameraman shuffled through the kitchen, their arms loaded with their personal effects. They spoke among themselves, paid little heed to the two people in the kitchen. Once outside LaMontagne announced, "We're ready."

"Are you coming?"

David looked into Joyce's eyes. *No*, he thought. *It's the last thing I want to do.* But Joyce was right about one thing. While he doubted Brian Andrews would be released, at least this quickly, it was possible. And if he found David alone there …

"Let's go," he said at last.

"That's m'boy!" Joyce clapped him on the back, nearly knocked him out of the chair. "Di will be fine, you'll see. Let's just get ourselves situated, and we'll go find her."

David said nothing. He allowed Joyce to lead him outside.

The rough gravel of the Andrews driveway gave way to smooth pavement as Jung turned the van onto the main road. The men in the front seat sounded relieved to have put the old Victorian in the rearview, and their conversation quickly turned to the heady topic of baseball. Joyce tuned them out. Her thoughts were of her clients, the one beside her, and the one whom Joyce had a good idea of her present circumstances.

David no doubt loved his sister, but he had gone blind to her problems. There was little doubt in Joyce's mind that Di had gone in search of a dealer. And in a college town like Lansing, there would be no shortage. The girl was probably high as a kite already. She had her doubts from the start that Di was clean. Her freak out at the cemetery and later at the guesthouse confirmed she was going through some serious withdrawal. David, of course, was too blinded by care for his sister and his own problems to see clearly. Anyone with an ounce of sense would know Di had gone under, and she would not resurface until she was good and ready. Judging by past experience that could be a few hours from now or a few months. Joyce scowled and hoped it was the former. She disliked the idea of David searching for someone who did not want to be found, growing more frustrated and anxious with each day's failure. And it was all her fault. She should never have dragged Di back into the field in the first place. As much as it bothered her, Joyce knew this was on her shoulders alone.

She opened her pocketbook and fumbled for her cigarette case. A minute later she felt much better.

Jung mumbled something from up front and rolled down his window. Joyce felt the breeze on her face and closed her eyes. It was another twenty minutes before they pulled into the parking lot of a Holiday Inn.

The hotel room was unremarkable in every way, identical to thousands of others from Brooklyn to Burbank. David had drifted in and out of sleep since their arrival, exhaustion overriding all else. After one particular stretch, during which he didn't dream, his eyes fluttered open and glanced about the nondescript room. The clock next to his bed read 12:35. He started to settle back in. The events of the past night came back to him all at once and he kicked off the covers and vaulted from the bed.

(*Di, you there?*)

How could he have fallen asleep? He remembered checking in to the hotel, the elevator ride up to the fourth floor, getting into his room ... Nothing after that.

(*Di?*)

He paced around the room, using his Inside Voice, aware that voice was becoming more frantic with each unanswered attempt. The small writing desk provided an opportunistic target, and he kicked it with everything he had. His resulting howl was equal parts pain and frustration. David limped back to the bed and sat on the edge and massaged his bruised toes.

When the pain subsided, he walked to the window and glanced outside. Some people went about their business and a few cars occupied the street, but there was little in the way of activity out there. *Just a sleepy college town during summer recess.*

David checked his phone but found no new messages. He tossed it onto the bed. He needed to find Di. Having lost half the day already—how the hell had he managed to fall asleep?— angered him in a way he could not explain. He was going to go out and find his sister, and he would not come back until he did. But what he needed now more than anything was a shower.

He spent a little longer than usual in there, letting the hot water drive the cobwebs from his mind and the anxiety from his head. It was a full forty minutes before he emerged from the shower and toweled himself off. He felt better immediately. Even the dry, cracked skin on his neck felt better to the touch. A few minutes after that he was dressed and heading for the lobby.

He was in the elevator when the flash hit him. For a moment he found himself standing in front of a large building. People, mostly young, milled about in groups of varying size. Someone stood in front of him, a young man in a white tee shirt. His skin was browned by the sun. He was saying something to David, but his words were unintelligible. Something about the scene made his eyes hurt so David closed them. When he opened them again he was back inside the Holiday Inn elevator, slumped in the corner of the car.

The elevator door was open, and an elderly couple stood at the threshold, staring at him and muttering to each other about today's generation.

David pulled himself to his feet and stumbled from the elevator. The old couple was admonishing him, that much he knew, but he paid them no mind. He staggered a few more feet until he found a chair. He did not so much sit down as he collapsed.

(Di? Di, where are you?)

There was no response. And still, he could get no sense of her. But he knew their minds had linked, if only for a moment. She was alive.

He tried to stand, failed. His legs and arms would not work. David closed his eyes again and steadied his breathing. Feeling returned to his limbs with glacial speed. He may have remained in the chair for an hour, maybe two, before he regained the ability to move.

The first thing he saw was the front desk and the three employees behind it. They went about their business oblivious to him. His eyes focused on the large round clock on the wall behind them. 1:40. Was that all? Good. Lots of daylight left.

He was nearly to the front door when he spotted LaMontagne at the hotel bar. The cameraman sat next to someone David took to be a traveling salesman. They chatted amicably, but David could see the boredom LaMontagne was trying so hard to hide.

Good. Keep talking to your new buddy. Just don't look this way for another few seconds. David headed for exit.

LaMontagne's head turned and caught sight of him. "David!" he called.

David stopped as if he'd run into an invisible wall. *Fuck.* He turned in LaMontagne's direction and waved and made for the exit. He was outside and looking at the rather diminutive parking lot that served the hotel. Despite its small size it was still nearly empty. David headed for the street.

"Need something?" LaMontagne asked from behind him.

"Just going for a walk," David replied without looking over his shoulder.

"Looking for your sister, right?"

"No, just for a walk." Jesus, he needed to work on his lying.

"I'll come with you."

"What for? I'm only gonna go around the block."

"Uh huh."

David's lips compressed into a thin line. He glanced about the parking lot, saw no one. *Just lay him out and be done with it. By the time he gets back on his feet you'll be too far ahead for him to catch up.* That thought appealed to him for a few reasons. But there was another, more pragmatic side that stopped him from launching a surprise attack on the cameraman. Instead, he said simply, "Fine."

"Just wish I had my camera. Filming you finding Diane would be gold." LaMontagne nodded in the direction of the street. "Teddy took the van to go find an electronics store. One of those idiot cops fucked up the recording equipment when they searched the van."

David couldn't give shit one about the recording equipment or the van, and he trusted LaMontagne to read that in his expression. "You have an iPhone, right? Use that."

Without awaiting a reply, David strode across the parking lot.

CHAPTER NINE

DO YOUR THING, MAN

They walked past several businesses one would expect to find in a college town. Every other storefront belonged to a coffee shop, a used book dealer, or a laundromat. Comic book stores and hookah lounges were well-represented. Bars of varying degrees of seediness stood on every corner. There were still plenty of students present in the city, taking summer courses instead of spending two solid months at Debauchery Beach. LaMontagne spent most of the time ogling some of those students and making comments under his breath. David ignored him.

Every so often he would use his Inside Voice but Di never picked up the phone. If not for that brief flash he received in the hotel elevator he would not be certain if his sister was even alive. He kept at it anyway, all the while glancing into every alley, every parking lot. He received no impressions that Di had ever been near any of them.

At 5:30 LaMontagne suggested getting something to eat. As much as David wanted to continue the search he had to admit he, too, was hungry. They chose a small café with sidewalk seating and ordered some food. LaMontagne offered to buy the first round. As much as a beer or three sounded like heaven David refused. He drank an iced tea and ate his quesadillas while LaMontagne checked his phone.

"You know we've walked almost twelve thousand steps since leaving the hotel."

"Good exercise," David replied.

"I don't think I've walked twelve thousand steps in the last week."

"Uh huh."

"Five texts from Joyce. She wants to know where we are and what we're doing."

"Tell her we're having dinner."

"She's sending Teddy to the cemetery, see if their records can ID whoever is in that old grave."

"That's not a bad idea."

David tried Di. He was becoming used to receiving no reply. There was no sense of his twin, just a void where she should have been. She may as well have been back in Paris.

"I'll get this one," LaMontagne said and pulled a Visa card out of his wallet.

"Thanks."

Once their bill was paid and the waiter tipped they resumed their trek across Lansing. The shops and stores were in various stages of closing down for the night. David glanced at his watch. 6:45. The sky had yet to show any signs of dusk.

"This town rolls up the sidewalks early, huh?"

"I suppose," David replied.

"Lots of noise and lights over there. Wanna check it out?"

David looked to where LaMontagne indicated. The lights of a sports stadium blazed a block away and the sound of cheering fans reached their ears. David looked more closely at the large building. Was that—

He took off running. LaMontagne offered a surprised grunt from behind him but David was already twenty feet ahead. He kept his eyes on the building and as he got closer he saw it was indeed a small stadium. A couple hundred people milled about outside; most appeared to be college-age. They drank from brown paper bags and smoked their cigarettes and joints.

This was the place. Di had been here. Perhaps she still was. *(Di? Di, can you hear me?)* Still nothing. He tried again, all the while moving amongst the crowd and scanning faces.

LaMontagne finally caught up. He was panting and his shirt was plastered to his torso with sweat. "I am way too fucking old to run in this humidity," he said through quick gasps of air.

David worked his way through the throngs of young people. He saw no sign of his sister, no sign she had ever been here. But he knew otherwise. This was the building behind the man in the white tee shirt in his vision …The man in the white tee shirt.

David had a new objective. This time it took him only a moment to locate the target. The tanned man in the white tee was still there, still moving among the crowds, chatting with anyone who came into his orbit.

Almost immediately David witnessed a hand-to-hand transaction between him and a woman who looked to be about twenty. She pocketed whatever he handed her and walked away trying—and failing—to appear nonchalant. David's eyes narrowed. "Bingo."

David moved in closer to the dealer keeping several people between them. He didn't want the man's attention. LaMontagne followed behind him. He seemed to have guessed the object of his companion's attention. David got as close as he dared and then closed his eyes.

LaMontagne placed a hand on his shoulder. "What's the plan?"

"Don't touch me," David hissed. When the cameraman stepped back, clearly surprised, David turned in his direction. "Physical contact really scrambles everything and this is hard enough as it is."

LaMontagne looked from David to the man in the white tee shirt. "What exactly are you trying to do?"

"Just be quiet and back up a few steps. I need to concentrate."

"I thought you couldn't read the living."

"Would you shut up?"

LaMontagne opened his mouth to reply but apparently thought better of it. He backed away, hands up. "Do your thing, man."

David refocused on the drug dealer. He expected nothing and in this he wasn't disappointed. A few steps closer. The man glanced his way and regarded David with open suspicion. He tilted his head and placed his hands on his hips. A second man joined the first. They spoke to each other without taking their eyes from the new arrival.

David closed his eyes, focused everything on his target. His head began to pound. He could feel fresh sweat break out on his forehead, his arms. Even with Di next to him this would be difficult if not impossible. Alone—

He pushed harder. David got a vague impression the man's name was Jenkins or something close to it. Even that was more than he expected. The pounding in his head picked up the pace. His heart joined in and David felt the double-bass heavy metal rhythm that now threatened to derail the whole attempt. He gritted his teeth and threw everything he had at the man.

For a brief moment the pounding subsided, and David could feel a link between him and the dealer. He knew the young woman who had just bought an eighth of coke from him was a regular customer and was named Christine or Kristen. The man had also done business with a few people now enjoying the game inside the stadium as well as a few passersby. Then the pounding returned. It blinded him, nearly severed the tenuous connection to the man in the white tee. David bit down and forced the connection to remain open.

He became aware his breathing was fast and ragged. It took everything he had to maintain contact. All at once his head was filled with fire. He tried to scream; he wasn't sure if he ever made a sound. The connection let go and David's knees buckled. He grabbed for a concrete planter, missed, and wound up on the ground. A bolt of lightning ripped across his chest and this time he did scream.

At first, he thought he was paralyzed. He tried to place his hand over his heart but couldn't control his limbs. It took him several attempts, but he managed to get one hand on his chest. His head still swam in fire, but he could feel the heat beginning to drop off. At the same time his heart switched tempo from Megadeth to merely Aerosmith. David knew enough to remain still until his body finished punishing him for trying to solo what had always been difficult for a two-person act.

As the world began to solidify again, he could hear someone nearby shouting. David opened one eye, saw only a red haze. He wiped at the blood and looked at it with his other eye. He lay on the cold concrete, his hair covered with sweat. It mixed with the blood coming from the cut just above his eye.

LaMontagne knelt beside him, shouting his name, looking into his eyes. The cameraman looked about frantically and shouted some more. David got the impression there were several people nearby scrambling about. For a brief moment he couldn't remember how he came to be here. He tried to speak, failed. Instead, he coughed and tasted copper.

David winced when he pushed himself up. He got as far as his knees and stopped, not trusting himself enough to be fully upright. One hand found the planter and the other went to his forehead and came away bloody. David looked at the blood dumbly for a moment before concluding he was not likely to bleed to death. His heart had moved on from Aerosmith and was now providing a steady beat for Simon and Garfunkel. His breathing was returning to normal, as well, and the pain was mostly gone from his chest. His head, however, pounded merrily along. He pushed himself the rest of the way to his feet.

"David, you okay? Talk to me, man. Christ, is anyone out here a doctor?"

LaMontagne was not the only one shouting. David looked about, found the drug dealer flat on his back, his buddy knelt over him, and shouted for help. A small crowd of people had gathered in a semicircle around them. The dealer's buddy was busy emptying the fallen man's pockets and filling his own. Several small bags filled with white or green tumbled free only to be stuffed into pockets a moment later. David could see a thin stream of blood had run from the dealer's nose. The man at first appeared dead but David noticed his chest rising and falling.

"And stop those motherfuckers!" the dealer's partner shouted. He pointed at David and LaMontagne. Several bystanders looked in their direction. "They did this!"

David struggled to stay on his feet. The world spun in a complete circle around him and he would have gone down again had LaMontagne not been there to grab him. They stagger-stepped away from the fallen dealer and his partner. The cut on his forehead had mostly stopped leaking blood into his eye and David could see the far side of the parking lot and the tree line that bordered it. He pointed and coughed out, "There."

"You read my mind," LaMontagne replied seemingly without irony. He led David in the indicated direction.

There was still a lot of commotion from behind them and now several bystanders were shouting for them to stop. David wanted to tell LaMontagne to keep moving but he could not speak. Bile threatened to erupt from him with each step. Fortunately, he didn't vomit, and LaMontagne knew enough to keep going. It felt like months before they reached the tree line but at last it stood before them.

The bright lights of the stadium could not penetrate more than ten feet into the darkness of the woods. More shouts from behind him. David dared not look back, fearful even that that simple head movement would send him crashing to the ground again, with or without LaMontagne propping him up. Instead, he took his first step into the woods.

The darkness hid a sharp decline and the ground disappeared beneath their feet. David's sense of balance gave up the ghost and he tumbled down the hill. Branches tore at his skin and his clothes. He cried out with each impact. He had time to wonder, *How fucking far down does this go?* before at last he came to a stop at the bottom of the hill. His head and hands splashed into cold water.

He lay still for several moments, willing his heart to slow and the world to stop spinning. This time he did vomit. The stream helpfully carried away the former contents of his stomach. The water helped with the dizziness, too, and brought him back to full alertness. He was instantly aware of LaMontagne calling for him. He needed only a moment more to regain control of most of his limbs. His hand scooped water into his mouth to mitigate the taste of the vomit.

David rolled onto his back, sputtering. The thin stream meandered past him and disappeared into the darkness of the woods. He pushed himself onto his knees and looked about tentatively. He was alone in the darkness for a few more seconds before LaMontagne materialized and took him by the arm. David stood on legs that still felt like putty. He took a deep breath, released it and watched it frost the air. "I'm okay," he said, and coughed again.

"We need to put some distance between us and everyone up there," LaMontagne said with a look toward the stadium. "They don't know what happened but they're pretty sure we had something to do with it. Which way we going?"

"Surprise me," David replied and spat onto the ground.

LaMontagne looked about frantically before settling on a direction. "Come on, this way."

David allowed himself to be led into the darkened woods. They started north along the bank, slowly, feeling their way. The canopy above shielded them from the early-evening sky. LaMontagne had his phone out and tried to navigate by its light. Every few steps he would look to his left, toward the noise of the stadium. So far no one had come after them.

The branches scratched their skin and David learned quickly to shield his eyes with his free hand. Their progress felt slow but they managed to put a good deal of distance between them and the stadium. David couldn't hear anything now but the sound of the stream. He caught only intermittent flashes of the sky through the branches above them. They slowed and stopped when they came to a rock large enough for both of them to sit down.

David's legs still shook a little but most of the weakness and disorientation he experienced at the stadium were gone. He was tired, yes, but it was a normal tired, and he could deal with that.

He knelt beside the stream and scooped up some water with his cupped hands. He splashed it onto his face, rubbed his forehead and neck. "Stupid, stupid, stupid," he said as much to the river as to his companion.

"What, exactly?" LaMontagne asked, panting.

"Trying to read the living almost never works. What the hell is wrong with you?" He scrubbed his arms and said, "Don't drink, because that'll make you do stupid things. See, Joyce? I can be just as stupid without the alcohol." When he finished cleaning himself he sat back down on the rock.

The sounds of the woods finally penetrated his self-preoccupation. The stream babbled its song, the crickets joined the chorus, the dead leaves rustled as something or other loped about the darkness. David took it all in. It helped with the pounding in his head and stilled the tremors in his limbs. His companion remained silent, glancing furtively about, trying to gauge their surroundings.

At last, David offered, "I had to try. Diane was standing in front of that guy earlier."

"Did you at least get anything from him?" LaMontagne asked.

"Not much, no. He saw Di, but she didn't try to buy anything from him, so I suppose that's good news. I didn't get much else."

LaMontagne's feet shuffled uneasily in the carpet of old leaves and pine needles that covered the ground. He started to speak, stopped, tried again.

"Spit it out," David told him.

"I know you think I sold to your sister back then," LaMontagne said after a few moments of silence.

David did not look at him. "You saying you never did?"

"One time, David, just one time."

David's hands curled into fists. Despite his exhaustion an image leaped into his head. LaMontagne meeting with Di in a dark, secluded area and slipping a small baggie into her hand. His sister would favor him with a smile before she wandered off to indulge. Had anything else occurred between them? What he and his friends had called "a little sumpin-sumpin" when they were teenagers? The idea of his sister paying for her coke with sex—and the thought had occurred to him a few times in the past—suddenly seemed even more repulsive when he pictured her with the man who stood beside him currently.

He thought about jumping up, grabbing LaMontagne and just beating him into the ground. Tremors in his legs and arms reminded him physical exertion was not a good idea at present. "You are so fucking lucky you waited until now for your confession."

"It was a favor, okay? I don't deal in that shit. She was desperate, she came to me. I didn't wanna do it. She was in bad shape. I'm sorry!"

David still wanted to throttle him, pound the smaller man straight into the dirt. He didn't. It wasn't this man's fault Di was a drug addict. And LaMontagne's eyes were full of regret, not deception. Perhaps it had been only that one time. The urge to break his jaw remained, but some of David's anger had burned off. He shrugged.

"I'm really sorry, man," LaMontagne added.

"Shut the fuck up." David looked up at the canopy above his head. The sky was still bright but it was growing darker to the east. He took deep breaths, slowing his heartbeat.

LaMontagne continued to peer into the darkness around them. "What do we do now? Where to?"

David didn't know.

CHAPTER TEN

ALMOST 9,000 MORE STEPS

The woods continued for what seemed like miles. Both men stumbled repeatedly in the near-dark. The canopy of branches and leaves effectively screened out whatever was left of the day's light, allowing only a sliver here and there. Both men used their phones as flashlights but somehow the woods seemed even darker around them. The stream wended its way beside them, whispering gently. Night critters had begun to make their presence known, although they stopped moving and making noise at the approach of the two men, resuming once these intruders had moved beyond their immediate area. A few mosquitos managed to find them and dine on them, and the two men walked into more than a few spider webs strewn across their path. LaMontagne waved his arms and cursed each time, drawing a wry smile from his companion.

David had recovered from his attempt to read the dealer outside the stadium, although his head still throbbed. The rest of the physical symptoms were gone and he was grateful for that. God knew he was having enough trouble navigating in the woods without having to lean on LaMontagne for support. Despite the man's help in getting them away from the stadium crowd he still wanted to throttle the son of a bitch. When his mind conjured the image of LaMontagne handing a small baggie to his sister David squashed it right away. This was not the time. But it might be, eventually.

They could see faint light to their left coming from somewhere on the other side of an embankment about 150 feet away. David listened but could hear nothing aside from the stream. He stopped, looked at LaMontagne.

"What do you think?" the cameraman asked.

"I think I'm sick of these fucking woods," David replied. He turned and headed toward the embankment. He didn't know how much distance they had travelled from the stadium but they had to be far enough away by now, and he hadn't lied to LaMontagne. He really was sick of these fucking woods.

He slipped a little bit on the tall, slick grass that covered the embankment. As he neared the top, he caught his first glimpse of the darkened sky. He stood at the edge of a large parking lot. A strip mall made up of perhaps twelve different storefronts loomed in the distance. The lot was barren and the storefronts posted giant signs that read CLOSED or THIS SPACE FOR LEASE. What looked to be a main road bordered the strip mall to their left. A single car drove past blasting something by Nirvana.

"Where are we?" LaMontagne asked when he crested the hill.

"Got me. Call Jung, tell him to come get us." David got them an address from the front window of a former pizza joint. He found a conveniently placed bench and sat down as LaMontagne called his partner.

David rubbed his temples. Despite what it would do for his headache he wanted a beer. No, that might not be enough this time. Tonight might call for Johnnie Walker, at least. After everything that had happened tonight, he deserved a few rounds. Hell, even those small watering holes they had walked past earlier would do. He just needed Jung to show up.

"He's not picking up. No answer to texts, either. Joyce texted nine more times, though. She's demanding to know where we are."

"Tell her to calm the fuck down and ask her where Jung is."

LaMontagne worked his phone. After another moment, he said, "She thinks he's still at the cemetery. She's gonna call him to pick us up."

David leaned forward, face in his hands. The throbbing in his head continued unabated. In addition to the Johnnie Walker, he was going to need a giant bottle of Excedrin or Tylenol to go with it.

"Okay, he's not answering her, either. She just texted me. She left him a voicemail."

"For Christ's sake." He closed his eyes. All he wanted was a stiff drink and something to get rid of this goddamned headache. "Can you find out if he's still at the cemetery? Maybe track his phone?"

"I think so." LaMontagne went to work on his phone. After a few minutes of swearing under his breath and furious button stabs to the screen he said, "Got it. He's at the cemetery, like Joyce said."

"How far is Mount Olive from here?"

LaMontagne consulted his phone again. His shoulders sagged. "Three-point-six miles. Now wait just a minute."

David stood on legs that felt better and stretched.

"We are *not* walking to the fucking cemetery! It'll take forever! And what if he leaves before we get there? Then what do we do?"

David smirked. "Think of it this way. You'll get even more steps in today. It'll be a personal record."

LaMontagne blinked at him. He stuttered before finally spitting out, "Uber. I'm gonna call Uber."

David placed his hand over LaMontagne's phone. "Look at us. Look at me. You think any of these college kids with their Priuses are gonna want my filthy ass in their car? We can walk. It's not that far."

"Three-point-six miles! How many steps is that?"

"How the hell do I know? Google it." David started across the parking lot.

LaMontagne Googled it. He swore quite loudly before taking off after his companion.

The sky was a deep purple when the gates of Mount Olive Cemetery came into view. They had passed several bars and taverns along the way. David glanced into each and every one of them. No Di—he had long since given up the notion that he would find his twin inside one of them—but, good God, how he needed a drink. The sidewalk cafés were the worst. Several times all it would require was an outstretched hand and he could finish off some kid's beer and deal with the consequences after. Somehow, he avoided the temptation each time. If they had to do any more walking tonight, though, all bets were definitely off.

"I just did almost 9,000 more steps," LaMontagne told him. He plopped down on a bench to the side of the main cemetery entrance. He took a deep breath, held it, exhaled. Then he kicked off his sneakers. "My feet are fucking killing me."

In truth David was in much the same shape. Seeing as how LaMontagne was not going to get up for at least a few minutes David joined him on the bench. His own feet hurt and his back was starting to act up. The throbbing in his head had mostly faded and for that, at least, he was grateful.

During their trek from the strip mall LaMontagne had kept an eye on Jung's location. The soundman remained at the cemetery. David couldn't imagine what was taking him so long but he was dammed glad to know their ride back to the hotel was just a short distance away.

After several minutes of watching LaMontagne massage his feet and complain about everything under the sun, David stood and stretched again. "Come on, let's cross the finish line."

LaMontagne swore again and put his sneakers back on. He accepted David's offered hand and followed him into the cemetery.

The lights of civilization faded behind them. The cemetery itself lacked anything in the way of streetlights. Headstones were oddly shaped monoliths sprung from the ground at unusual angles. The trees, comforting in daylight, served only to blot out the last of the purple light from above.

The two men followed the blacktop up a short hill and around a bend to the main office. The building was small with an attached garage and a narrow driveway. Parked in the driveway was Jung's van.

"Thank Christ," LaMontagne muttered. He ran to the van, looked inside. "No Teddy," he announced.

Light spilled from the office windows. David strode to the front door and swung it open. He had never been inside the cemetery office, but he knew it had never looked like this. The four chairs inside the waiting room were overturned; one of them was smashed to kindling. The hairs on David's arm stood at attention.

A small TV mounted to the wall showed the action at Comerica Park. The Tigers trailed the Rockies 3-0 in the bottom of the fifth. For some reason David would remember that detail.

LaMontagne gasped as he got his first look inside the office.

"Umm, hello?" David called. Aside from the low volume of the TV the office was silent.

"David, this ain't right."

No shit, he wanted to say. Instead, he made for the counter.

It was low and David peeked over the top. Several binders full of papers littered the small desk and the floor. The computer monitor hung by its power cord off the edge of the desk like the dangling head of a dead serpent. The lone chair was lying in pieces in the corner. A small pool of blood marred the carpet in front of the far wall. Beyond the counter and the desk was a single closed door. David exchanged a look with LaMontagne before he walked around the counter. David pushed open the door just a crack.

"Teddy?" LaMontagne called.

David started at the unexpected noise behind him. He hissed, "Quiet!" before he returned his attention to the door.

On the other side was a short hallway that led to another door. The light in the ceiling was smashed but there was enough light from the office for him to see it was empty. David glanced over his shoulder at LaMontagne before he headed for the second door.

It opened into the garage. Several small landscaping vehicles took up most of the space. A large workbench stood to their left. Above the workbench and tacked to the drywall was a Detroit Tigers calendar. July's hero was Miguel Cabrera launching a moon shot against the Red Sox. Numerous tools of varying sizes hung from hooks on the walls.

"Teddy?" LaMontagne called again. When there was no

reply, from Jung or anyone, LaMontagne looked at David and asked, "Where could he be?"

David walked around a small backhoe and stopped as if he'd run into an invisible wall.

A body knelt on the concrete floor. The head was several feet away. Its face was turned away from David, a fact for which he was grateful. A large pool of blood covered much of the floor. The dead man's hands were tied with bungee cord behind his back.

"Holy shit," he whispered.

"What the actual fuck!" LaMontagne yelled. "What the fuck is going on here?" He backed away toward the door that led back to the office. "We gotta call the cops right fucking now!"

"Wait."

"Fuck that!" LaMontagne retreated through the door.

David followed him back into the office. LaMontagne was pressing almost every button on the office phone before he gave up and pulled his cell out of his pocket.

David grabbed him. "Wait a minute. Hang on a minute."

"What the hell for?" His eyes were wild. They darted every which way as if he expected whoever was responsible for the body in the garage to step out of the walls and finish the job.

"Just one minute, okay? Jim, that wasn't Jung back there. I don't know who it was, probably the poor bastard who works here. But it wasn't Teddy, okay? We're gonna call the cops. Obviously, we will, but just give me a second here."

LaMontagne's eyes traveled from his phone to the door which led to the garage and back before he refocused on David. He nodded quite vociferously. "Okay. Okay, I'm cool."

"I know you are. First, we're gonna check the van. If he's not in there, then we'll come back in here. I want to check something before you make that call. Okay?"

LaMontagne nodded again.

They exited the building and walked around to the driveway. David didn't look in the direction of the open garage. He didn't want to think about what was inside. The van was unlocked. It was also empty. David breathed a long sigh of relief.

"Okay, let's head back inside."

Once they were back in the office David bent down behind

the counter and looked at the computer monitor. The screen was still alive and displayed a map of the cemetery. "This isn't tampering with evidence or anything," he muttered as he angled the monitor for a better look at the screen. A single spot on the map was highlighted in yellow. "That's what I thought," he told his companion. LaMontagne nodded absently and looked nervously out the window.

David aimed the mouse at the highlighted spot and clicked it. The area enlarged to take up the screen. The small rectangle made of dotted lines sat right next to what he took to be a large tree. The words beneath the rectangle read SILAS CALDER, 1843. David nodded. "And now we have a name."

"Get what you wanted?" LaMontagne remained by the window. His hands clenched and unclenched. His feet shifted on the old carpet.

"Teddy did come by here to find out about that grave, like Joyce said. It looks like he succeeded."

"Uh huh. So where the fuck is he?"

"He's probably up there, taking pics or something. We can find out for sure."

LaMontagne scanned the area outside the office one last time before he opened the door. David followed him outside.

"You know," LaMontagne told him as they began to ascend the hill, "if he went up there to see the grave, why didn't he drive? Why leave the van down here? That's a hell of a hill to climb by foot."

"We'll ask him when we get there."

That's a load of shit, he told himself. *I don't know what we'll find up there but it won't be Jung taking pictures with his phone.* He couldn't say that, of course. Despite their physical exhaustion he had no doubt LaMontagne would set a speed record getting to that grave if he suspected his friend was in trouble, so David kept quiet as they made their way up the hill.

They paused at the top. The large tree under which Silas Calder was spending eternity hid every sign of the grave. If not for a single pinprick of light that reached David's eyes from within that zone of darkness he wouldn't have known there was anything there at all.

"Someone's in there," LaMontagne said, and pointed to the light. "Teddy! You there?" His voice echoed off the hills around them. It was the only reply he received.

David pulled out his phone and instructed LaMontagne to do the same. The meager light was enough, and they advanced toward the grave. David kept his eyes fixed on the small dot of blue light that somehow existed within the absolute darkness beneath the tree. It was how he nearly missed the shovel.

It lay on the ground directly at his feet. Had he not seen it at the last second he would have tripped over it. David knelt and waved his phone slowly over the instrument. Fresh dirt covered the tip of the business end, and more loose dirt was scattered about to the edges of his phone's light.

"Oh, this doesn't look good at all," LaMontagne said. "Teddy!"

David stood and advanced toward the grave. The small blue light grew in size until David recognized it as a cellphone. It was on the ground amid a pile of fresh dirt. He was about to kneel down to retrieve it when LaMontagne surged past him and scooped it out of the dirt.

"It's Teddy's," he said, his voice flat.

David waved his phone slowly in front of him.

A small rectangular object glinted at his feet. David knelt and retrieved the item. The nametag read *M. O'Leary.*

David looked up. The dark form of a mound of dirt stood a few feet before him. David approached it. He looked over the side, into the hole where Silas Calder was laid to rest in the year 1843. There was indeed a body within. It lay within the rotted remains of a plain, wooden casket. The cadaver's arms and legs dangled outside the ancient box. The body glistened in the light from his phone but it seemed wrong. David couldn't recognize it. Or perhaps his conscious mind refused to allow him to recognize it. He took a step back without knowing he had moved at all.

"Any sign of Teddy?" LaMontagne called from somewhere back in the real world.

David backed away from the open grave until he was at last out from beneath the tree. He turned to LaMontagne.

Red and blue flashing lights bounced off the trees and headstones around them quite suddenly. Both men turned and saw a police cruiser making its way slowly up the hill. The car's spotlight swept along the gentle slopes of the cemetery ... and it was getting closer.

"Split! Go, right now," David told LaMontagne. "I'll handle this."

"What? No! Where's Teddy?"

David eyed the approaching cruiser. "If you don't go right now, they'll see you. If they've already been inside the office, and I'm pretty sure they have, they won't leave here until they've found what they're looking for. No need for both of us to be thrown into a cell. Now go!" He shoved the other man.

LaMontagne stumbled. He righted himself by bracing against a tall headstone. His eyes darted from David to the flashing red and blue lights. "Fuck!"

David tossed the nametag to him. "Take this for now. Go!"

LaMontagne caught the small object and disappeared into the darkness.

When David was sure LaMontagne was gone he stepped onto the road, arms raised above his head.

THEN

The flight from Newark International took forever. Including the layover in Atlanta they were looking at over thirteen hours sitting in the cramped seats of economy class. David, at least, could boast an aisle seat. Di sat next to him, sandwiched between him and their mother. Their father sat across the aisle from David, snoozing in his chair and missing the inflight movie, *The Iron Giant*. In truth, David wasn't paying close attention to the movie, either.

There was a very attractive girl seated directly in front of his father. He noticed her when they boarded. He had even managed to bump into her on his way past. She had smiled politely and apologized for her clumsiness. David laughed a bit too loudly, especially considering he'd gone out of his way to make physical contact. He caught her sneaking a look at him when the flight attendant brought the drinks cart around. She took a Sprite; David wanted, more than anything, a can of Bud. But it seemed unlikely in the extreme the lovely woman with the nametag that read LAURIE would provide him with one. He was obviously underage, and they weren't yet in Europe, where, David heard, kids were allowed to drink. He settled on a Sprite. He didn't particularly care for it, but if the girl across the aisle saw him with the same drink, well …

They had made eye contact when he caught her looking. He smiled. She smiled back. That would be the extent of their interaction. David imagined one of them following the other to the bathroom. He'd heard of the Mile High Club and wanted very much to be a member. He did eventually join, but it would be on a private jet sixteen years later, when they were flying to Germany for a special episode of *The Cemetery Game*. For sixteen-year-old David Walsh, sharing a look with the girl seated in front of his father was as close as he would come.

Di was reading a magazine. David glanced at it but looked away quickly. He couldn't read while inside any type of moving vehicle without becoming violently ill. That included, unfortunately, jetliners. He envied his twin. Not that he particularly enjoyed reading, but anything would be better than watching a kids' movie while he contorted his body to fit in the ridiculously small space of row 47.

The plane hit a patch of turbulence. There were a few gasps from the more nervous passengers. Di took one hand off the magazine and placed it on his.

David found himself no longer in his seat. The area was dark but there was enough light for him to see. He stood in a large space filled with pallets of suitcases and other bags. The floor beneath his feet rumbled much more deeply than it had when he was seated next to his sister. At first he thought it was smoke lying low to the deck. His heart leaped into his throat. If the plane was on fire—It took him a moment to realize it was fog.

Thank God for that, he thought.

Di stood next to him. Her eyes were wide as they moved over every inch of their new surroundings. "David," she whispered, "it's happening again."

"I know," he replied, with much more confidence than he felt.

He heard a low-key growl, then a whimper. David turned and saw a beagle in a crate. The small dog looked directly at him. Its head was down but it wagged its tail with much enthusiasm.

"Hey, boy," David said in his most soothing tone. He knelt in front of the crate, held a hand toward the animal. It leaned forward as if to sniff his hand but quickly recoiled. It whimpered again. "It's okay. I'm not gonna hurt you."

"Stop playing around," Diane scolded him. "What if it bites you?"

(I don't think it can), David thought. *(Not right now,*

anyway.) He had no idea how he knew that, but he was sure he was correct.

"Don't bet on it," Di replied.

David flashed back to their grandfather's funeral. He couldn't remember the details, not from two years ago, but he felt a jolt of *déjà vu* when Di replied to him.

Before he could respond his eyes fell on a large, long crate fastened to the deck with thick black straps. Without realizing it he had taken a few steps toward the object. He hadn't realized he moved until he felt Di fall into step beside him.

"I feel it, too," she remarked when he looked at her. "Something's in there."

David found he had no curiosity regarding the contents of the box, yet he was powerless to stop himself from advancing toward it. They got close, within five or six feet, before they halted their approach.

"Now what?" he asked the baggage compartment.

A woman sat on the other end of the crate. She looked around the room, her blue-green eyes moving lazily from spot to spot. She didn't look directly at the twins, not even when she spoke to them. "What are your names, children?"

"I'm Diane, this is my brother, David."

David would have preferred the woman not know their names, although he couldn't explain why. He squeezed his sister's hand with a bit more strength.

"It's okay," Di told him. "She's not going to hurt us. Like you said, I don't think she can."

"You'd better be right," David whispered.

"I would never hurt a child," the woman told him. She had yet to look directly at them. "My name is Grace Tzepos. I teach math and science for grades ten through twelve. It is nice to meet you, Diane and David."

"Likewise," Di replied.

David cast a look at his sister. It was not nice to meet Grace Tzepos. He wanted nothing to do with any of this. He would never admit it to his sister but he was scared, just as scared as he was two years earlier in that cemetery in Shreveport.

"My sons are taking me home," Tzepos told them. "I came

from a small village in the mountains. Eptahori, it's called."
She smiled at a memory. "I haven't been back there in eighteen
years. It will be nice to see it again."

David swallowed. "Yeah, that's great." He turned to his
sister. "We need to go, Di."

Di indicated the woman with a nod of her head. "Wait."

"For what? To get murdered? I say we get outta here right
now, while we still can!"

Tzepos slid off the crate and approached them.

David stiffened. He tried to back up, found he could not
move. As had happened two years ago, he was rooted to the
spot. The woman closed the distance between them. David
winced and looked away.

"You're dead, aren't you?" Di asked. Her tone was soft,
gentle.

"I believe so," Tzepos replied. Her tone was the mirror
image of Di's. "I don't remember how it happened, but I don't
believe I suffered. My boys are bringing my body home." She
patted the large crate. "I always said I wanted to be buried in the
same village where I grew up."

David finally looked at her. She stood before them, no more
than a foot or so away. She had finally turned her eyes on them.
David prayed his sister was right. If Grace Tzepos decided to
grab for them she couldn't miss.

"Did you have a heart attack or something?" David
surprised himself with the question. Why would he ask this
woman anything? Why prolong the encounter? When Grace
tilted her head a bit, he swallowed and continued. "You look
young, is what I mean."

"I'm eighty-seven," she replied with a smile.

David and Di exchanged a glance. "Like Grandpa," his sister
whispered. "He didn't look old, either."

"Can you give my boys a message from me, please? I didn't
get a chance to tell them myself before, well, before I left them."

Di smiled. "Of course, Mrs. Tzepos."

"Please, dear, call me Grace."

"Grace, then."

David wanted to leap out of his skin. How could Di be so

calm in front of this ... what? Ghost? What else could she be? Had he known how to escape from the baggage compartment he would be out of there right now, the woman's message be damned.

Grace looked at the twins' hands, still clasped. She placed hers over theirs. Her touch was warm, soothing. It made David think of warm breezes in September. The tension left his muscles all at once. "Tell them there is a will. Tell them to look in the bottom left drawer of the desk in my husband's old study. I hid it in an envelope that contained all our old passports and airline tickets. Their uncle plans on fighting them for the estate. They don't have anything to worry about, now."

"We will tell them," Di replied. Her voice was soft, solemn.

Grace smiled. "Thank you, my dear. I'm going to rest now." She released their hands and retreated a few steps. The fog rolled up from the deck and surrounded her.

David tugged on his sister's hand. "Di, we need to go."

Di smiled again. "I get it, now. This." She indicated with a sweep of her arm. "I think I know what all this is."

"Great. You can tell me when we're out of here."

David stopped. He realized he had no idea how to make it happen. "Umm."

Di released his hand.

David found himself back in his seat in row 47. He blinked, shook his head to clear it. Di sat next to him, the magazine in her lap. Their mother snoozed next to her. No one near them reacted in any way to their sudden reappearance.

"Just like the funeral," David whispered.

"Yeah," Di replied. "Just like that."

CHAPTER ELEVEN

SLEEPING DOGS

"Mr. Walsh, how good to see you again."

Ahmad looked even more like he just stepped out of a Humphrey Bogart movie than he had in the Andrews living room. He took the chair on the opposite side of the small table. His clothes were wrinkled, his hair a rat's nest. He grunted as he eased his bulk into the small chair and placed a manila folder on the tabletop. He flipped it open and examined the papers inside. His expression cycled through annoyance, feigned surprise, and, finally, feigned awe. He closed the file and laced his meaty fingers together in front of him. "People sure do have a way of winding up dead around you."

David kept his expression blank and his mouth closed.

"I should be home watching a Bond marathon on BBC America. Instead, I'm here. Why am I here? Would you care to guess?" When no answer presented itself, Ahmad continued. "Two dead. One, Scott Alexander, aged fifty-three, divorced father of one. He maintained the equipment at Mount Olive. He also had a wonderful singing voice and went to church every Sunday. He was beheaded with what looks like a small-bladed weapon, possibly a hatchet. The other, well, going by the license in his wallet he's one of your people, one Theodore Jung. But we don't know for sure because he was skinned. Facial ID is impossible and so are fingerprints. So we'll have to use DNA." Ahmad leaned a bit closer. "The M.E. said it's possible the man was skinned while still alive. Now what kind of sick fuck would do something like that?"

David's poker face faltered just a bit. He had seen the body in the grave belonging to Silas Calder, had seen the blood and muscle glistening in the moonlight. He'd suspected all along it was Jung. And if that wasn't bad enough, to be skinned alive …

David swallowed. He kept his eyes on the tabletop, but he could feel Ahmad's eyes drilling into him.

After a moment he looked up. "I didn't do it."

Ahmad leaned back and spread his arms as if to give David a hug. "Well, shit! Why didn't you say so earlier? I guess we can let you go, then! So sorry for detaining you, sir. Have a safe and pleasant flight back to L.A." The detective's eyes hardened. He folded his arms across his chest.

The men stared at each other across the table for several minutes. David used the time to reinstall his poker face. It wasn't easy given what he had just been told. In fact, he couldn't be certain he succeeded in anything other than looking scared and guilty. He swallowed again.

"You have a fresh wound on your forehead," Ahmad stated matter-of-factly.

Yeah, I fell down while trying to read the mind of a drug dealer who saw my sister.

"Slipped in the shower."

Ahmad nodded. "I hate when that happens." He shifted in his chair. "You know, after our last meet-and-greet, I did some research on you. There's a ton of videos online starring you and your sister. Most of them are old episodes of *The Cemetery Game*, but there are also quite a few about what went on in North Platte. Seems the old lady's suicide the other night wasn't a unique experience for you."

David glanced past Ahmad to the two-way mirror on the wall and was surprised at how neutral his expression remained. He did not feel neutral at all.

"Hey! Maybe Misters Alexander and Jung killed themselves, too! It would certainly fit with Mrs. Andrews and the man in Nebraska." Ahmad pulled out his phone, began tapping the screen. "What was his name again? I saw it earlier …"

"Higgins. Mike Higgins."

Your wife says she's sorry for having that affair.

"That's the guy!" Ahmad returned his phone to his coat pocket. "Saw a whole lot of online rantings by fans of your show, demanding you and your sister be held responsible for that man's death. Lots of them seemed to think you two drove him to it."

Darcy said you suck and she's glad she's dead.

We did, David thought.

Ahmad leaned as far across the table as his gut would allow. His voice was barely a whisper. "Come on, you can tell me. Just between friends here. Did you really make up all that shit for Higgins? His dead wife having an affair with his business partner? That was it, wasn't it? There are a couple versions of the story out there. And you know how the internet is. Can't believe a goddamned word you read. So c'mon, tell me."

David's poker face slipped. His eyes narrowed until Ahmad took up his entire field of vision. It wasn't the detective he saw. Instead, it was the living room of a modest home in North Platte, Nebraska.

He saw himself sitting on the man's sofa while Di paced slowly about the room. David was drunk, Diane was high as a kite and jonesing for more. LaMontagne and Jung were there to record for all posterity what would happen next. Mike Higgins sat on the sofa, his hands welded together in his lap, his expression anxious. His feet tapped an unsteady, rapid beat on the carpet.

Neither twin was in any condition to be in front of the camera. They had likewise been unable to get anything from his wife. It was not that the dead woman was unwilling to speak to them; they had been far too out of it to do more than go through the motions for both the camera and Mr. Higgins. So they did something they had vowed never to do.

"We lied." David spoke almost without realizing he had said anything. He looked at Ahmad with complete surprise, his stone expression gone.

"No shit. You lied."

David swallowed. "We lied. We didn't know the guy would react the way he did. The only reason we were there in the first place was because our manager thought we should hit some small towns instead of working just the big cities." *Because maybe a small town will provide fewer distractions,* is what Joyce had told them. He and Di both knew what she meant. Joyce's plan failed miserably. There were plenty of bars in North Platte, Nebraska, and no shortage of illegal substances. The twins managed to find what they needed with little effort. "The whole point was to do something different. Let the fans see something other than just another murder mystery."

"That went well. And did you lie to Mrs. Andrews, too?"

David's hands curled into fists. Just as quickly he unclenched them. None of this was Ahmad's fault. Were David seated on the other side of the table he might have asked that question himself.

"We didn't get anything out of her husband, and we told her as much."

"I see."

David held up both hands. "Look, Mr. Ahmad, we didn't have anything to do with Mrs. Andrews killing herself. I swear to you."

Ahmad's fingers tapped the manila envelope on the table. "There's still the matter of the two dead men at the cemetery and your presence there."

"I already gave a statement to the officer."

Ahmad opened the folder again. His finger traced its way down the second page. "You were looking for your sister." He looked at David again. "Does she usually spend her free time in cemeteries after hours? I mean, I know people are into some freaky shit, but, seriously."

David shrugged.

Ahmad stood and scooped up the manila folder. "We'll be holding on to you until preliminary forensics tells me whether or not I can charge you with a crime . Have you made your phone call yet?"

David shook his head.

"Desk sergeant will hook you up. Now if you don't mind, I'm gonna go back home and try to catch the end of *Live and Let Die.*"

"I'll save you the trouble. Bond kills the bad guy and gets the girl."

"Doesn't he always?" Ahmad knocked on the door and a cop on the other side opened it. David was alone in the room for some time.

He called Joyce, of course. She was completely freaked out and quite indignant at David's detention and the Lansing PD in general. David said little. The intermittent beep on the line reminded him the call was being recorded. He even pointed it out to Joyce when she started to describe what the agency's lawyers were going to do to the city's police department. He asked about Di even though he knew what Joyce's answer would be. He wasn't wrong. She promised to have him out in a couple hours. David hung up and waited for an officer to escort him to a holding cell.

He had caught the barest impression of the cells the night before when he and Di had probed Brian Andrews. His perception of them had been way off. There were four cells and they were quite large. He couldn't quite resist the temptation to glance into each one as he walked past. Most of the residents of the lockup looked to be college kids sleeping off the latest bender. Some were awake but most were either asleep or passed out. Some looked up as David was escorted by, more grateful to have something new to look at rather than out of any genuine curiosity.

David breathed a sigh of relief when he didn't see Brian Andrews among the cell block residents. *Must have made bail. Or was released.* Either was fine with him. The last thing he wanted was to spend a night next to the man. He wasn't likely to have calmed down since the previous night, not that David could blame him. And despite his present situation David wouldn't be able to stay awake all night waiting for Andrews to make his move. A man that size and with that much rage could do an awful lot of damage before the cops managed to open the cell door and come to David's rescue.

The cop stopped him at the last cell. David looked inside. Three college-age kids and two older gents were asleep—or pretending to be—on the benches therein. A single toilet sat in the far corner. The toilet paper roll was empty.

The cop opened the door and David crossed the threshold.

He watched the guard lock the door and return the way he'd come. David found an empty bench and sat down.

He tried Di with his Inside Voice again. Of course, she didn't respond.

The images from the cemetery creeped slowly back into his head. The kneeling, decapitated body in the garage. The blood. The nametag that seemed to have no connection to anything. The unearthed grave of Silas Calder, died 1843. The mutilated body of Teddy Jung in the rotted remains of that ancient box.

Facial ID is impossible and so are fingerprints.

Teddy.

David realized he never really knew the soundman. He'd worked on the show since the first season, three or four episodes into the series. David couldn't remember any incidents with him, unpleasant or otherwise. He was friendly, professional, never caused any problems for anyone. He showed up every day and did his job. And David had ignored him. He had no ill will toward Teddy. David had, in fact, had no feelings about him at all. He was just *there*. Now he wasn't.

Despite his present surroundings David found he couldn't keep his eyes open. He glanced at his cellmates again. None had moved a muscle since his arrival. *Keep it that way, boys,* he thought. With the image of Teddy Jung's corpse still in his mind, David drifted off to sleep.

He dreamed of his sister, as he knew he would. They were young and standing near their grandfather's final resting place. This time when they were pulled into the fog it was no surprise to him. They spoke with their grandfather, a pleasant conversation made all the better because in the dream, neither twin was the least bit afraid. Di willed them back to the real world.

Then he found himself on the flight to Greece. Their first time on a plane since returning from Shreveport. This time, however, there was no fear. They spoke with the old teacher and the conversation was just as pleasant as the one they shared two years earlier with their dead grandfather. David couldn't remember the name of the village where Grace Tzepos was to be buried. For some reason he felt guilty about that. Di had gotten them back to the land of the living that time, too.

The next dream they were in college. David could see his younger self standing next to his twin as the cops investigated the accident scene. Di's dorm mate—what the hell was her name?—being loaded into the back of the ambulance. The destination was not the hospital but the morgue. They were once again in the mist. The dead girl asked them to explain to her mother what had happened. This time it had been David who got them out of the mist.

Then a whirlwind as the twins practiced this new ability. Meeting Joyce. Signing the series contract. His drinking getting worse. Di suddenly disappearing, sometimes for hours, sometimes for days. Then North Platte. And after that ...

David awoke so suddenly he toppled from the bench. He struck his head on the cold, concrete floor and yelped. It took a moment for the stars to clear from his vision. He expected one or more of his cellmates to awaken but he heard nothing from them. Good.

Sleeping dogs and all that, he thought. He pushed himself first to his knees and climbed back onto the bench.

He shook his head like a prizefighter who'd just taken a haymaker from his opponent. Dizzy and suddenly out of breath, David gripped the edges of the bench to keep from falling again onto the cold floor. He closed his eyes and counted back from ten. When the countdown was complete, he opened his eyes and took a long, slow breath. He felt better immediately. That was when he noticed the mist.

It rolled slowly across the floor of the holding cell. Thin tendrils reached out as if they were searching for something. David's eyes scanned the corridor on the other side of the bars and the adjoining cells. He couldn't see from where the mist originated. A fire in the building? No. He smelled no smoke, and surely the officers on duty would have reacted by now.

As the mist advanced farther into the cell David regarded it. He sat back on the bench and reached out his hand. The mist produced another tendril. It wafted slowly toward David's outstretched fingers.

"What are you?" David whispered.

The tendril divided itself and reached David's hand. There were five of them now and they snaked around his fingers before making their way to his wrist. Just as David was about to pull back the tendrils became long, skeletal fingers. They grabbed David's wrist and pulled.

David yelped as he was wrenched from his perch. He landed hard on the cold stone floor of the holding cell. He scrambled back on hands and knees. The boney fingers no longer held him. He expected to feel the bench behind him, but it seemed to have vanished along with the holding cell. David's whipped his head around, eyes wide and taking in his new surroundings.

He was back at Mount Olive. The cold concrete floor of the Lansing Police Department had been replaced by the soft dirt beneath a large tree that hid the grave of Silas Calder. The grave was open, the dirt formerly covering the casket displayed in large piles scattered around the gravesite. Despite the absence of any light source David could see quite clearly the numerous footprints in the dirt. Quite a few people, it seemed, had visited this grave in the recent past.

Against his will he found himself crawling on hands and knees toward the open grave. His rebellious limbs refused to stop or even slow their advance. The hole in the ground grew larger until David finally came to a stop before it. His head and eyes joined the insurrection begun by his arms and legs and David peered over the rim of the hole and into the black earth.

He expected to see Ted Jung's body within, or perhaps it would be Silas Calder himself. Instead, he saw nothing but ancient dirt and the rotted remains of a wooden coffin. David released a breath and, surprising even himself, he giggled. "Jesus Christ, man, wake the fuck up. Enough with this bullshit."

David found he could move once more. His body, it seemed, had ended its rebellion. He pushed himself back from the edge of the grave and got his feet under him. Once he cleared the tree he looked about. The fog was thick out here; it blanketed the ground and rose to a height of perhaps four feet. Many of the headstones were obscured although some of the taller specimens managed to poke through. They resembled swimmers struggling to keep their heads above water.

"So now what?" he asked the empty cemetery. When he received nothing in the way of a reply, he announced, "Okay, I can wake up n—"

(DAVID!)

The bomb exploded deep within his brain. David screamed and clutched his head with both hands. He staggered in random directions, colliding with headstones and trees, a human pinball bouncing from bumper to bumper. His knee struck a low headstone and David was on the ground again. Lightning lanced up his thigh and took up residence at the base of his spine. He probably let loose another scream but he could hear nothing but the sledgehammer shattering the inside of his skull.

He caught an image of Diane through the featureless white that was now his universe. She was on her hands and knees on what looked like a linoleum floor. Blood covered much of her face. There was something next to her; the image coalesced into an overturned chair.

(David, I need you now!) she screamed, her Inside Voice was hoarse and cracked as if it belonged to an elderly, lifelong chain-smoker.

He wanted to reach for her, wanted to pull her close and get her the hell out of that room. He found he was not capable of even a reply. David lay on the ground of Mount Olive, blind, deaf and paralyzed.

No, not Mount Olive. The cold ground of the cemetery had given way to the cold concrete floor of the holding cell. David sat bolt upright and immediately regretted it. The sledgehammer was still inside his skull banging merrily away. David groaned and his hands went to his head.

"What the fuck happened to you, man?" someone close by asked.

The last thing on Earth David wanted to do was open his eyes. He opened them, anyway, just a slit. A college kid knelt on the floor in front of him. The rest of his cellmates regarded him with everything from concern to aggravation.

"You might'a hit your head," College Kid told him. "You probably shouldn't move. I'm sure a cop will be in here any minute," he added with a nod toward the security camera in the corner.

"I need to get to Diane," he mumbled.

"I got to Diane, already," one of the older men chimed. "She was fucking excellent. Now shut the fuck up so I can get some sleep."

David ignored him.

He reached a hand toward College Kid. With a disapproving scowl and another glance toward the corridor College Kid helped him back onto his bench.

III.

DIANE

CHAPTER TWELVE

THE BARRIER

Diane had no idea where she was. She stood on a deserted street with dark storefronts. The street was devoid of any vehicles. No sounds reached her ears save for the litter skipping across the blacktop, propelled by a slight summer breeze. If not for the streetlights, few and far between, she might have been in some post-apocalyptic city, the last surviving person on Earth.

She looked one way, then the other. She took a step forward, stopped. Which way to go? *Trust in Google Maps*, she thought and reached for her phone. Her back pocket was empty. She cursed when she realized she left it in the van. Just before she and David tried to contact Emily Andrews …

David.

It hit her all at once. Diane staggered until her shoulder found the side of a building. She nearly slumped but her legs refused to buckle. She stayed that way for several moments, panting, legs and arms shaking.

They had managed to make contact with Emily Andrews, she remembered that much. Everything else was a blur.

(David?)

She got the merest impression of him. She could feel he was out of the fog but not much more. He didn't answer.

She tried again and a third time with no reply. Could she have wandered that far from him? She had no memory of leaving the fog—nor of the reason—and she couldn't remember how she came to stand on this deserted street. She assumed she was still in Lansing. Beyond that she couldn't begin to guess. He should still be close enough to pick up her call. So why didn't he answer?

Because he can't. He might have made it back to the real world but that doesn't mean he's okay. He's probably face down in the street somewhere, about to become a spirit himself.

"Shut up," Diane mumbled.

Her legs and arms were steadied. She pushed herself away from the building and once again examined both ends of the street. "Six of one, half-dozen of another," she whispered, and chose a direction.

She stayed close to the buildings as she passed them. She felt much better than she had even a few moments before, but she didn't yet trust her legs not to dump her onto the sidewalk. Her right hand brushed the brick and stucco facades of the buildings and glided across the glass windows as a cross street presented itself roughly 150 feet ahead. She heard no traffic, saw no lights. Still, it had to lead back to civilization.

A man stepped onto the sidewalk at the corner ahead of her. He stood directly in her path, between her and the cross street, which seemed at least a mile distant.

Diane froze. Gooseflesh rose on her arms and her heart skipped a beat. The man—she could see no features but something about the figure suggested a male—remained perfectly still. He simply stood in her path. He appeared to be dressed in a long coat; it undulated in the breeze, shortening and lengthening the shadows around him.

Diane backed up. Perhaps it would be better to try the other end of the street. She walked backwards, unwilling to take her eyes from the man. He remained where he was, said nothing, and made no gestures. When Diane found herself back to her starting point, with enough distance between her and the stranger, she turned and quickened her pace.

She made it fifty feet before she glanced over her shoulder. The man stood perhaps twenty feet behind her. She still couldn't make out any features, cloaked as he was in shadow, although now she got the impression the long coat was really a robe. Diane's breath caught in her throat. Adrenaline flooded her bloodstream. Her heart pounded in her chest, her breath came in short, quick gulps. She ran for all she was worth.

She reached the end of the street. The cross street on this side seemed like more of a main drag, or, at least, what passed for one in Lansing. Her head whipped first left, then right. There were no pedestrians, no cars. A fence on the other side of the street cut off access to an open field. Beyond that field, a great distance away, Diane could hear the sounds of a highway.

Without checking to see where the man was behind her Diane raced across the street. She reached the fence, a chain-link and weather-beaten monstrosity, and hurled herself at it. She scrambled up and over the fence and crashed down to the ground on the other side.

The man stood on the opposite side of the fence. He was a shadow, his features hidden in the near-complete darkness around them. Diane screamed and shrank back. The man made no move to follow her over the fence; in fact he made no move at all. He might have been a statue for all she could tell.

Diane pushed herself to her feet and raced into the open field. The grass and weeds were high but she had no problem keeping her feet under her. No more than a minute after she scaled the fence Diane caught her first glimpse of the highway ahead. It was on much higher ground so she could see no cars. She could, however, hear plenty of them. Diane sprinted in that direction.

She reached the base of the hill and looked up. The brush was thick and tall. Diane took a tentative step onto the hill. She could feel no ground beneath her feet, only vines and leaves. Sharp thorns cut deep into the flesh of her hands and knuckles. Diane yelped and pulled them back.

She moved ten feet to her right and tried again. If anything, the brush was thicker in this spot. She ran along the border between the field and the hill. Each time she tried to force her way into the brush she was repelled. Her hands and forearms were slick with blood. She wiped them on her jeans and continued moving.

The border of thick brush began to angle away from the highway. "No, no, no, no," Diane shouted in ever-increasing volume. When the field gave way to more thick brush on the side,

Diane stopped. She gasped for breath, felt her heart smashing against her ribcage. She placed her bloody hands on her knees and gulped air until she felt some semblance of strength return to her limbs. As her breathing slowed she turned, ready to try the other direction.

The man stood directly in front of her.

Diane gasped and fell onto her back.

The man said nothing, and didn't move. His black robe rippled in the breeze. He was so close Diane could hear the rough, heavy fabric scratch against itself. She peered into the shadows that hid his face, and still saw nothing.

Sudden anger replaced the fear that had consumed her since she first spied him at the end of the street. Diane's lips curled back and revealed her teeth. "Fine," she breathed. "You want this? Let's go!"

She threw herself at the man , bloody fingers scratching for purchase on anything she could touch. The robe felt old and brittle. Her fingernails punctured it easily; deep cold penetrated her hands. Diane gasped. She threw her whole body against his like a linebacker pushing through for a touchdown. Her momentum carried them both to the cold ground.

Diane screamed into the black that concealed the man's face. She ignored the numbness working its way up her arms and toward her shoulders. Her hands smashed his arms into the ground again and again. The man didn't struggle, and didn't make a single sound. Was he out already?

Diane let go of one arm and swung with all she had at the where she imagined his jaw to be. She connected, although the blood covering her fist made it more of a glancing blow. Still the man offered no resistance. Diane rolled off him and came up in a crouch. She coiled her legs beneath her and prepared to launch at him again if he tried to rise. He did not. In fact, he did not move at all.

Diane inched closer. She raised her fist, and looked for any sign the man was conscious. He lay still on the ground, a shadow among shadows. The mist thinned and parted as her fingers reached for him ...

Diane stopped.

Where had the mist come from? Had it been there the whole time? No, she didn't think so. Her head whipped from side to side. The entire field, as far as she could see, was blanketed by the mist. It seemed to thicken as she watched.

At the same moment, she realized she could no longer hear the sounds from the highway. Diane turned and looked up the hill. The hill was gone, as was the highway and all its traffic. The field was perfectly level in all directions. She also couldn't see the fence she'd scaled or the buildings beyond. The cold in her hands and arms, too, had left her.

"Oh, Jesus," she whispered.

She turned back to the man on the ground. The darkness remained but he was gone. Her hands probed the area where the man had fallen and came up empty.

"Where did you go?" Diane asked aloud.

She pushed herself to her feet and once again wiped her hands on her jeans. There was no blood. Diane held up both hands in front of her. There were no wounds, no scratches from the brush, just two perfectly unremarkable hands. She checked her jeans, saw no crimson stains. "What the—"

I was right, she thought. *I'm in the fog. How the hell did it happen? Was I here the whole time?* No, she didn't believe she was. Back on the side street, that was real. The field, the highway, they were real, too. How could she have entered the fog? The transition had always required her willingness to enter and the presence of her brother. Neither had been present in the open field by the highway. So how …

Diane stood straight and willed herself back to the real world. Nothing happened. She tried again. For the first time in her life she felt something blocking her way. It felt like a wall, although she could see no barrier. Why couldn't she leave?

She tried again, but something was different now. Something had changed after this final attempt to leave the fog. The wall, or whatever it was, held firm. Diane's head began to throb. She grimaced against the pain and forced herself against the barrier. Still, she couldn't break through.

A hole appeared in the air in front of her. Beyond it, Diane could see the field across which she had fled. At first, she thought the field was moving. It took her a moment to realize someone was walking through it.

The view changed. The camera through which she viewed the real world panned down. Two bloody hands appeared and displayed themselves for her to see. The hands disappeared and Diane could now see her blood-stained jeans. The camera panned up again and she glimpsed the fence she'd climbed to escape from the man. It seemed her body was walking back across that field but she was no longer in the driver's seat.

Diane pressed her hand against the window. The image rippled but the barrier remained solid. She pounded her fist against it. More ripples cascaded across the image.

"Let me out of here!" she screamed.

Diane watched herself climb the fence again. When her body reached the other side it started to walk along the fence line. The sky was brightening above the deserted streets. Diane could only wait to see where her body took her.

Diane realized she'd been mistaken at first. She wasn't in the fog, not completely. Nor did her current whereabouts feel like the Waiting Room. This was some strange amalgamation of both, as if she had one foot on each side of the border. The fog was light, more of a mist, but it was present. As her physical body moved through the physical world Diane tried to figure out exactly where she was in this one.

The room in which she found herself, although there were no walls or ceiling or any other feature to suggest a confined space, gave the impression of just that. The mist rippled at her passing and curled itself around her legs and her waist. That she could see through it suggested she wasn't in the fog. But where the hell was she?

(David? David I could use a hand right about now.)

She waited, not really expecting a reply and not receiving one.

Diane regarded the mist. Might it be thick enough to provide at least a small comfort? She thought of her favorite chair from back home. The mist coalesced into the form she pictured. "At least there's that," she said to no one. She plopped herself into the chair and thought.

Manipulating the mist was an ability she hadn't used in years. When they were still teens, she and David realized they could manipulate the fog to create simple objects. David had once created a hammock when the spirit they were speaking to droned on endlessly about his service during the First World War. She had giggled, finding humor in her brother's impatience. When he did the same thing during her conversation with Oscar Wilde she was less amused. She found she had the same ability, although she'd used it only twice, and not for at least a dozen years. Diane sat in the mist-chair and watched the show through the window.

The sky brightened as the sun crested the eastern horizon. It was still early-morning but now she could see a few cars zipping along. There were still no pedestrians, but they'd soon be in evidence. She could see more buildings in the distance. Office buildings, by the look of them. Where was she going? Diane wished she knew the layout of the city, but she had simply not made any effort to do so before she left New York.

She tried the window again. It was as solid as before. The ripples were slight this time. She smacked her hand against it more forcefully. The impact barely affected it at all. Diane took a long, slow breath and sat back in the chair. This, at least, brought her a modicum of comfort. *As if you're not really trapped in here, seven hundred miles from the real chair and the real world.*

She guessed an hour had passed judging by what she could make out of the morning sunlight. Street traffic increased the closer her body moved toward the office buildings. She saw the first pedestrians of the day far ahead. They congregated outside the office buildings and smoked their last cigarettes and drank their coffee before beginning their work day.

"Help me!" Diane shouted.

They took no notice of her. Why should they? She hadn't spoken in the real world, she knew. *It was worth a shot*, she thought.

Most of the office workers had gone inside by the time Diane drew close enough for her to see any detail of the people. One woman lingered on the side of the closest building. Her eyes were on her phone and she took no notice of Diane at all.

Diane willed her hand to reach for the woman. "Grab her, grab her," she shouted at the window.

Her hand didn't obey. The woman, however, looked up. Her expression changed from amusement to confusion to concern.

"Oh, honey! Are you okay? What happened to you?"

Diane's brow furrowed until she remembered the blood on her hands and clothes. *Yes,* she thought. *Call the cops! Call somebody!* And then, to the thing in charge of her body, *You blew it, asshole. I look like an assault victim. There's no way the cops don't show up.*

The woman's face took up the entire window. She was looking into Diane's eyes, waiting for an answer. But there would be no answer coming, Diane knew. *Now just call the cops,* Diane thought. *And when David's close enough I bet* he'll *hear me, even in here.* The window shook, just a little, as if her body had received a mild shock.

The image panned down, lingered on the woman's gold nametag. *M. O'Leary,* it proclaimed.

"I think I need help." Diane was unsure who spoke. It took her a moment to recognize the voice as her own. "I'm hurt."

"What?" Diane asked the window.

The woman reached for Diane, and guided her in the direction of the building's front door.

"No, not in there," Diane's voice told the woman. "I think I just need a minute. Can you stay with me? I don't wanna go in there. Too many people."

The woman eyed the front entrance, then looked again at Diane and offered what was probably meant as a supportive smile. "Of course, honey. Here, there's a bench on the other side of the dumpster. It's where they force the smokers to sit but it'll do us just fine for us."

Diane watched the woman guide her body around the dumpster on the side of the building. There was indeed a bench there, situated between two tall, plastic receptacles for cigarette butts.

"Here, sit down," M. O'Leary told Diane. "Catch your breath. Do you want to tell me what happened?"

"No, lady, no!" Diane stood and smacked the window with both hands. "Get back on your goddamned phone and call the fucking cops, for Christ's sake!"

"Just have a seat, honey," M. O'Leary advised. Her tone was soft, the practiced tenor of a mother who had soothed away the nightmares of her children on more than one occasion. She pushed a stray lock of Diane's hair from her eyes. "Do you want to tell me what happened?"

"Well," Diane heard her voice say, "there was a man."

Then Diane's hands were around the woman's throat. M. O'Leary's own hands reflexively tried to free herself. Diane saw her fingers dig themselves into the soft flesh of the woman's neck. O'Leary gasped, her eyes wide. She clawed at Diane's wrists but she could not move them.

"No! Stop!" Diane shouted. "Jesus, you're killing her!"

Diane watched as M. O'Leary's body was forced down to the bench. Her struggles were enough to tumble both of them to the ground but no more than that. Diane's hands remained wrapped around the unfortunate woman's neck. After another moment M. O'Leary's arms dropped away. Diane heard a rattle in the woman's throat before her eyes dimmed.

"My thanks," Diane heard herself say. "I had not considered our appearance. I suppose a woman covered with blood would draw attention."

Diane took a step back from the window. Her eyes remained fixed on the dead woman even as she watched her hands begin to remove the woman's clothes.

"You ... you heard me?" she asked the fog.

There was no reply. Diane watched her body undress the dead woman and strip off her own bloody clothes.

I hope they don't fit. I hope they look so ridiculous someone notices.

"No one will care," her voice told her.

Diane started.

You heard that?

"Oh, yes," her voice replied. "Once again, I thank you."

Diane's jaw dropped.

She watched herself slip into the woman's outfit. Her bloody hands wiped themselves on her old clothes before she flung them into the dumpster. Her body grunted when she lifted the woman's body off the ground. It took everything she had but she managed to get the dead woman into the dumpster, as well. Then she closed the top. M. O'Leary's left arm hung outside. Diane saw her hand go to the woman's fingers. A diamond and a wedding band adorned her finger. Diane held the dead woman's hand in front of her eyes, examining the rings for a moment before she placed the arm inside the dumpster.

Diane's body took a step toward the street, stopped. Her hand went to the nametag on her lapel and tore it free. Diane got the impression whoever was controlling her body had stuffed the nametag into her pocket.

Diane's body emerged from the alley between the buildings and continued on her way. No one took notice of her in their rush to get to work.

CHAPTER THIRTEEN

THE FIRE-AND-BRIMSTONE KIND

It was probably around noon, judging by the position of the sun in the sky. Diane's view out the window was of a crowded sidewalk. No one looked up from their feet or their phones to notice her. Shops of all kinds lined each side of the street. People entered and exited those shops and went about their day.

"And here I am, stuck in here," Diane remarked at the people who passed by her window. "You didn't hear that, did you?" she asked the current occupant of the driver's seat. "No, you can't hear what I say, only what I think. I'm gonna have to be careful with that."

She needed to draw attention to herself. But how? She had no control over her physical form. Her one chance had been the bloody clothes and they were out of the picture, at least until garbage day.

She thought of the woman in the alley. Had she been in the real world she would cry but that was something that simply wasn't possible in the fog. Instead, Diane said a silent prayer for the poor woman. "I couldn't help you, but maybe I can see to it that this son of a bitch pays for what he did."

"I feel strange," she heard herself say.

Diane sat up, casting all thoughts of revenge from her mind.

"I think I'm hungry," the thing told her

Diane chewed her lip for a moment. *Yeah, umm, I haven't eaten anything since early last night,* she thought. *You'll need to eat. And when you can't pay the bill because you didn't take that poor woman's purse, they'll call the cops,* she added.

"I see," the thing replied.

"Fuck!" Diane stood and paced a few steps away from the window. "Goddammit, I can't believe I did that!" She had him. She had him set up and she let him off the hook.

"I guess we'll have to remain hungry for now," her voice informed her. "Don't worry. We'll think of something."

Diane paced about the mist for a few more minutes before she returned to her chair. The view outside the window had changed. The storefronts gave way to what looked to be a sports stadium ahead. Even from a distance she could see dozens of people, most of them college-age, milling about outside.

The thing in the driver's seat seemed headed in that direction. Diane tried to scream, to do anything that would attract attention. She drew a few casual looks from the college kids but no one took any real notice of her.

"Come on, guys. Woman in her thirties, hanging out with kids almost young enough to be her children. Someone look at me, goddammit!"

No one did. In another moment they found themselves a part of the crowd. Diane looked out the window, saw faces pass by, saw kids in groups talking and laughing and drinking. None took more than a cursory interest in her.

The view outside the window panned lazily from left to right. Two girls stared at her momentarily before they turned away and giggled. "I probably look like shit," Diane remarked. "The ultimate example of the walk of shame, kids. Stay in school. Study hard."

The man in the white tee shirt caught her eye. He stood alone, watching the kids mill about. He offered smiles and shook a few hands. If he were better dressed he might be a political candidate trying to secure votes. "White Tee Shirt Guy for president," Diane said to no one. But she knew exactly what he was and what he was doing here. One year ago, hell, six months ago, she would have been talking to him and slipping some cash into his hand as he slipped something more valuable into hers. The thought sent a shiver through her body, as it had uncountable times while she was using. She could very nearly taste it. She looked away from the window.

Diane gave it a few minutes. When she looked back, White Tee Shirt Guy was front and center. He looked her over. Despite the practiced smile and friendly demeanor he was clearly suspicious of this older, disheveled woman in front of him. Still, his skills as a politician won the day. He leaned forward a bit.

"What can I get you, sweetheart?"

"I do not know," Diane heard herself say. "What are your wares?"

"What are my what?" He licked his lips and cast a quick eye about the crowd. He scratched under his lip with his thumb before he turned away from her. "Maybe you better run along now."

An image flashed before Diane's eyes. It was so sudden it buckled her knees and dropped her to the ground. David. He was in a small room. No, not a room. An elevator? The kind you find in any hotel in the country. That seemed right. Diane reached for him, but the image was already gone.

"David! David! Where are you?" She waited for him to respond. She called for him again, tried to reestablish whatever link they shared for that brief moment. It was gone. "No," Diane whimpered. "No, no, come back!" She closed her eyes, thought of nothing but her brother and the elevator. She felt nothing. "Goddammit!" She used the chair to pull herself back to her feet.

"Look, lady, split now. You're fucking up my shit," the dealer told her. He turned his back to her in the age-old stance of every dealer who realized the customer had no money.

The view changed as Diane's eyes scanned the crowd. Two boys halted their approach to the dealer and instead began what they probably hoped appeared to be a casual conversation. Their eyes, however, returned repeatedly to the dealer and the older woman next to him.

White Tee Shirt Guy turned back in her direction. He leaned in close, a move Diane had seen a few times from various dealers when she didn't have enough money. "Get the fuck outta here right now," he hissed. "I got bitches who'll fuck you up so bad your mama won't recognize you."

To back up his claim he nodded slightly to the left. The

window moved in that direction and Diane saw two girls standing perhaps fifteen feet away. Their eyes and body language suggested they were waiting for a signal from White Tee Shirt Guy. "Last chance," he whispered before backing up a step. He looked away, trying to get his politician's mask back into place. When Diane still hadn't moved, he shrugged and walked away.

The two girls approached, already making threats and clearly looking forward to what they were about to do. "You fucked up, gramma," one of them said, lacing her fingers together and cracking her knuckles.

"Young ladies such as yourselves are never to address adults in this manner," Diane heard herself announce. Her tone was angry, even indignant. "Clearly your parents have been neglectful."

"Bitch, *what*?" The first girl, the one who had made the threat, grabbed Diane's arm and began leading her away from White Tee Shirt Guy, away from the crowd. Her companion took hold of Diane's other arm. From the view outside the window it seemed they were taking her toward the wooded area that bordered the stadium lot.

"This twunt just talked about your momma," the second girl exclaimed. "Bitch is crazy!"

"Remove your hands from my person," Diane's voice told them. The woods loomed in front of her. She seemed to be struggling to free herself, but the younger girls held her firmly.

"I'm'a remove your head from your shoulders, you dumb ho," the first hissed in reply.

They reached the edge of the lot. The ground sloped steeply and vanished into the dark of the woods. Diane's body struggled more fiercely now but there seemed no way to escape the iron grip of the two girls. They nodded to each other and heaved Diane over the side.

Her body tumbled down the embankment. Diane felt nothing from the fall; her status as a spectator in her own body seemed to serve as insulation from the physical world.

Upon the first impact, an image flashed before Diane's eyes. A man, an old man, wisps of white hair clinging to his scalp.

He was looking down on her, his expression grim, eyes filled with rage.

When her body struck the ground again Diane received another image. He had something in his hand. A hammer? Maybe. He brought it down several times, his expression becoming more hostile with each downward stroke.

The third and last impact and Diane was inside the spirit's mind. She had time to realize what was happening before she was cast out once more.

The window returned. Diane saw her arms and legs strike the ground as well as a few rocks poking up through the carpet of dead leaves. At last, she came to a stop at the bottom of the hill. Diane heard herself groan and the window went black.

Am I unconscious? If she were it might give her a chance to get back into the driver's seat. Diane closed her eyes, willed herself out of the mist. She expected to feel the bruises as she regained control of her body, but she felt nothing. When she opened her eyes again, she was still in the mist.

Come on, come on. She tried again.

This time she felt something. She couldn't quantify it; the sensation was too fleeting for her to receive anything but the vaguest impression. The old man in the black robe once again flashed before her eyes. He banged his hammer and held it still long enough for Diane to recognize it. A gavel. That was all she got, and she could barely see that. But there was something, if only for a moment. Diane bore down.

The mist around her began to dissipate. Wisps and tendrils vanished or moved farther away. *This is it,* she thought. *Almost there.*

"I hardly think so," she heard her own voice announce.

The mist closed in, and rolled around her in drifts so thick she couldn't see anything below her knees. The window opened again but Diane saw only red. One of her hands awkwardly blotted out the window for a few moments and then her view was clear. She was looking at the thick canopy of trees that obscured much of the daylight. She saw her hands grasp a large tree and use it to pull her body back onto its feet.

"That was unpleasant," the spirit told her.

Maybe for you, Diane thought back. *I thought it was hilarious.*

"Those malcontents will pay dearly for their transgression," the spirit replied.

Yeah, keep telling yourself that.

This time the spirit didn't reply.

You were a judge, Diane thought.

The image outside the window froze.

Yeah, you were. Looked to me like you were the fire-and-brimstone kind, too. Do I have that right?

"Keep silent," the spirit told her.

Diane dug deep, trying to recall what she'd touched in that brief moment when she found herself within the spirit's mind. It took a few moments to find what she was looking for. *Calder. Your name was Calder.*

"How did ..." Her body's voice faltered. Diane could picture the look on her face, brows furrowed, lips pursed. Finally, Calder said, "You're more gifted than I thought. I shall have to be mindful of that." His tone had returned to its previous level of haughty hostility.

The window showed Diane the hill. As it panned up she expected to see the two girls making their way after her but they were nowhere to be found. Apparently tossing her over the side was punishment enough. Diane didn't know if she was thankful or disappointed.

Her body began to walk into the woods. Her gait was awkward, slow. "We're limping." That was good. Despite the injury which she couldn't feel she decided anything that slowed down the spirit was a good thing. "Just don't do any permanent damage," she advised no one. "That's what you get for fucking with a drug dea—"

Wait.

Why had the spirit sought out the dealer in the first place? Had he been an addict in life? "Use your head, idiot," she admonished herself. The date on the headstone was 1843. Diane doubted there were dealers in his time. At least, not as she knew them today. So why go to him?

"Because he caught my attention." The idea struck her all at once. Without realizing it Diane began to pace. The mist swirled around her legs, sending puffs and tendrils into the air.

"You have no idea why you went to that particular man, do you? No. I bet you don't. You walked over to him because I was thinking about him. That's it, isn't it?"

She realized for the first time she was pacing. She stopped, looked at the window. She saw woods, heard birds chirping and squirrels squawking their protest at her presence. She caught the sound of a stream somewhere close by.

"One way to find out." She envisioned the stream, pictured herself drinking from it. "I have to be thirsty," she reasoned. The image she conjured of the stream filled her head until she could see nothing else.

She watched the window, saw herself change direction. Her hands moved tree branches out of her way and swatted at insects that buzzed around her head. The view panned down and she saw fresh droplets of blood on her white sneakers and a tear in the slacks Calder removed from M. O'Leary. The window panned up again, moving more branches out of the way. The sounds of the stream grew louder until at last she came upon it.

A shaft on sunlight penetrated the canopy overhead and illuminated the stream before her. It looked pretty much as she imagined. It was perhaps ten to twelve inches deep and no more than five or six feet wide. She could see rocks and dead leaves at the bottom.

Calder knelt in front of it and Diane got her first look at their appearance. The reflection was anything but clear but she could see enough. Blood had caked on her forehead and her cheeks. Her arms and hands were covered with fresh contusions and lacerations. Her stolen blouse was torn in several places and spotted with dirt and blood. Her hair was a rat's nest and held several leaves and other forest debris.

She watched her hands cup some of the water and bring it to her mouth. Diane tried not to think about what might be in that water and what effects it would have on her body. Instead, she watched, fascinated, as her body reacted to her direction.

"My God, that's it," she whispered, hand on her mouth. "I can't control you, but I *can* aim you, can't I?" Diane began to pace again. It took her less than a second to come up with the next experiment.

She thought of her brother in the elevator. He was no longer in the Andrews guest house, obviously. That made sense, all things considered. So which hotel? He had to be close, or she doubted she'd have gotten anything at all. There were plenty of hotels in Lansing and the surrounding area. Which hotel had Joyce selected for their stay? She could not remember.

Diane focused on the image of the elevator. It had been a flash, nothing more, and she had looked at nothing other than her brother. A number of placards were mounted on the wall behind him. Diane tried to home in on them. The writing was far too small to read, although it doubtless listed the steps to take in an emergency, the number for the front desk, etc. Above it all, top center of the whole thing, was the hotel's logo. Diane lasered her eyes to that precise spot and it swam into sharp focus.

The Holiday Inn.

If she could get Calder to go to the hotel she knew her brother could help her. Even in the mist she felt she could get a message to David if she could just get close enough. Diane cleared her mind of everything but the hotel and her twin. She waited.

Her hands continued to scoop water and bring it to her mouth. She could hear herself slurping and swallowing. Droplets of blood fell from her forehead and were carried away by the slow, steady current of the stream. After another few moments of this Diane watched herself regain her feet.

She returned to the general direction in which she had been headed before the diversion to the stream. The woods were plunged into semidarkness once again as she left the stream and its shaft of sunlight behind. The view outside her window darkened considerably before her eyes adjusted and she could see more clearly.

"That's it," she whispered, "the Holiday Inn. Go to the Holiday Inn. It's somewhere downtown. Just look for the sign. And when we get there ask them to call up to David's room." She put this thought on repeat, thinking of nothing else. "Jesus, if this works …" She stopped herself. "Think of nothing but the hotel, bitch. Let's see if our luck holds."

They walked the woods for what felt like hours. Intermittent sounds reached her ears, the stream, snaking its way through the woods, traffic moving along on the streets and highways of Lansing. Diane ignored all of it. She continued to think of the hotel and her brother.

Her body emerged from the woods onto what appeared to be a main road. Cars whipped by. Several office buildings and storefronts occupied the other side of the road. Dozens of pedestrians filled the sidewalks going about their daily business. Farther down the road the woods ended, and more storefronts and buildings appeared. Diane watched herself set off in that direction.

It was difficult to tell if she was heading for the hotel. She assumed so, as she could see more buildings and more people ahead. "We're definitely heading toward civilization," she said to the window. "Good. That's good. Keep going."

Once the woods were in the rearview, she encountered foot traffic. Diane watched through the window as people reacted to her appearance. A few of them asked if she was all right, did she need help? Diane heard herself tell them she was okay, nothing to be concerned about. They appeared skeptical. Some of them asked if she needed to call someone and even offered their cell phones. Diane suspected if she suddenly changed direction and tried to get the thing controlling her body to take one of the phones she might lose the image of the hotel. She did nothing.

"Might you know the route to Mount Olive?" she heard herself ask a woman in a power suit who had stopped to inquire if she was okay.

"The cemetery?" the woman asked. "Honey, are you sure you're okay?"

"I am well," Diane's voice told her. "I need to reach Mount Olive Cemetery."

The woman appeared unconvinced. After a long stare at Diane, she pointed ahead of them. "Go two more blocks in this direction. Then turn right onto Hawthorne. Follow that street for, I don't know, maybe a mile and a half. Columbus Boulevard will be on your left. Take that and follow it all the way to the cemetery."

"Thank you," Diane's voice replied.

"Are you sure you're all right?"

But Diane's body had already left the woman behind.

"No, no, no," Diane whispered. "The hotel. The Holiday Inn. Why are we going to the cemetery?"

The thing controlling her body did not reply. Of course, it didn't. It couldn't hear her.

Diane filled her head with images of the hotel and David. She watched their progress outside the window. After a couple blocks the thing looked up and Diane could see the street sign for Hawthorne Road. Her body made the turn and continued walking.

Diane could do nothing but watch.

CHAPTER FOURTEEN

A PROPER LADY

Hawthorne Road went on for what seemed like forever. She walked past restaurants and shops, department stores and small office buildings. More people asked if she was all right, more cell phones were offered. Diane heard herself decline their assistance in a very personable tone. Lansing's older citizens didn't offer their assistance so much as they scowled in her direction. One of them, an old man in a tweed suit and fedora, labeled her a "tramp" to his companion, an equally old man who surreptitiously added whiskey to his coffee at a sidewalk café. On a normal day Diane might have had something to say in response to that. Her present circumstances, however, were anything but normal.

"Why are we going to the cemetery?" she asked. "What's there? What do you need?"

Since her plan to guide Calder to David's hotel was apparently by the boards, Diane instead tried again to use her Inside Voice to call her brother. The reply she received was not the reply she wanted.

"He can't hear you," her voice told her. "I won't let him hear you."

"What was that, honey?"

Outside the window Diane saw two older women standing to the side of a Starbucks entrance. They were dressed professionally if a bit too warmly for the weather. Each held a Starbucks cup in one hand and a cigarette in the other.

"Nothing, ladies," Diane's voice replied. "Talking to myself, I suppose. Enjoy the day."

They asked if she was okay, but they were already gone from the window.

You know, it's pretty fucking rude to ignore people like that, Diane thought.

Diane's voice admonished her. "A proper lady does not speak in such a manner."

Is that how it was in your time? Women were seen but not heard? Didn't have the right to voice their opinions?

"Indeed," her voice replied. "And please, stop trying to talk to your brother. It's like an itch in the back of my brain that I can't scratch. But that's all it is, an itch. It won't work."

Says you.

Diane contemplated a continuous call to David. An endless loop that might not get through but would annoy the hell out of the thing in control of her body. But no. Their Inside Voice almost always drained them if used too often, and Diane felt she would need to save her strength for later. So she gave up trying to contact her twin. For now, anyway.

Columbus Boulevard finally appeared, and the thing turned left onto it. There Diane saw more people walking by, heard more inquiries about her well-being. Calder either brushed off their concerns or ignored them. Her pace was a bit steadier now. The limp they'd acquired after the fall down the embankment was mostly gone. Diane didn't know whether to be pleased or worried.

Once past a block of apartments, Diane watched the thing duck into an alley. The window went black, but she could hear the sounds of her body vomiting onto the ground. Diane smirked. *That water was pretty disgusting, wasn't it?*

Her body was struck by another round of her stomach purging whatever was left of its contents. That was the moment Diane was hit with another image. Her knees buckled and the mist washed over the top of her head. She didn't wind up flat on her back this time, merely on her hands and knees.

She saw Calder again as he had been in life. The robe he sported as a spirit was wrapped around his thin frame. His expression was stern, hostile. He was looking up at someone dressed identically to him and shouting at the man. This other judge banged his gavel upon the bench.

Diane winced at the throbbing in her head. It took up residence behind her eyes and blinded her to all else. "Jesus, fuck!" She had never felt any physical symptoms on this side of the divide—pain nor pleasure. She felt now she was close to passing out.

The image was gone in an instant. The pain departed with it. Diane waited, still on her hands and knees, the mist undulating around and over her. When she was convinced it was gone for good, she grasped the chair and used it to haul herself to her feet.

"You were in trouble," she stated.

The window was still black but after a few more seconds it opened again. They emerged from the alley on unsteady feet. Calder kept one hand on the building next to her, much as Diane had done after coming to on the dark, deserted street the night before.

A couple kids walked by and made rude comments and gestured in her direction. One of them called out, "Crackhead!" and laughed.

It was hardly the first time someone hurled that name in her direction, although it had been months since the last. Diane shrugged.

The sun had already begun its downward trek when Diane caught her first glimpse of Mount Olive. It was still far ahead, perhaps a mile or two distant. From here she could see the upper hills. Gravestones appeared as small black dots on the landscape.

They encountered no more people the rest of the way to the cemetery, although several cars slowed as they drove past, the drivers either shouting something obscene at her or else throwing her a look of pity. None stopped.

The sun had sunk below the tallest hills of Mount Olive when the thing in the driver's seat reached the cemetery gates. She crossed the threshold without breaking stride. She stopped, however, at the first crossroads. The view outside the window looked left, then right.

Don't know where to go, do you? That's a shame, Diane taunted.

"No, I do not," her voice answered. "But all is well. I'll get us there, don't concern yourself."

Diane watched her body take the path to the left. After several soft turns she spotted the cemetery office on her left. The garage doors were open, but she saw no sign of any workers. She likewise saw no mourners or visitors as her body made its way up a hill. They had the cemetery to themselves, it seemed.

She could hear her body's labored breathing as they crested the top of the hill. Outside the window Diane saw the large tree in the far corner that obscured an old headstone within its shadows. They headed in that direction.

Diane sat up. "This could be my chance," she told the mist. "Maybe I can push the bastard right into his own body, assuming there's anything left of it."

She watched as they drew closer to the hidden gravestone. The shadows of the tree enveloped them and for a few moments. Diane saw nothing but black as her physical eyes adjusted to the sharp contrast of darkness. Then the headstone appeared. Diane swallowed as she saw the torn ground atop the grave. She looked at her hands and thought of David pulling her away from there, even as she herself fought him. No, not herself. She was no more in control of her body then than she was now. *You son of a bitch,* she thought.

"Language, my dear," her voice responded.

Go fuck yourself.

Diane got a close-up look at the headstone when her body knelt in the dirt before it. She could make out the date, saw the worn and pitted surface. *They must have loved you,* she thought to the thing. *Not even a name.*

Calder ignored her. Diane watched her hands begin to claw at the dirt. The inch or two of topsoil gave way easily but her progress slowed considerably after that. Her hands dug into the hard dirt and clay but did little to remove any of it.

Easy on my hands, dickhead. You'll never get through all that and you know it.

The digging continued for several more minutes without comment from the old judge. Diane watched her hands finally pull themselves from the dirt. The thing held them in front of the window as if to show her. Fresh cuts on all her fingers and her palms produced beads of blood. They stood out against the black of the dirt covering her skin.

"Yes, this will take entirely too long," the thing announced. It stood and walked back into the dying sunlight. Through the window the world appeared as solid white; even with the sun now hidden behind a few of the taller buildings in the distance its light was a magnesium flare compared to the darkness beneath the large tree. As the image cleared, she saw they were walking back down the hill.

Giving up?

Diane's own voice giggled before answering, "No."

Eventually the main office came back into view. Its outside lights had come on although there was still plenty of daylight left. Diane saw the maroon van, Ted's van, parked at the edge of the small driveway.

Her heart leaped into her throat. She began pacing again. "Ted," she said. "Ted's here. Maybe with David. This could be my chance." All she had to do was get close enough and she might be able to contact her twin, even separated as they were by the mist.

Immediately, Diane cleared her mind of any thought of her twin, of any thought at all. She pictured a brick wall and held that image. She closed her eyes, permitting herself only a quick glance at the window every few seconds to track their progress. Diane steeled herself as best she could and waited.

After a few moments she heard a man's voice. It was unfamiliar and the tone was harsh. "Jesus, would you look at this? What the hell happened to you, lady?"

Then, a second voice, familiar. Ted. "Di! Oh my God, *Di!* We've been looking everywhere for you!"

Diane permitted herself a quick glance at the window. Ted was rushing to her as a second man she didn't know stood at the open garage doors. She willed her eyes to look for David but the thing in control of her body kept her gaze fixed on Ted.

"What happened?" he asked as he grasped her arms. He looked her up and down. "Jesus, Di, what happened to you? Your brother's been worried sick! We all have!"

"I need help," Diane heard herself say.

"You got it," Ted replied. He wrapped one arm around her shoulders and led her toward the garage. "Scott, I need to use your phone."

"Yeah, of course," Scott replied. His tone had softened somewhat from his initial reaction to Diane's appearance. He led the way inside.

The view in the window took in the garage. Landscaping equipment both mechanized and manual filled the space. The window lingered on a hatchet hanging from the wall before they left the garage behind and entered a short corridor. On the other side was Mount Olive Cemetery's main office.

Diane couldn't hide her disappointment that David wasn't present. Her shoulders slumped and she returned to her chair. With her brother she might have had a chance but there was no possibility of contacting Ted. Even if she weren't in the mist it wouldn't work. "Goddammit," she whispered.

"Phone's right there," the other man said when they entered the office, pointing to it. He stepped out of the way but not before another long look at the new arrival.

Diane saw his eyes for but a moment but that was enough to tell her the man's thoughts regarding her. *Fucking white trash,* his eyes told her. *Might be good for a fuck but that's about all. Too bad she didn't show up before her friend got here. Woulda made for a good night at work.*

A desktop computer and monitor sat on the counter. The monitor displayed a map of Mount Olive. A single grave was highlighted. Beneath it was displayed the name SILAS CALDER, 1843.

Ted reached for the phone on the counter.

Diane saw her hand grab a pair of scissors next to the phone. She swung her arm in a long arc and buried the scissors in the cemetery worker's abdomen. The man grunted and stumbled back and tripped over the chair behind the counter. He slumped against the wall, his hands clutching his midsection as blood seeped between his fingers. "What the fuck ..." he shouted.

Ted froze, his hand inches from the phone.

Diane screamed, *"No!"*

The cemetery worker slid down the wall, still clutching his abdomen. Diane's hand grabbed a glass vase filled with plastic flowers that sat atop a filing cabinet and swung it at her soundman. Ted got his hands up, but Diane's arm eluded them. The vase connected solidly with the side of Jung's head. He staggered back from the impact, holding his head. His hip smacked the side of the counter and the computer monitor tumbled over the side. His feet became entangled and Jung landed on the floor. His hands covered his head and he groaned.

Calder vaulted the counter. He reached Jung and raised the vase again.

"Don't do it!" Diane shouted.

Calder brought the vase down on Jung's head a second time. Droplets of blood flew in all directions. Jung rolled away, both hands clutching his head. "Di, no." His voice was weak, his words, slurred.

"You'll keep for a few minutes," Diane's voice announced.

She returned her attention to the unfortunate cemetery worker. Diane watched herself grab the man's shirt collar and then drag him back down the corridor to the garage. Their progress was slow and Diane could hear her ragged breathing as her body struggled with the man's weight. When they at last entered the garage Diane saw the man tossed roughly to the concrete floor. He whimpered while he did what he could to stop the bleeding. His shirt and work pants were saturated with blood, and she could see some of it was now dripping from the corners of his mouth.

"Fucking bitch," he gurgled. "You fucking stabbed me."

Diane watched her hands take up a bungee cord from the work bench. The worker was dragged into a seated position on the floor.

"Kneel," she heard her voice tell him.

"Fuck you!" Blood and spittle flew from his lips.

Diane's hands grasped the scissors still protruding from his abdomen and twisted them. The man screamed. When Calder at last released his grip on the scissors the man pulled himself onto his knees. One hand braced his body against the floor, although the blood made his hand slick and it took him three attempts to get it to support his weight.

"Please, please don't kill me," he pleaded. More blood gurgled up from his insides and pattered on the floor. "I got a kid …"

"Leave him alone!" Diane screamed at the window. Her fists beat on the image, causing weak ripples across the surface.

Diane watched as Calder tied the man's hands behind his back with the bungee cord. Then he stepped away and surveyed his work.

Let him go! Don't do this!

"Quiet, woman," her own voice replied.

Diane watched her hand take a hatchet hanging from the wall.

Please, stop!

The hatchet was raised. Diane turned from the window. Her hands covered her ears but she could still hear, quite clearly, the sound of the hatchet finding its mark. When the sounds at last ceased Diane looked out the window once again.

Thankfully, she was looking at the corridor again and not the body of the poor man in the garage.

Not Teddy! Leave him alone, Diane screamed at the thing. *He didn't do anything to you! Stop,* please!

Ted was still on the floor, but he began to push himself back when he saw Diane reenter the office. He held out a hand as if to ward off another blow. "Di, please, I'm trying to help you."

"And you will," Diane heard her voice tell him.

Her hands, covered with the cemetery worker's blood, grasped one of the chairs. She brought it down on top of Jung. The chair splintered; Jung screamed and curled into a fetal position.

Diane looked through the window, scanning for anything that might help Jung. Her eyes settled on the phone. "Let's see if you can still be steered in the right direction." She thought of the phone and nothing else. Jung, the cemetery office, the cemetery itself, she drove all from her mind and zeroed in on the phone.

She watched herself change direction. Her hand reached for the receiver dangling by its cord.

"Yes, yes! Pick it up! Hit the button to open the line." She watched her hand do as she directed. Diane concentrated on David's number, repeating it like a mantra. Her fingers pressed the first four numbers before they stopped.

"No, no, keep going!"

Her finger hovered in the air above the number keys. Diane repeated her brother's number several more times, her eyes glued to the phone.

At last, one hand dropped the receiver and the other pulled back from the keypad.

"Make no further attempts to delay me," her voice ordered.

She watched herself grasp something from the floor, something her hands had dropped when she aimed for the phone. At first Diane didn't recognize the object. It took her a moment to get a good look at it. She brandished the hatchet from the garage, waving it slowly in the air in Jung's direction. "On your feet, Chinaman."

"Di ..."

"On your feet, I said!" She banged the hatchet on the counter for emphasis.

Jung scrambled to his feet. Just as quickly he stumbled. He would have gone down again had the wall been a few inches farther away. He braced himself, back to the wall, one hand still protecting the side of his head. "Di, please! Why are you doing this?"

"Be silent," the thing ordered. "Outside. That way." It indicated the corridor with a nod.

Leave him alone, you fucker! Diane shouted at it.

"Silence!" Calder replied.

"I didn't say anything," Jung told her as he stumbled down the corridor.

They entered the garage. Jung stopped short when he saw the body kneeling on the cold floor. Diane got her first look at the decapitated corpse kneeling in a pool of the dead man's blood. She turned away from the window.

She heard her body take something from the wall. When

Diane looked again she saw Jung walking ahead of her, Calder prodding him forward with the business end of a shovel.

"Di, please! I'm hurt!"

"You'll be worse if you don't keep walking."

They ascended the hill. The sun was long gone and dusk had at last arrived. Calder prodded Jung toward the large tree, ignoring the wounded man's pleas. The impenetrable darkness surrounding the tree swallowed them and this time the image in the window remained black.

"Go for it, Teddy. He can't see shit. Run! Run right now and don't stop!" Diane could see nothing out the window and she heard no sound of Jung taking her unheard advice and sprinting away.

"Dig, Chinaman" she heard her voice order. The sound of something being tossed upon the ground. "The spade is to your left."

More pleas from Jung. More threats from Calder. Then the sound of a shovel stabbing into the earth.

Diane didn't know how long they stood within the shadow of the great tree. It felt like hours and may have been. The rhythmic sound of the shovel striking the ground and then loose dirt being tossed aside seemed to last forever. Until the sound changed.

"I think I found something," Jung announced. His voice was weak and unsteady. He no longer sounded like himself at all. More like a drunken stranger who had just run a marathon.

"Out of the hole," Diane's voice ordered him.

The view outside the window was still mostly black but Diane saw a shape that might have been Ted staggering out of the way.

"Yes," her voice announced. "Yes, this is what I require."

"Glad you approve," Jung retorted. His voice was unsteady, weak. "Di, please, I need to get to a hospital. I think I'm hurt pretty bad."

Let him go, Diane pleaded. *He did whatever you wanted him to do so let him go. Please.*

"Be silent, both of you," Calder told them.

"Run, Teddy! Run right now! Hit him with the shovel and run like hell!"

Jung did neither. His breathing was ragged and shallow.

Diane could see almost nothing, but she got the impression her body was now crawling out from the hole dug by Jung. Something rattled in the darkness. The sound reminded Diane of a craps player at Foxwoods grinding the dice in his hands before tossing them onto the table. Whatever it was it was close by, perhaps even being carried in her arms.

"Now, Chinaman, kneel."

"I'm Korean," Jung protested weakly.

Oh, Jesus. No! Let him go! He did what you asked. He's no threat to you. Please stop!

Light suddenly filled the world. Calder shrank from it; Diane focused on it.

Jung had taken his phone from his pocket. He was trying to enter his security code but Diane could see his fingers slipping on the screen. "Come on, come on," he prodded himself.

Calder recovered from the unexpected assault on his eyes. He backhanded Jung. The phone flew from the soundman's hand. Jung backpedaled but somehow remained upright. The effort seemed to take the last of his strength.

Jung looked at Diane. "I don't feel so good. I'm gonna lie down for a bit." In the meager light from his cell Diane watched Jung's body strike the ground and lie still.

"Just as well," her voice replied.

Within a few minutes Diane heard someone whistling and realized it was Calder. It was low-key, a dirge Diane had never before heard. The tune was interrupted several times by the sound of grunting and deep breaths being taken. After a while the whistling stopped. The sound of something wet being lifted from the ground followed by the same object being thrown down. The rattling of dice again and a moment later they were out from beneath the tree.

Diane was happy to have something to look at other than pitch darkness. Calder looked down and Diane saw the bones cradled in her arms. The skeleton appeared complete but it was difficult to say for certain in the meager light. Her clothes were now saturated with blood and her sneakers made squishy sounds when she walked.

Diane held a hand over her mouth.

What did you do?

Calder did not reply. The whistling resumed and they headed down the hill.

Where's Teddy? What did you do to him?

The old judge ignored her.

He had to stop several times to scoop up a stray bone that dropped from his arms. He grunted with the effort each time.

You don't sound so good. Maybe you should lie down and take a nap. She received no reply.

At the bottom of the hill they turned into the driveway of the cemetery office. Calder sidestepped the pool of blood in which the headless cemetery worker knelt and moved to the workbench. There he pulled a duffel bag hanging by its strap and opened it. The bones went inside; Diane noted how her hands gently folded the bones and took care with their handling. The hatchet, covered with blood, followed the bones into the duffel. Then he zipped the bag and walked outside. Calder paused at the van. Diane saw her hand move to the door handle and then stop.

Diane smirked. *Don't know how to drive, do you? Yeah, I bet you have no fucking idea. They didn't have these things in 1843.*

To herself, she said, "Good. There's no way we can walk out of here looking like this. If a cop doesn't drive by someone will call them and report us. Then you're fucked. You'll regret what you did to Teddy and that man back there."

"Show me," her voice ordered.

Go to hell, Diane replied. *You killed him, didn't you? Teddy. You murdered him. He was harmless, wouldn't hurt anyone. And you killed him anyway. You can go fuck yourself. And when I get my hands on you—*

"Your threats do not concern me." It moved away from the van and started walking. The whistling resumed. They headed for the cemetery exit, the duffel bag slung over their shoulder.

THEN

It was Diane's idea to use their ability to make money. A murder, even a child murder, was not unheard of in Paterson. The case, however, had gone cold. The cops had nothing, the newspaper proclaimed. The child's family, while not wealthy, were not paupers, either. They'd offered a reward of $10,000 for information leading to the conviction of those responsible for their son's death. Diane heard the story first from the local ABC affiliate. The papers hyped the hell out of it, a new headline appearing almost daily. The child's family was crying out for justice, a reporter exclaimed. Diane sat at the kitchen table in her small apartment in Jersey City, sipping her morning coffee and smoking a joint, when she decided they could help the family.

"If we take the reward, we'll look mercenary as hell," David warned. "This kid's dead and here we are, taking money from the family."

Diane waved him off. "We'll be helping them. We'll be helping the cops. Hell, we'll be helping the community. That's not mercenary, David."

He took convincing. Diane provided it.

The twins marched into the Paterson Police Department and asked to see the lead detective on the Espinosa murder. As expected, they got the runaround from the desk sergeant. It was only when Diane told him they had information about the case that they were allowed to speak with someone.

Detective Lieutenant Faith Coughlin was skeptical right off the bat. She regarded the twins with open suspicion and contempt. "So, if I have this right, you two are psychics. Is that it?"

Diane and David exchanged a glance. David shrugged.

Diane nodded. "Yes. Of a sort. It's hard to explain. But I think we can help you. And the family, too. Listen, if it gets a murderer off your streets isn't it worth a shot?"

Coughlin folded her hands on her desk. "What am I thinking right now?"

Diane smirked. "It doesn't work like that. We can't read the living, only the dead."

"How convenient," Coughlin replied dryly. "So we'll take you out to the cemetery and dig up this poor kid and you two, what? Read his mind?"

"Thank you for your time," David said and stood.

Diane placed her hand on his arm. "No one has to be dug up. We just need to get close to the body. Look, Detective, we didn't even need to come here. We could have gone straight to the cemetery and found out what we needed and gone to the family ourselves, without you or the Paterson P.D. We're here out of courtesy, nothing more."

"Uh huh." Coughlin sounded bored. She leaned back in her chair and regarded the twins. "Okay. You know what? I'll take you out there myself. And when you give me some bullshit excuse why you couldn't come up with anything, I'll haul your asses in for interfering with a police investigation and giving a false statement to a detective. Cool?"

"It doesn't always wo—"

"Deal," Diane said a bit too loudly. She exchanged another look with her brother.

Coughlin was as good as her word. She drove the twins to Cedar Grove Cemetery. The police unit pulled off to the side and the detective escorted them to the grave of Manuel (Manny to his friends) Espinosa.

(*I hope this works,*) David told her.

(*It will,*) Diane replied.

(*It better!*)

They clasped hands. Day became night and the twins entered the fog.

It worked. They located Manny and the child held nothing back. The man who had taken him and raped him and ultimately murdered him was a friend of the family. The murderer, additionally, liked to keep trophies.

Diane provided Coughlin with the name and address of the murderer. Obtaining a warrant was difficult, Coughlin told them later. The judge nearly demanded to meet the twins. Had Coughlin not enjoyed a good relationship with the judge it was likely the murderer would have gotten away with his crimes. As it turned out, Coughlin served the warrant. Physical evidence was collected, including the shorts worn by Manny Espinosa the day he disappeared.

After that it became a media circus. The murderer was tried and convicted. The twins were cast into the spotlight. The family handed them a check for $10,000.

Diane continued hunting for stories of unsolved murders. David did, as well. His initial reluctance to the entire endeavor fell by the wayside as his bank account grew fatter.

They assisted in three more unsolved murders, each time collecting the offered reward. They even worked with Coughlin again when a fat banker turned up dead in a crack house.

With each case their names appeared in the papers and in online articles. The CBS affiliate ran a story about them that was picked up by nearly every outlet in the Northeast.

Joyce Clark called them and set up a meeting.

"This could be good for us," Diane stated as she paced about her brother's living room. "Come on, our own reality series? Isn't that what everyone wants these days?"

David sat on his sofa clicking his TV remote and drinking another beer. He remained quiet.

"You think we're making money now? Wait 'til that first network check hits your bank account. I'm telling you, David, this is our chance. We could make so much money on this we'll both be retired and living in the Bahamas before we turn forty."

David emptied the beer can and placed it on the coffee table next to its brothers. He withdrew another from the small cooler next to him. "Uh huh."

Diane sat next to him, took the remote from his hand and turned off the television. Then she took the beer can from him for good measure. David groaned. "Look, let's just meet with this woman, okay? It won't hurt to hear what she has to say. If we don't like the deal, we walk. No harm, no foul. What do you say?"

"I say I want my beer back."

Diane brought the can a little closer to him. When David reached for it she pulled it back. "Promise we'll meet with her."

"For Christ's sake!" He reached for the cooler, found it empty. "You gotta be kidding me." His eyes went to the can in Diane's hands. "If I say yes to this bullshit can I have my beer, please?"

"Of course," Diane replied. She smiled her most beautiful smile and batted her eyelashes.

"You're a dope," her twin told her. He sighed. "Fine. I agree. Happy now?"

Diane's smile widened and she offered the can to her brother. David grabbed it and chugged. "Thank you, big brother." She planted a kiss on his cheek.

David waved her off and reached for the TV remote.

CHAPTER FIFTEEN

WELL BEGUN IS HALF DONE

The sky transitioned from purple to black not long after they cleared the gates of Mount Olive. Calder moved from shadow to shadow. When a car approached, he would use anything nearby for cover. Businesses closed for the night, parked cars. Diane couldn't believe no one had reacted to the sight of this woman covered with blood walking down the street of a major American city. She had expected them to make it no more than a few hundred feet beyond the cemetery gates before someone stopped them. No one did. Nor did she see any police cars. For the most part, the thing carrying the duffel bag had the streets of Lansing to itself.

Diane had remained silent throughout the trek thus far. Her thoughts were of Teddy Jung. What might his last moments have been like, she wondered against her will. She was happy that the darkness had obscured everything. She was certain if she'd been forced to watch what happened the memory of that would send her mind over the edge, perhaps forever. She thought of his family, whom she met only once. His wife, Joanie, his son, Teddy Junior. She even thought of the dog, a chocolate lab named Biscuits. And she thought of the vase connecting with his head. That image replayed over and over in her mind, despite all her attempts to squash it. Diane wanted, needed to cry but that was impossible in this place. She wasn't capable even of shedding a tear for the man whom she murdered. *You didn't murder anyone*, she told herself. He *did*. Diane nodded to herself. "And there's fuck-all I can do about it."

The whistling had long since stopped, replaced by the sound of her ragged breathing. Diane noticed her gait had changed around the same time. Her pace was slower, as well. "What's wrong with you?" she asked quietly. She puzzled over the changes until the answer came to her. "We haven't had a thing to eat since yesterday. Well, lack of food isn't going to kill us in only one day, but with all the walking around and physical exertions we've been going through I bet you're feeling pretty weak right about now. If we pass out it's game over for you, you son of a bitch." Diane rubbed her temples and kept close watch on their progress.

They came upon a park. The baseball diamond was lit up but no game was being played. The basketball and tennis courts were likewise illuminated but deserted. Calder found a bench and sat down with a huff. Diane could hear her lungs sucking air in great gulps.

You're not in good shape, are you, Your Honor?

"I need food," her voice replied.

Mm hmm. And how do you plan to accomplish that?

"That will be my secret," the old judge replied.

I bet that bag is getting heavy. How much does a human skeleton weigh, anyway? Twenty pounds? Twenty-five? Not much, really, but look at the shape you're in. Maybe you should take a nap. We could use the rest, I'm sure.

"Silence, woman."

They sat on the bench for perhaps another fifteen minutes before Calder put Diane's body back on its feet. He slung the duffel over his shoulder and entered the park.

Streetlights illuminated the walking trails. The sounds of kids partying reached Diane's ears but she couldn't see anyone. Wherever the party was it wasn't close by. She spotted a few people walking on the trails but no one came close and Calder did his best to avoid them. He was forced off the path only once when two college kids, walking arm in arm, approached. Calder watched them pass from his place of concealment behind a row of bushes. Once they were gone he stepped back onto the path and continued walking.

Starving. Don't know where you are or where to go. You really didn't plan this through, did you?

"I know exactly where I'm going," Calder replied. "Your attempts to provoke me will not succeed."

Diane smirked. *Can't blame a girl for trying.*

They crossed the rest of the park without seeing another soul. The street looked to be another main road. Calder waited at the edge of the park until the street was clear. Then he raced across. Beyond a row of houses Diane could see another wooded area. Calder entered without breaking stride.

Leaves and dead twigs crunched beneath his sneakers and tore at his clothes and skin. The view outside the window was of a dark landscape filled with darker shapes. Her body stumbled repeatedly. Each time Diane expected to see herself fall over. A conveniently placed tree or rock always seemed to present itself at the right time, however, and Calder managed to keep upright.

What troubled Diane the most was this new feeling of purpose. No longer were her footfalls chaotic or halting. Calder was moving much more surely now, as if he had a specific destination in mind and was closing in. "Where are you taking me?" Diane asked the window.

Their sojourn through the woods continued for what felt like hours. Diane spent the time thinking about Ted, the poor woman whose clothes she now wore, and the unfortunate asshole at the cemetery office. She also thought about Emily Andrews and what became of her. "Everybody would have been better off if we'd just stayed the fuck home."

She blamed Joyce for dragging them out here. Just as quickly she knew none of this was her manager's fault. Joyce had done what anyone in her position would do: take care of her clients and try to further their careers. Or, in this case, resurrect them. She blamed David. She blamed herself. She blamed her sobriety. Had she been high when Joyce arrived, she suspected the plan would have died a quick death.

Of course, all of that was bullshit. There was only one person—if that term could even be applied to him—who bore responsibility for everything that had occurred since their first visit to Mount Olive, and he'd been dead for almost two centuries. "Cops will totally buy that story," she remarked to the fog.

At last, the woods disappeared, and Diane saw they stood at the edge of a road. It was narrower than the streets near the center of Lansing. It was almost pitch dark; Diane could see no streetlights in either direction when Calder scanned their immediate surroundings.

Diane leaned closer to the window, and asked, "Where the hell are you taking me?"

Her body walked along the side of the road. Calder had to jump into the woods only once when a single car passed. After it was gone, they were walking again. His stride remained measured and unbroken. Diane could hear the labored breathing and Calder switched the duffel from his left shoulder to his right every few minutes.

"You're exhausted. Or maybe I should say, *I'm* exhausted. How much longer can we go on like this?" She hoped the answer was something like, *Not long at all. In fact, we're at the end of the road now.* But they weren't. Not yet. Her body continued walking.

She saw a narrow side road ahead on the left. When they reached it, Calder turned and continued walking. The road snaked through the woods that bordered it on both sides.

Gravel crunched beneath its sneakers. Diane realized where they were.

"Oh, shit."

As if aware of her sudden epiphany, Calder turned his eyes up and to the right. Barely visible above the trees Diane could just make out the top of the Andrews residence.

"Why are we coming back here? Haven't we caused this family enough grief?"

Her body navigated the twists and turns of the driveway until at last they stood before the house. Light spilled from several windows within the residence. Brian Andrews's Cadillac was parked close to the front door. Diane watched the house grow larger in the window. Her body paused near the Caddy. Her eyes scanned each window facing the driveway.

Diane spotted no movement within the house, but she knew all the same Brian Andrews was somewhere within.

Then Calder was on the move again. He mounted the steps and approached the front door. Diane's hand grasped the door handle and turned it over. The door opened easily and silently.

What are you planning to do, Calder? Leave this man alone!

"But, my dear," her voice whispered to her, "we have unfinished business within this domicile."

What unfinished business? What are you talking about? Calder!

This time there was no reply. Diane's body entered the home and closed the door behind it.

The foyer was deserted, as was the living room. The sounds of the television reached Diane's ears but there was no sign of Brian Andrews. Her body crossed into the living room, advancing slowly but steadily. It knelt on the large rug and placed the duffel bag upon it. Then it peeked around the corner of the living room. Brian Andrews didn't present himself.

Her body moved across the living room and neared a short hallway that led to a brightly lit room—the kitchen, if she remembered correctly. Now she could hear something. Diane recognized it as the unmistakable sound of a utensil scraping the bottom of a glass jar.

Andrews, run! Get out now!

Diane's eyes were glued to the window. Her body moved silently toward the kitchen. At the threshold it stopped and looked inside. Brian Andrews stood with his back to them. A plate with two sandwiches—they looked to be peanut butter and jelly—sat on the counter. He got whatever was left in the jelly jar and applied it to the sandwich before he placed the jar and the butter knife into the sink. Then he turned around.

(David, I need you! Please hear me!)

Calder crossed the few feet that divided him from Brian Andrews. The man's eyes widened and his mouth hung agape at the sight before him. Before he could react, Calder was on him. His fingers wrapped themselves around the portly man's throat and squeezed. Andrews staggered back against the counter, his hands going to his throat on pure instinct.

(David, where are you?)

Unlike M. O'Leary, Brian Andrews recovered from his surprise quickly. Also unlike the unfortunate woman, he was far stronger than Diane. His fingers clamped down on Calder's wrists and pulled them away from his throat. He gulped in air and threw Calder aside. The view outside the window spun crazily out of control.

"You fucking bitch!" Andrews roared. He surged forward and grabbed Calder's arms and lifted him from the floor. "You killed my mother! Now you think you're gonna kill me? Fuck you!" He heaved him to the side.

Diane knew her body had crashed into something solid. The window went black for a moment before she saw Calder was lying on the floor. Her body gasped for breath.

(David, please!)

Andrews sucked air as he hefted her off the floor and threw her across the small kitchen. Diane caught a glimpse of the kitchen table before her body slid across it and wound up on the floor again.

Outside the window Diane saw the man's feet as he crossed the room toward her. Then he lifted her from the floor, probably by what was left of the stolen shirt.

"*Fuck you!*" Andrews screamed. Spittle flew from his lips. He drew back his fist and it flashed forward. The window went black but only for a moment. When the lights came back on Diane saw him draw back his fist a second time. The window darkened again. Then her body was looking at the floor.

"Think you're gonna kill me, too," Brian Andrews huffed. His feet moved away from her.

She heard the phone lifted off its wall mount. Calder stood but slowly. His legs must have buckled because he very nearly wound up the floor again. Diane watched her hand reach for the rather large and solid-looking tea kettle which sat on the stove.

(DAVID!)

For the briefest moment she could sense her brother. It was as if she stood in a dark room and someone flicked the light switch on and then off immediately. Diane bore down.

Andrews's meaty fingers stabbed buttons on the phone.

Calder approached him from behind. Andrews turned at the last moment, eyes widening again. Calder swung the tea kettle much as he had swung the glass vase in the cemetery office. Andrews staggered back, holding the side of his head. Calder swung it again. And a third time. Each impact was accompanied by a dull *thud*.

(*David, I need you now!*)

This time she saw her brother, if only in a flash. He appeared to be lying on a concrete floor, asleep or unconscious, she couldn't tell. She tried to push the connection, but the path closed as if a giant wall had sprung into being. The force of the disconnection caused Diane to stagger back.

Brian Andrews slumped to the floor. He looked up at her through the blood which covered much of his face and head. "Fuck you." Blood bubbled from his lips.

Calder brought the tea kettle down one more time and Brian Andrews didn't have much to say after that. Diane recovered just in time to hear the kettle land on the linoleum floor. Then she watched as her body stumbled across the kitchen to the counter.

"Well begun is half done," her voice announced. She watched her hand pick up the first sandwich from the plate.

You sound funny, Diane told him.

"Yes, I'm afraid the ruffian did quite a bit of damage to your face." Her body stepped in front of the sink and looked into the window above it.

Diane took an involuntary step back when she saw the reflection. Blood streamed from both nostrils and the sides of her mouth. Her face was covered with it, as were the remains of her stolen shirt. Her left eye was swollen and the skin beneath it was already turning black. Her eyes looked down and she watched herself spit quite a quantity of blood into the sink. Against the stainless steel basin the blood appeared as bright as neon.

Diane couldn't see Andrews's body. Was he still alive? She thought so. It seemed unlikely the tea kettle, as solid as it was, could kill him, not with so few blows. "Please be alive, please be alive," she whispered.

She kept her thoughts away from her brother. She knew she'd made contact with him, but she didn't know if he was in any condition to receive it. She hoped so. If she could see his surroundings, maybe he could see hers? Would he recognize the place? Maybe. He might be on his way here already. "I hope."

When her body finished the first sandwich it started on the second. "There," her voice announced after the second sandwich had followed the first, "That hit the spot. Don't you agree?"

I'm going to fucking kill you, Diane thought.

Her own voice laughed at her. "Oh, no, dearest, I am afraid you will not. But I will most certainly kill you."

The view outside the window blurred for several seconds before it snapped back into focus.

"I don't feel well," her voice informed her.

You don't look well, either.

The window blurred, then dimmed. "I may need to sit down."

It was difficult to see but Diane thought her body was moving toward one of the kitchen chairs that had somehow maintained its position during the fight with Andrews.

"Just for a moment, mind you. We still have a bit of work to do before the new day."

Diane's view changed and she realized her body was now on its hands and knees. It crawled across the kitchen floor, her hands finding small puddles of blood and leaving streaks of it in their wake. She wished she could see more but the image was blurry and the edges were already dark.

"Just a bit of work," her voice repeated.

The window went black.

IV.

THE CEMETERY GAME

CHAPTER SIXTEEN

THE VOID

David walked out the front door of the police department to see Joyce and LaMontagne standing on the lower steps. The early-afternoon sun was bright and David shielded his eyes. Joyce ran to him and nearly knocked him down when she threw her arms around him. The breath exploded from his lungs when she pulled him close.

"Jesus, Joyce, take it easy. I wasn't on death row."

Joyce released him and stepped back. She looked him up and down. "You're okay? They didn't step out of line with you? I mean, other than taking you in in the first place."

David waved her off. "No, I'm fine. Really."

"Because you look like shit."

"Thanks."

She hooked her arm in his and almost dragged him down the steps.

LaMontagne held out his hand and David shook it. "Thanks, man," the cameraman said. "That was huge."

"They won't get away with this," Joyce announced before David could respond. "They had no cause to arrest you!"

"They didn't arrest me," David corrected her, "just held me on suspicion. And given their point of view, I'd say they had a lot of cause. I'm actually pretty surprised they released me this quickly."

LaMontagne nodded in Joyce's direction. "Thank her. She got you out."

"Most of the prints they found belonged to Teddy or that

poor bastard who worked there. I told them I knew a legion of Los Angeles lawyers who would love to come out here and crawl up their asses if they didn't let you go immediately!" She smiled, sounded quite pleased with herself.

"Thanks again." He swallowed. "Teddy. Ahmad gave me the rundown. I'm really sorry, man."

LaMontagne did not meet his gaze.

Joyce guided them the rest of the way down the steps and stopped before a silver Sienna. She opened the backseat door for him.

"Rental?" David asked.

"They impounded the van," LaMontagne replied. "Evidence."

"I guess that makes sense," David remarked. He slid into the backseat and rubbed his knee. The desk sergeant had given him a couple Tylenol and asked if he needed the fire department to come examine him. David decided the pain wasn't so bad and he was right. The Tylenol did its job well enough. When Joyce took her spot in the passenger seat, David leaned forward and asked, "You have anything in that bottomless pocketbook of yours for joint pain?"

Joyce regarded him suspiciously. "I thought you said they didn't harm you."

"They didn't. I fell off the bench last night and whacked my knee on the floor."

Joyce seemed skeptical of his explanation. Nevertheless, she rummaged through her pocketbook until she came across a bottle of Aleve. She handed it to him.

As LaMontagne guided their rented minivan into traffic, he asked, "Anything about Di?"

"She's alive," David answered. Joyce started to react. "Calm down. That's all I know." He related what happened during the night down to the last detail. He ended with, "So she's alive. Or, at least, she was ten hours ago. I haven't been able to get anything from her since."

Joyce turned her head and regarded him. "That doesn't mean anything, honey. She could be incommunicado for any number of reasons. I'm sure she's okay."

David shook his head. *No, she's not even within visual range of okay.* He said nothing, merely watched their progress through the city.

After several blocks during which no one spoke, Joyce again turned and faced him. "We have some news about that spirit from the cemetery. Jim here did a great job investigating." She paused. Although David didn't look at her, he knew her expression was grim. "It's not good, David. This guy was a piece of work in his time."

"I printed what I could find online," LaMontagne chimed in. He took a manila envelope from above his visor and handed it to David.

David placed it on his lap. "I can't read in a moving vehicle. Never could. Makes me throw up. I'll wait until we get to where we're going." Then, "Find anything about that nametag?"

"Yeah. At least, I think so. On the news this morning they talked about a missing person. Megan O'Leary is her name. Showed up for work yesterday morning but never made it into the building. Cops are looking for her."

David frowned. "They'll find her eventually. Di, or this spirit, I should say, doesn't seem to care too much about hiding bodies."

Joyce's brow furrowed. "What are you saying, David?"

"Nothing for now. Forget it." A pause. "Where are we going, anyway?"

"The hotel," LaMontagne replied. "You know, to regroup."

No, David wanted to scream. *We're gonna find my sister and we're not doing anything else until we do!* That had been his plan since Di's sudden blast hit him in the cell. In the cold light of day, however, it was unrealistic. He could get no sense of his twin, had no idea where she could be. She'd been in someone's kitchen, that much he knew. Beyond that he had nothing. As much as he hated to agree with LaMontagne he saw no other course. At least, not until he heard from Di again.

"Sure," David told him.

They drove in silence the rest of the way.

Diane existed in a void. When her window to the world went black so did everything around her. Her mist-chair was gone and, although she couldn't see it, she knew the rest of the mist was gone as well. She felt nothing, heard nothing. She tried to speak but even her own voice was gone. She felt neither warm nor cold. Even the ground was denied her, she simply floated through the void. All she could do, she found, was think.

What if I'm dead? she wondered. *What if Brian Andrews succeeded in killing me? What if that last punch he threw broke something inside my head? Gave me an aneurism or something. Or he could have woken up and seeen me lying on his kitchen floor and decided to finish the job. I could be on a slab in the coroner's office right now. Or buried somewhere on his property.*

No. She rejected that idea. He was still a suspect in his mother's death, as far as she knew. It was always possible the cops would search the property and the surrounding area. A freshly dug grave would certainly not help his cause.

So, yeah, I'm in a freezer drawer somewhere. Hell of a way to go. Killed by some doofus in a nowhere town in the Midwest. If I had known I'd go out this way I'd have stayed in Bridgehampton and never bothered to get clean.

The void bore a vague similarity to the Waiting Room, the true Waiting Room, or a close approximation of it, anyway. It didn't feel like it, however. The Waiting Room had always been fleeting, a one-tenth-of-a-second pause between the real world and the fog. In that respect, at least, this was much different.

She tried her Inside Voice several times. Not only did her brother not reply, she realized she couldn't sense him at all. In fact, she could sense nothing. Her universe was gone, replaced by an endless expanse of … nil.

At least Calder is out of the picture. The thought made her smile. She didn't know what his endgame was but she could at least take some comfort in knowing he'd fallen short. *Hell of a price to pay, though. At the very least I'd have liked to see him—*

Diane stopped. What, exactly, would happen to the old spirit if her body was indeed dead? Would he return to the fog to await someone else with the same ability as her and David?

Would he become nothing, as seemed to have happened to her?

He could be in here right now, she realized.

The thought would have sent a shiver down her spine had she possessed one at the moment. Her head whipped about, eyes scanning the void. She saw nothing but black. *You're going about this all wrong, Di. You don't need to see him with your eyes. Not in here, you don't.*

Diane closed her eyes and imagined herself taking long, steady breaths. As she had done so often throughout her life, Diane reached out into the void. It was a somewhat different sensation, flying solo instead of having her brother beside her. There was a sense of weightlessness, of being able to breathe even with the absence of anything resembling air. These were familiar to her. What wasn't familiar was the perception of pins-and-needles all over her body, as if all her muscles were awakening at the same time. The hair on her arms stood at attention, the corners of her mouth turned upward.

There.

Diane's eyes snapped open. There was someone in here with her. The consciousness was simultaneously close by and light years away. Diane spread her arms and took flight. The gesture was both ridiculous and unnecessary. She wasn't truly flying. She wasn't moving at all. It helped her, however, to reinforce the impression that she was flying through the endless black and toward a specific destination. Her perception of time was as gone as the real world. She might have flown for days or milliseconds. She decided it didn't matter.

She saw him ahead of her and a little below her plane of flight. Diane came to a landing next to the spirit. At first she didn't want to look at it. This was the thing, after all, that had killed at least three people using her body as its means of murder. If anything, the thought enraged her. Diane placed her hand on Calder's shoulder and spun him around.

He appeared much as he had during their first encounter in the fog. An old man in a black robe, white wisps of hair still clinging to his skull, his skin thin and hugging his bones. Diane noticed his eyes for the first time. They were pools of black, as dark as the void around them. They were also expressionless.

The spirit took no notice of her. She might as well have not been there, her hand on his shoulder, looking into his black tar-eyes.

Diane shook his shoulder. *Wake up, asshole. We have business to settle.*

Calder didn't react.

Diane shook him and slapped his face. The old spirit remained oblivious to her presence. She went so far as to slug him, a haymaker right across his jaw. His head moved with the impact but he seemed otherwise unaffected.

This is stupid. What I need is to get inside there. She stood in front of him, hand on her chin, looking into his eyes. *Okay, I've never tried this before so bear with me. I hope like hell it hurts you.*

Diane placed her fingers against his temple. She closed her eyes and pushed, ever so gently, against the spirit's head.

The world exploded into color. Diane staggered, not quite prepared for such a result. The void was gone, although she and Calder remained. She saw her fingers had penetrated the side of the spirit's skull; Calder remained unresponsive.

She was in the shower. She felt neither heat nor cold but steam filled the space. It took her several seconds to recognize it. This was the shower in the Andrews guest house. Calder stood next to her. Diane noted the water seemed to fall straight through him; the judge was bone dry.

She watched herself step from the shower, Calder following a step behind. She exited the bathroom naked and looked both ways. The hallway was empty. Diane walked down the stairs. At the bottom she peeked into the living room. Joyce sat on a recliner, smoking and watching television. A check of the kitchen showed it to be clear. Diane crept past Joyce without making a sound. She snuck through the kitchen and out the front door.

There was a light drizzle outside. It should have felt cold on her naked skin but again Diane felt nothing. She watched herself ascend the hill toward the main house. Calder matched her pace step for step.

Then she was inside the Andrews residence. She could hear the television in the living room but she paid it no mind. On the second floor she found Emily Andrews. The elderly woman sat on her bed. Her eyes were wet and her hands held a framed photograph. She looked up when Diane entered the room.

"Ms. Walsh?" Her voice was weak and surprised.

Diane knelt in front of her and took the photo frame from her hands. The image was of Emily and George Andrews and it was old. Diane tossed it onto the bed.

"Your George is waiting for you, Emily," Diane heard the judge tell the frail woman. "He cannot stand to spend another minute away from you. He wants you to join him."

Tears spilled from the woman's eyes.

Diane pulled the sash from Emily's nightgown, slowly and gingerly. Her smile remained in place. She eyed the ceiling fan rotating lazily above their heads. "That will do, I think," she announced. "Here, let me help you."

Emily Andrews cried as Diane lifted her from the bed. The woman's legs were jelly, useless; Diane heard herself grunt with the effort of supporting her.

"No," Emily told her. "George would never want this."

"Sshhh. I spoke to him, remember? I did not want to say anything in front of your son. But this is what George wants. It is what you want, too. Do not be afraid. You will see him again in another minute."

The sash was flung over the ceiling fan. Diane knotted it and shaped the other end into a noose .

Jesus, no, Diane thought, watching herself. She turned, saw Calder standing behind her. He remained oblivious to what was happening.

Diane fitted the noose around the old woman's neck while still supporting most of her weight. "You coveted Sam Wilkes while your husband was overseas. Oh, I know you couldn't bring yourself to complete the act, but the temptation was there just the same. You might have lain with him if your husband did not return home when he did. You are guilty, Emily Andrews." Diane leaned in until her lips were nearly toughing the old woman's ear. "The sentence is death."

Emily tried to speak. Her arms flailed. She managed to strike Diane several times but her blows were weak.

No!

Diane released her hold on the woman. The sash stretched taught. The ceiling fan managed to hold the weight long enough for Diane to hear a *snap*. Then the contraption pulled away from the ceiling. It and Emily landed on the bed. The withered body bounced once. Neither the fan nor the old woman moved after that.

There was a sudden *whoosh* and they were now in a courtroom, an *old* courtroom, by its appearance. The walls were rough, unpainted wood. Two simple tables stood before the bench, two equally simple chairs had been allocated to each table. A wood barrier separated the front of the room from the spectator benches that went all the way to the rear wall. They were occupied with faceless figures dressed in a wide variety of fashion. Some of them appeared wealthy, the women in elaborate dresses and the men in ancient suits. Others wore simpler, rougher clothing. They sat in silence. The room sported a single window; it was large and took up the center of its wall. Diane couldn't see anything outside the window but the featureless black of the void. The witness box was small and looked anything but comfortable. It stood to the side of the bench. Behind the bench sat Judge Silas Calder.

He appeared no different than his spirit. He was old, his expression hostile and commanding. He brought down his gavel and shouted at someone, but Diane could hear nothing.

Diane wanted to sprint across the room and leap at Calder. She thought she could land several haymakers across his face before anyone could stop her. The memory of what he'd done— what *they* had done—to Emily Andrews had burned itself into Diane's mind. Yet she couldn't move. Just as in the old woman's bedroom, Diane was no more than a spectator watching an ancient man's memories.

You son of a bitch! You killed her! And you used me to do it! I swear to God I'm going to fucking kill you!

Calder didn't react to her outburst in any way. He regarded a faceless man dressed in simple, nondescript clothing, who stood before the bench. The condemned had no expression to read but his shoulders slumped and he quivered with every strike of the gavel.

There was another silent *whoosh* and the courtroom vanished. Diane found herself outside. She was part of a crowd of faceless spectators. Before them was a gallows. Judge Calder stood on the raised platform. He held a book in his hands and seemed to read loudly from it. The faceless man who had stood before the bench now stood beside the judge. His hands were tied behind his back. A noose hung around his neck.

When Saint Sepulchre's bell tomorrow tolls, the Lord above have mercy on your souls. The phrase leaped into Diane's mind. She remembered it from a book about medieval England she had read years before, although the context eluded her. If any of the faceless people heard her speak they gave no indication. Nor did the condemned man or Judge Calder.

The judge finished intoning from his book, closed it and stepped aside. No one moved. No lever was thrown. Still the doomed man fell through a trap door that opened suddenly beneath his feet.

The crowd vanished as did the scene. Diane looked about. She was still outside, perhaps even in the same spot she occupied for the unfortunate's hanging. The gallows was gone. In its place sat a large bed of what looked to be small logs and branches. A faceless woman was secured to the bed with heavy ropes. The crowd reappeared around Diane. Calder stood at the head of the crowd, facing them, reading from the book once more. Once again, he finished and stood aside. The bed burst into flames, although no one had approached it with torch in hand. Thick, black smoke immediately filled the air. The spectators bowed their heads all at once, as if they shared the same mind.

Jesus, I don't want to see any more of this. Diane closed her eyes and turned away from the pyre.

The next *whoosh* deposited Diane inside what appeared to be a private residence. It was luxuriously appointed with very old furniture. Thick drapes adorned the windows. The chairs were richly upholstered. A staircase of solid oak led to a second floor.

Calder stood by a window. He held a rifle of some type in

one hand and an elaborate pistol in the other. He peered through the glass. His feet shuffled nervously on the hardwood floor as he moved from window to window.

The front door, made of oak and at least four inches thick, burst open. Thick splinters flew through the air; some pelted Calder and forced him to shield his face. Several faceless men stood on the other side of that door. Many carried torches. Calder shouted something and fired the rifle at them. The faceless men seemed not to move at all but somehow they crossed the threshold and were inside the home. Calder switched to the pistol and emptied it into the nearest of the intruders.

The next thing Diane knew she was standing in an open field. A large house, nearly a mansion, burned a few hundred yards away. Flames leaped from every window turning the black sky to orange.

The crowd of faceless men stood before a large tree. A rope was slung over the lowest branch. The end of the rope was tied into a noose. Inside that noose was the neck of Judge Calder.

He sat on a horse as black as the night air. His hands were bound behind his back. He shouted at the faceless men gathered before him. Spittle flew from his withered lips. The old man's eyes blazed with a light that rivaled the fire consuming his home. Diane took an involuntary step back. The hatred and rage behind those eyes, while not focused specifically on her, threatened to set her afire if she looked at them too long. She half-expected the crowd around her to burst into flame, so powerful was the old judge's fury.

The horse leaped forward and ran as if someone had struck it from behind, although Diane saw no one move. The rope went taut. Calder's legs kicked at suddenly empty air. He must have been struggling for breath but somehow he still cursed at the assembled crowd. The men stood in place, watching without eyes as the judge slowly strangled.

The old man's struggles seemed to last hours. However long it took, eventually his legs stopped scissoring the air. His body swung gently from side to side. For the first time since she found herself in the courtroom a sound reached Diane's ears. It was the creak of the rope against the limb of the tree.

Yes. Die, you bastard! Die and burn in hell!

Diane took her first steps since finding herself in 1840s Michigan. She walked slowly to the tree and its grisly ornament. The old judge's body was silhouetted against the fires consuming the mansion in the distance. As Diane drew near she looked into Calder's eyes. They bulged from their sockets and, somehow, still held the last moments of the old man's rage. Diane reached a hand toward the swinging body but she pulled it back at the last moment. She half-expected the judge to suddenly come to life and grab for her. He did not. The fire behind his eyes remained but it had been extinguished within the rest of his body.

Diane looked about. The faceless crowd had vanished. She found herself alone with the dangling corpse. Even the mansion was gone. All of existence had winked out save for herself, the body, and the tree. She expected another scene shift. Instead, she remained where she stood. *Okay, what now?*

She received no reply but the creaking of the rope upon the branch.

CHAPTER SEVENTEEN

NOWHERE

David tried Diane again while he put on fresh clothes. There was no reply, of course. He was disappointed but not surprised. He'd tried to contact her multiple times since Joyce and LaMontagne met him outside the jail. Each time he was left waiting for a reply that never came.

She wasn't dead, of that much he was certain. He didn't know how he knew, but there was no doubt he'd sense his sister's passing, if it had come. Di was alive. But where? Well, that was the ten-million-dollar question, wasn't it?

A kitchen. That certainly narrowed it down. Wherever she was she had not gone willingly. She was bleeding, although now he couldn't remember how badly or from where. The details of the memory were fading, as they usually did when the twins communicated in that manner. She needed him. While he'd been in jail with a bunch of drunk college kids and a few adults who should know better. Even now, what good was he to her sitting on the bed in his hotel room, hair still wet from the shower?

Don't do that, he told himself. *You won't be any good to her at all racing around Lansing. What are you supposed to do? Knock on doors and ask if anyone is holding your sister against her will?* He needed a starting point. He just did not know how to find one.

Once he was dressed, he headed down to the lobby. As expected, Joyce and LaMontagne were at the hotel bar. David joined them and ordered a sandwich and a Coke. Joyce raised an eyebrow at his drink selection but said nothing.

David told them how Di had reached out to him the night before. The details were becoming fuzzier but he related what he could remember. The kitchen, the overturned chair, the blood. He told them how he'd been trying to contact her but as yet she hadn't replied. When his two companions exchanged a look of dread he said, "She's alive. I know she is, so get that look off your faces."

The waitress, a young woman with long, black hair, brought his food and drink to the table. David devoured the sandwich in no time. Until it was in front of him, he'd had no idea he was so hungry. He could have ordered another; thoughts of his sister and what she might be going through quelled the rest of his appetite.

When the sandwich was gone and the glass of Coke empty, Joyce placed her hand over his and said, "Honey, I hate to say this. Really, I do. And I think you know where I'm going with this." She took a deep breath. "What if she fell off the wagon? You said her nose was bleeding. Doesn't that happen during an overdose?"

"Di's clean," David replied with a little too much force in his tone.

Several people seated around them looked in their direction before returning to their food and conversation.

David leaned forward a bit and lowered his voice. "She's not on that shit again. I know that's what you like to think but I'm telling you, she's clean. This was something else."

Joyce patted his hand. "Okay, okay. Forget I brought it up."

Look at you, he thought, *defending Di's honor. A week ago you didn't want to know anything about her.* On the heels of that, *People change.* The thought made him smile.

The waitress returned and refilled David's glass. Joyce ordered another coffee for her cameraman and a Jack and Coke for herself. When the waitress left LaMontagne asked, "Did you look through that folder I gave you?"

"I skimmed the highlights," David confessed. "Look, I wasn't in the mood to read some dead asshole's life story, okay? I have enough to deal with as it is."

LaMontagne frowned, looked at Joyce. She shrugged, nodded in David's direction.

"This guy, Silas Calder, he was a pretty serious dude," LaMontagne began.

"Yeah, I gathered that much," David replied dryly.

"There wasn't a lot of detail to be found online, not even on Google," LaMontagne continued, "but I did find out a few things. He was a judge back in the day, and he had zero fucks to give as far as that cruel and unusual punishment thing went. This guy was old school even back then. He'd execute people by hanging, beheading, drawing and quartering, burning them alive, even flaying."

David's mind immediately went to Jung inside the grave.

Going by the license in his wallet it's one of your people, one Theodore Jung. But we don't know for sure because he was skinned.

There hadn't been much light with which to see—a fact for which David remained grateful—but there was just enough to see it glint off the soundman's wet body.

Facial ID is impossible and so are fingerprints.

LaMontagne paused when the waitress returned with their drinks. After she once again departed, he continued. "He also wasn't a fan of due process. What he said, went. Reading between the lines, I'd say he bullied the juries into delivering the verdict he wanted. He might even have ignored their verdict if it wasn't the one he wanted."

"Sounds like a charmer," David remarked.

"Yeah, he was a peach, all right," LaMontagne replied. "Finally, the good citizens of Lansing had enough of his shit. Burned down his house and executed his ass. The accounts differ as to how. Some said he was hanged, some say he was shot. Whatever the method, it seems he met his end at the hands of the angry mob. That's where the internet info stopped. No mention of where he was buried or anything else."

"Well, we know where he was buried," David said. "'Was' being the operative word."

"And you're sure he's the old spirit you and Di saw in the fog?" Joyce asked.

David nodded as he polished off his Coke. "Yeah, it's him. But I don't think he's in the fog anymore, Joyce. I think he's out here now, in the real world."

Joyce blinked at him. "What?" Her voice rose a full octave. She looked at LaMontagne as if to confirm she had heard correctly. "How?"

David shrugged. "I wish I knew. But it has something to do with Di. He used her to get out, don't ask me how."

"How can you know that?" LaMontagne asked.

We don't know for sure because he was skinned.

"I know. That's all I can tell you."

"Could that explain why you can't ESP her?" LaMontagne asked. "Whatever you call it."

David's lips compressed into a thin line. "Yeah," he nodded. "Yeah, I think so. Look, Di and I, we don't know how this works. This thing we do, it didn't come with an instruction manual. It was all trial and error right from the start. So I can't tell you how this happened, only that it has."

"What's our play?" Joyce asked after the men fell silent. "We still need to find Di."

"I'm gonna keep the phone line open," David told her. "I don't think we can do much of anything until she decides to call me."

David looked away. Joyce said something else, but he no longer heard her. He thought of Teddy Jung. He thought of Scott Alexander, aged fifty-three, divorced father of one, headless inside a cemetery garage. He thought of the Honorable Silas Calder who flayed and beheaded the condemned, the Eighth Amendment be damned.

And he thought of Diane.

Calder was with her, David knew. He was helpless to do anything about it until Di picked up the phone. Assuming she was still able. *Come on, Di. Talk to me. Get past that son of a bitch and tell me where you are. This time I'll be ready.*

David waited.

Diane watched the body of Judge Calder hang motionless from the tree. The body was transparent now, as was the tree.

They had both begun to lose their solidity, if in truth such a term could apply in this place, shortly after the faceless crowd had vanished. Not for the first time since she noticed the slow fadeout, Diane wondered what would happen to her when both body and tree were gone completely.

Was she doomed to spend eternity in this dark place? She was not simply a prisoner of the mist anymore; she was inside Calder's mind inside a void inside the mist. The real world was so far from her it might as well have ceased to exist. Most troubling, Diane realized she could no longer remember how she arrived here.

She remembered entering Calder's mind. She remembered the black, featureless void. She even remembered sitting on a chair and watching the world outside the window. But she had lost some of the details, details she used to know.

That's it, isn't it? That's what will happen to me. I'll eventually forget everything, even who I am. I'll be a nameless, brainless ghost inside the mind of an old murderer who was himself murdered. Quite the ending for someone who made millions talking to dead people. Shit, even Joyce would find the humor in that. Whoever Joyce is.

The body and tree were almost gone now. Diane found she could actually see the change in their appearance. It took her several moments to remember why either was significant to her in the first place.

You'd better try something. And you'd better be quick about it.

Diane looked about. Who had spoken? Aside from the almost-gone body there was no one within her sight. So who—? "Jesus, it was me, wasn't it? Come on, get your shit together, Di."

Yeah, it's you. You're talking to yourself. And why not? You're all alone in this world. And pretty soon even that will be gone and you'll be nowhere. So whatever you plan to do you'd better get a move on.

"You're right," Diane answered herself.

She thought of her body. The last she knew it was on the floor in Brian Andrews's kitchen. Diane closed her eyes. She extended one arm as if she were reaching for something in the empty air before her.

For a minute or a day—Diane couldn't be sure which—her fingers felt nothing but air. Her brow furrowed in concentration. She gritted her teeth. "Come on, come on." She didn't need to open her eyes to know the body and tree had gone from this world. She was alone now. The thought terrified her and made her bear down.

Her fingertips brushed something. It was cold and smooth. The contact startled her enough that she nearly lost her concentration. She knew if her concentration lapsed she'd soon become nothing. She grunted with the effort of finding that smooth surface again.

"Stay. With. It," she hissed through clenched teeth.

The cold, smooth object appeared again. Her probing fingers felt it, rubbed against it. *Almost there. Come on, do it!* Something about the object caused her pain. It wasn't in her hands but it seemed every other part of her body felt it. Diane embraced the pain, the first physical sensation of which she'd become aware since the open field next to the highway.

Diane bore down with everything she had left. The pain transitioned to agony. It became difficult to breathe. Her head, her upper body, her legs—no part of her was immune to this newfound distress. A whimper made it past her lips. Diane bit her tongue and hoped the pain would force her to focus.

"Do. It. *Now,*" she ordered herself.

She felt weightless. Wherever her body was, it was now floating above the ground. Or perhaps the ground itself had vanished along with the faceless crowd and their victim. Was she too late?

The pain upped the wattage. Diane moaned and then screamed. The sound snapped her back to full consciousness. At first she couldn't open her eyes. Something cold and sticky covered them. She felt about her face gingerly, removed the semi-viscous substance from her eyes as best she could. Then she opened them.

She was looking at the ceiling in Brian Andrews's kitchen.

It came back to her all at once, Calder, Ted, Emily Andrews.

The memories of the last few days surged into her mind. The assault seemed to strike as if the memories were a physical thing.

Diane gasped, took in a breath as if she had been under water for several minutes. She felt the air flood her lungs. At the same time she rolled onto her side. Immediately she squealed with the pain in her arms and her ribs. "Fuck," she gasped.

Her arms shook with the effort, but she managed to rise to her hands and knees. Her hair hung in clumps in front of her eyes. There was more red than brown in those clumps. More of it dripped from her nose, from the corners of her mouth. Diane spat blood onto the floor.

Her hands slipped on the slick linoleum. Diane grabbed the nearest object to keep from falling. It was the table. Her fingers clamped down on the edge. She pulled until she got her feet under her. Diane stood.

She looked about the wrecked kitchen. Brian Andrews lay perhaps eight feet from her. He moaned softly. One hand swiped weakly at the air around his head. She took a step in his direction, stopped.

What the hell are you doing? When he comes to, he's going to want some payback. You'd better get your ass out of here before that happens. Right after that, she thought, *Then again, we're not in any condition to run or walk very far, are we? And after what you did to his mother, maybe you should be happy about that.*

Diane couldn't argue with herself. She took a few halting steps toward the doorway which led to the living room. She was nearly there when she remembered her brother.

"David," she called. She nearly tried again before she realized she was speaking aloud. "Idiot," she chided herself. Diane entered the living room. Her eyes went immediately to the duffel bag lying on the large rug. She remembered what was in there.

(David?)

She waited. When her brother didn't reply, she tried again.

(Di? Di, where are you?)

Diane allowed herself a smile. Droplets of blood dripped

from her lips and decorated the hardwood of the Andrews living room.

(I'm at the Andrews house. You'd better get here fast.)

(Are you okay?) came the immediate response.

(Just hurry,) she told him.

Diane eyed the front door. There was daylight on the other side, although it appeared to be already fading to twilight. She stagger-stepped in that direction.

Diane froze in mid-step. She felt a jolt travel throughout her body as if she had just touched a live wire. Her muscles contracted all at once. The bile rose in her throat and she vomited from a standing position. She felt her knees buckle but she was already back in the mist by the time her body landed on the floor.

David knocked loudly and continuously on Joyce's door until she opened it. She saw his eyes, read his body language. "Di?"

David nodded. "She's at the Andrews place. Don't ask me why. I need the keys to the rental and I need them right now. I have to go get her."

"I'll get my bag. Tell Jim. Let him drive."

David might have argued had the circumstances been different. Instead, he bolted for the next door and started knocking again. Less than five minutes later they were in the Sienna and leaving the Holiday Inn parking lot as quickly as LaMontagne dared drive.

(Di, we're on the way.) David told her. He waited, received only silence as a reply. *(Di, you there?)*

He looked at his companions. "Something's wrong. I've lost her again."

"I'm sure she's okay," Joyce replied. "Diane's tough, David. Certainly mentally, and you know from personal experience how tough she can be in the physical sense." She smirked at this last.

"She's in trouble, Joyce, whether or not you believe it. Jim, I need you to go faster, man."

LaMontagne eyed the speedometer. "I'm already going

forty-five in a twenty-five. And there's traffic ahead." He glanced sideways, and must have seen the expression on David's face. "I'll do what I can."

David looked out through the windshield, saw the traffic lights and the major intersections in front of them. People were getting out of work around now. Vehicle and pedestrian traffic seemed to increase by the moment.

David swore his frustration. "Just get us there."

"We're moving, bro, we're moving," LaMontagne replied.

"David, why would she go there? Of all the fucking places on Earth, why there?"

David shook his head. "How the hell do I know? Maybe she thought we were still staying there. We'll ask her when we see her."

(Di, whatever's happening, we're on our way. Just hang on.)
His sister offered no reply.

THEN

Joyce would be chewing her nails down to nothing if she hadn't already. She stood off-camera, a few feet behind and to the left of LaMontagne. Her feet shifted nervously on the carpet of Mike Higgins's living room. *This is because of me,* she thought. *This was my bright idea. Great job, Clark ! Let's haul them to the middle of nowhere because then maybe they could concentrate on their job and not derail the whole fucking enterprise.* She knew now it was a bad idea. It was compounded when she gave in and allowed the twins to try this. She should have put the whole thing on hold. She hadn't and now, here they were.

David might appear sober, but Joyce knew better. She saw the signs even if the others didn't. She knew her clients too well. David would need ten hours and as many cups of coffee to be regular drunk instead of shitfaced drunk as he was now. He stood straight as an arrow, didn't slur his words—although he tripped up any time he tried a word that began with *S*—and was generally polite and friendly. He managed to keep his smile in place as he spoke with Mr. Higgins.

Diane, on the other hand, was so high she could barely contain herself. Her eyes darted every which way. Her hands clenched and unclenched. She shifted her feet every few seconds. When she spoke, it was almost too fast for human ears to comprehend. And she sniffled. A lot. Every few moments she would rub her nose with the back of her hand. She might as well have hung a sign around her neck that read COKEHEAD.

Higgins, for his part, seemed oblivious to the twins' current state. Oh, he would glance at Diane every now and then, a flash of concern in his eyes. That was always after she'd spoken something too fast for him to catch. But most of his attention was focused on the urn on the coffee table before him.

"Are you ready, Mr. Higgins?" David asked. His tone was solemn, sincere, and spoken mostly for the camera.

Higgins, hands folded in his lap, turned his eyes from the urn to David and Diane. He nodded nervously. "Yes. Yes, I am."

David nodded. He held out his hand for Diane. She giggled before she accepted it and sniffled again.

Joyce couldn't see their faces from where she stood but she could imagine well enough. This wasn't the first time the twins had pulled this. David would be scowling but not overtly so. He was very much aware of the camera's presence. Diane would be biting her lip to stop from laughing. After a few lines of powder she found humor in everything.

Just don't lose it here, Di, Joyce prayed. *Please don't lose it here. Not in front of the camera.*

In theory any footage damaging to the show could be erased. But Joyce knew these things had a way of making it onto the internet regardless of precaution. The twins were already mainstays in some of the tabloids and she was hearing from the producers every other week about some scandal or other. If something happened now it could easily put the show in jeopardy. Joyce held her breath.

Each twin raised their free hand toward the urn. Joyce nodded. *Play for the camera. Let's make this the best episode yet.* It was something she'd say to the twins every time out. If she allowed herself to be truthful, she'd be forced to admit they hadn't had a great episode in nearly two years. Once David's drinking got out of control and Di started disappearing for days at a time, nearly every aspect of the show had gone downhill. *This is our chance to put one in the win column. Don't screw it up.*

David hummed softly, just enough for the boom mic to pick up. That had been Joyce's idea right from the start. "We have to give the audience the impression something is happening, because the two of you standing there in front of a grave isn't what you could call visually attractive to the eye, even with the reenactments," she informed them. In the years since the first episode the humming had become second nature to them, despite the complete lack of its necessity to enter the fog.

Joyce nodded. Maybe they'd get through this, after all.

Minutes elapsed with nothing from the twins. David's humming continued. Every few moments one or the other would shift their feet or tilt their head. Joyce watched them as intently as Higgins. His eyes were wide and unblinking. His hands shook. His feet played a double-bass drum on the carpet.

David's humming intensified.

It's not working, Joyce realized. *They got nothing from the dead woman.* Her lips compressed into a thin line. This would not play well for the camera, or for the producers. She could already hear their complaints on the conference call once she returned to the hotel. Immediately she thought of counterarguments to what she was sure they would say. Nothing she came up with in the Higgins living room sounded good enough to her. This was going to be bad.

"We have her," Diane announced. She waved her arm in an arc through the air. "Denise, right?"

Higgins shifted uncomfortably. "Debbie."

"Debbie, that's it," Diane agreed. "Yes, Debbie. She's here right now."

Joyce placed her hand over her mouth. Never in the history of the show, never even before there was a show, had the twins operated like this. They weren't conduits to the afterlife. They'd never updated a client while in the fog. Even Jung and LaMontagne cast a glance in her direction. Joyce fought against her instincts to tell them to stop recording. She wanted to grab David and Di and drag them from this man's living room before things got worse, Yet she seemed incapable of moving, a spectator to a bad car accident that was happening right in front of her.

"She says," Di began, "She says, she loves you and the kids very much. She's sorry for leaving you so soon."

David's arm dropped and the humming ceased. He turned his head in his twin's direction and stared at her. Even from her vantage point Joyce could see the utter shock in his eyes.

"She wishes you all the best," Di continued. "She says go live your life and she'll be waiting for you on the other side."

Higgins stammered. His hands and feet were still, now, but his eyes darted left and right quickly. "We didn't have any kids," he said, his tone weak and confused.

"Oops." Di stifled a laugh and wiped her nose again.

David placed his hand on her shoulder, but it was clear he was close to losing it, too.

"Sorry about that," Di told Higgins. "I must have misheard her. Lemme try again."

Di closed her eyes. After several moments of silence she nudged her brother. David started humming again.

Joyce's hand continued to cover her mouth. Was this really happening? Were they so fucking out of it they were no longer even trying to contact the deceased? Maybe *The Cemetery Game* had finally come to an end, right here in Bumblefuck, Nebraska.

"Maybe we should rest for a bit," Joyce offered. The twins ignored her. Higgins looked from them to Joyce, clearly anxious and miserable.

"You have to help me," the man pleaded. "Please!"

David continued humming, although several times he nearly broke into laughter. Di might have been a statue aside from the constant sniffling.

"We'll try again later," Joyce announced. She strode to the twins and placed her hands on their arms.

David tried to pull away. When he was unsuccessful, he stopped humming and turned on her. "Get off me, Joyce!"

Joyce pulled harder on his arm and on Diane's.

"Your wife says she's sorry for having that affair," Di blurted out.

Joyce froze. Everyone froze. Higgins's lips parted. He might have been trying to speak but Di's sudden declaration had robbed him of that ability.

Joyce was the first to recover. She yanked her clients toward the door. The twins pulled away in opposite directions as if the move were choreographed. Joyce managed to keep her hand on Di's arm but she lost hold of David. He stumbled, arms pinwheeling, and lost his balance. He crashed into the coffee table.

What occurred next happened in slow motion. Joyce watched, horrified, as the table splintered. The urn was launched into the air. It sailed across the room and crashed into the wall above Mike Higgins's head. The porcelain shattered like glass. Bits of it pelted Higgins. The ashes of Debbie Higgins fell like gray snow onto her husband's head, his shoulders. David's feet were straight up in the air. Jung moved toward him. Di had ceased her struggle and belly-laughed at her brother. Joyce's feet had grown roots into the carpet. LaMontagne shouted, "Holy shit!"

Real time reasserted itself. Joyce's numb fingers released their hold on the junior Walsh twin. Diane slapped her hands together and laughed. Jung got his hands under David's arms and lifted him to his feet. LaMontagne, still recording, looked at Joyce for instruction. Joyce's eyes moved from David to Diane to Mr. Higgins. He sat still the whole time, covered with his wife's ashes. His eyes were wide, horrified. He did not breathe.

"Get them out of here," Joyce commanded when her voice finally returned. The cast and crew of *The Cemetery Game* looked at her, at each other, at the room.

Di stopped laughing. She locked eyes with her brother. David lost it. He burst into laughter. Di couldn't hold it in any longer. She joined him.

"Do it now," Joyce hissed.

She moved as fast as she was able to Mr. Higgins. He had yet to move a muscle. When Joyce knelt in front of him his eyes moved slowly in her direction.

"I'm so, so sorry, Mr. Higgins," Joyce told him. She reached for the small pile of ash on his head but stopped herself. Was she really going to simply brush it off him? Her hand paused halfway to his head.

He whispered something.

"Excuse me?" Joyce leaned in closer.

He whispered again.

Joyce still could hear nothing. She leaned in even more. "I'm sorry, Mr. Higgins. I couldn't hear you."

Higgins stood so suddenly Joyce fell back. Ash tumbled from his head and his body, drifting down to the carpet, the sofa, the remains of the coffee table. "I said get out! Get the fuck out of my house! Right fucking now! I'm going to kill every last one of you cocksuckers!"

The twins stopped laughing. Jung and LaMontagne paused in their effort to move them toward the front door. Joyce pushed herself away from him. She didn't dare try to stand; if she got in his line of sight there was no telling what he would do.

David started to laugh again. Di patted his shoulder but he was beyond any such attempt. "Dude, calm down," he announced. He could no longer stop himself from slurring his words. "It was just a joke. Relax!"

Mike Higgins stood in the center of his living room. Every muscle quivered. It caused the ash to fall from his hair and his clothes in a continuous snowfall. "Get. *Out.*"

Di started laughing again. She stabbed a finger at Higgins. "Hey! Darcy said you suck and she's glad she's dead. It's better than being around you for the rest of her life!"

Joyce's heart stopped beating. Higgins's expression transformed from rage to utter hopelessness in the blink of an eye.

"Di," David began.

Diane turned almost too fast for Joyce's eyes to follow. She slugged her brother across his jaw. David reeled from the impact. He crashed into a standing lamp and it snapped in two. David rubbed his jaw, looked wide-eyed at his sister.

"This is *your* fault, you fucking asshole!" she shouted.

"You fucking bitch!" He started for her.

Jung intercepted him. He got his arms around David and lifted his feet from the floor. David struggled with a drunk's strength. Jung spun him in the direction of the front door and shoved him through it and out of the house. David stumbled down the steps and crash landed onto the front lawn.

LaMontagne placed his hands on Di's shoulders. "Come on, Di. Let's get you out of here. I think we're done." He seemed surprised that she made no effort to attack him. After a glance outside to be sure Jung still had David under control, he looked back from the door. "Joyce?"

Joyce pushed herself to her feet. Her heart thundered in her chest and she found herself short of breath. *This better be a heart attack because if it's not I'm going to strangle them both!*

She regarded their host. "Mr. Higgins, I cannot apologize

enough," she began.

His eyes moved to her. Within them Joyce saw nothing but agony. "Just go," he stuttered.

Joyce was reluctant to take her eyes from him. She felt along the wall nearest the front door until she found her pocketbook. She picked it up and was through the door as fast as her legs could carry her.

"I'm so sorry," she called over her shoulder.

Higgins made no reply.

CHAPTER EIGHTEEN

REALLY REAL

Diane found herself back in the mist. Her window to the real world had returned. She couldn't make out the scene on the other side. She thought she was in the Andrews living room but the window kept going dark. She pressed her hands to the window's surface as if she could wipe away the darkness. The image continued to strobe slowly, erratically. Diane thought she could make out the rug, and the dark mass to her left could have been the duffel bag. It appeared her body was lying on the floor of the living room. She could even hear the sounds of the television, although it faded in and out along with the view.

"You're out there again," she announced. "But you're not quite conscious, are you? Andrews really did a number on us. We probably have a concussion. Good. If you're lying on the floor then you won't hurt anyone else."

Diane heard herself groan. The window opened up again. It remained that way for several seconds. The view changed as her body tried to rise from the floor. It went black again but came back on a moment later. Diane could see she had regained her feet.

"Spoke too soon," she remarked to the fog.

Sounds from somewhere close by. The window spun to the right and Diane could see the hallway leading to the kitchen. Brian Andrews stood on unsteady legs. He'd propped himself against the doorframe. One hand was on the back of his head while the other massaged his jaw. He looked at Diane with hatred.

"Gonna kill you, bitch." Blood and spittle dripped from his lips. "For everything you did you have to die." He took his first lurching step into the hallway.

Diane watched the scene through the window. Her first instinct was to run. Andrews was easily twice her size and weight. He might not be at 100-percent but then, neither was she. This time she had no access to a tea kettle.

"Calm down, Mr. Andrews," she heard her voice tell him. It sounded wrong to her own ears. Wet and clumsy, as if she'd forgotten how to speak, or was trying to enunciate with swollen lips and a very bruised throat. "I have no desire to fight you."

Andrews had made it almost to the living room. He was still unsteady; from what Diane could see it seemed the man was being driven forward by hatred alone. "Gonna end you, bitch," he announced as if she hadn't spoken at all. He emerged into the living room.

Diane watched herself retreat but she was moving too slowly and unevenly. There was no way she could avoid the man. He reached for her with both hands.

Andrews went down with a yelp. He tried to get his hands under him but he was too out of it. His head struck an end table on the way down. He sprawled on the rug, both hands covering the side of his head. Fresh blood seeped between his fingers. He groaned something and rolled onto his side. Diane caught a quick glimpse of the duffel bag that caused him to trip.

She heard herself laugh. It was an ugly, wet sound. Then, "Just lie still, Mr. Andrews. I shall take excellent care of you."

Leave him alone, Diane shouted into the window. *Haven't you done enough to this man? He's no threat to you. Just leave!*

The view outside moved slowly from right to left as Calder shook his head. "I need him," her voice announced. "And when I am done, I will not need you anymore. That thought should not comfort you, Diane Lynn Walsh. You have much to answer for."

Diane took an angry step toward the window. *Come and get me, you son of a bitch. I'm ready whenever you are.*

Diane heard herself giggle. Then Calder got to work.

He unzipped the duffel bag. Gingerly, almost with reverence, he began to remove the skeleton. He placed the bones on the rug next to Brian Andrews. The man had stopped moving and groaning. His chest rose and fell with labored breaths; it was the only sign he was still alive. Calder removed the hatchet, regarded it for a moment, and placed it back inside the duffel. The blood was dry now and looked like nothing more ominous than rust. But it wasn't, Diane knew. She thought again of Teddy and the poor man who had the misfortune of being on shift at Mount Olive tonight. She would have cried had she been able.

(Di, can you hear me?)

Diane started. Her brother's Inside Voice was strong. It resonated all about her as if it had originated within the mist itself.

(David!)

She held her breath, her eyes darting in every direction as if her twin were about to emerge from the darkness and embrace her.

(Di, we're almost there. Just hang on. Are you okay?)

(I'm most definitely not okay,) she replied. *(Hurry!)*

Diane began to pace. She waited for her brother to say more. Then she looked at the window.

Calder had stopped arranging the bones even though several remained within the duffel. His hands hung frozen a few inches above the rug.

"Are you...Was that ..." A pause. "That was your brother, was it not?" her voice asked. "I heard something. It was most peculiar, like the voice of a dream."

Diane froze.

"Fascinating means of communication," her voice continued. "I assume that means he is close by. Why else would he be able to talk to you?"

Diane didn't move and didn't speak. Her eyes remained glued to the window.

"I cannot permit that. I shall have to deal with him immediately. I require no distractions."

Diane watched her hands go limp. They fell to her sides. The window went dark again.

"I just got through to her," David announced.

LaMontagne did a quick double take before returning his eyes to the road.

Joyce leaned forward. "What? What did she say? Is she okay?"

David shook his head. "She's in trouble. Jim, we really need to go faster."

LaMontagne glanced at the dashboard panel. "Already doing fifty. I go any faster on this twisty-ass road and we'll be in the woods."

David looked out the windshield again. They had left Lansing behind. The sky, transitioning to navy blue, could barely be glimpsed through the canopy of branches and leaves above them. He knew they were close to the Andrews residence but most of this road looked the same as the rest of it. The lack of anything resembling a landmark certainly did nothing to help.

"Just get me there as fast as you can."

"What do you think I'm doing?"

Joyce reached back and patted David's knee. "How did you get through? I thought she was shut off from you somehow."

"She was. I think it's because we're close. I still can't get a good reading on her. It's like there's something in the way. But I can sense her, which is more than I could do before."

Joyce nodded. "She'll be okay, honey. We'll get to her and you'll see everything will be fine."

David wanted to say, *Are you sure about that? Because I'm not. I think we're pretty goddamned far from fine.* What he actually said was, "I hope so." He tried to reach his sister again but this time he could not get through. *There's something in the way, all right, and I know his name.* David chewed his lip. *Just hang on, Di. We're almost there.*

They rounded a particularly sharp turn in the road. LaMontagne gasped. Joyce shouted something. David drew in a quick, short breath.

An ancient man in black robes stood in the center of the road, illuminated perfectly in the Sienna's headlights. He smiled at them.

LaMontagne swore and slammed both feet onto the brake

pedal at the same time he turned the wheel to the left.

Everything that followed seemed to happen in slow motion. The minivan swerved wildly across the blacktop. Joyce screamed and braced herself against the dashboard. LaMontagne's arms extended fully, his muscles corded. He all but stood on the brake pedal. David's eyes remained on the old man. Calder didn't move a muscle, simply stood his ground. His smile remained in place as if it were sculpted. The Sienna missed him by inches on its way past. Calder's eyes remained locked on David.

David pulled his own gaze away from the old man in time to see the woods leap up to meet the minivan. The vehicle shook with several impacts. David could hear tree limbs cracking even above the squeal of the brakes. The windshield shattered but the safety glass remained in place. His seatbelt hugged him tightly, nearly cutting off his breathing and his circulation. The Sienna bounced off the forest floor several times and more tree limbs flew in all directions before its uncontrolled advance.

The vehicle came to a sudden stop when a limb stabbed through the shattered glass of the windshield. Beyond the limb was the rest of the tree. The Sienna smashed into it. The sound of breaking plastic and metal filled the universe. The airbags deployed and for a moment David could see nothing but white.

The horn sounded its protest, taking the place of breaking limbs and the rending of plastic. The minivan's rear tires bounced one last time and came to a stop.

David struggled with the airbag for several moments before the thing deflated enough for him to see. He took his first breath since sighting the old man in the road. The air inside the minivan smelled of burned plastic and smoke.

The tree limb that punched through the windshield had missed Joyce by at least a foot. It had not, however, missed LaMontagne. Blood ran freely from the torn skin of his upper arm. His shirt and the driver's seat were already covered with it. The limb had continued past him and into the back of the van. It had missed David by no more than six inches. He stared at the jagged tip of the spear, imagined what it would have felt like entering his body. The image churned the bile in his stomach.

"Everybody okay?" Joyce shouted above the blare of the

horn. Her voice was high, her breaths coming in quick, shallow gasps.

"Jim's hurt," David replied. He unbuckled his seatbelt and beat down the airbag as best he could.

LaMontagne had one hand on his wounded arm. Blood ran freely between his fingers. He sat as far back in the seat as physics would allow. He said something but David couldn't make it out. David tried to examine the wound but LaMontagne's hand was welded to his arm.

David tried his door. It opened with a loud creak that overwhelmed the horn. He stepped out of the vehicle and braced himself against the tree. His legs and arms trembled and it was a full minute or two before he trusted them enough to move.

Joyce's door refused at first to open. It took everything David had to get it to cooperate. He reached over, unlocked Joyce's seatbelt and helped her from the wreck. She leaned against the side of the vehicle. Her breathing was ragged and her arms and legs shook.

David staggered to the front of the Sienna. The bumper was gone, the hood had folded back like an accordion. David reached into the space where he expected to find the battery. His fingers probed until he found it. The positive terminal was held fast but its twin was wobbly. David tore at the cable until it came loose. The Sienna's horn ceased blaring. The sudden absence of sound filled his world. David actually looked around to convince himself he was still conscious.

Joyce had worked her way around to the driver's door. David stagger-stepped to her; his legs still shook although he was regaining control of his muscles quickly now. He grabbed at the door and pulled with Joyce.

The driver's door opened with a shriek of metal against metal. David stepped back to allow Joyce past him. She threw her arms around LaMontagne and squeezed the air from his lungs. Together they were able to push the airbag down enough to release his seatbelt. She helped him exit the minivan.

His hand remained clamped on the wound. Blood continued to seep through his fingers and down his arm but the flow was reduced considerably. He placed no weight on his right leg.

"Jesus, that looks bad," Joyce said. "I'm gonna see if there's a first aid kit in there somewhere. Aren't all rental cars supposed to have them?"

"We'll need to get him to a hospital," David remarked.

"Assholes, I'm right here. I can hear you, you know." LaMontagne spoke through clenched teeth. "Jesus fuck, this hurts." He pulled his hand a millimeter from the wound, looked at it, and covered it up again. "That's gonna leave a scar."

"Chicks dig scars," David told him. He craned his neck but he couldn't see Joyce within the minivan. He could, however, hear her tearing the inside apart. "How's the first aid kit coming?"

"I don't see one," came the reply.

"Check under the seats," David advised.

"No shit! Why didn't I think of that? Just shut up and let me look."

David shared a glance with LaMontagne. Neither could suppress a laugh.

"Where'd that old guy come from?" LaMontagne asked through clenched teeth. "Just standing out in the middle of the road like that. Was he crazy?"

David started. He'd forgotten the old man entirely. He looked back toward the road but couldn't see it or any sign of him. "I don't think that was a man. It was Calder."

"Oh, that's just wonderful," LaMontagne replied. "So he's real now? Like, really real?"

David shook his head. "He wasn't actually standing there. I mean, I don't think he was. I don't know. But make no mistake. He's real, all right."

Joyce returned to them. "I couldn't find anything." She looked at LaMontagne again. "How is he?"

"He's a pretty bad driver, all things considered," David told her.

LaMontagne grimaced and raised his wounded arm a few inches. "You know, my ears do work. You two need to stop talking about me like I'm not here." With effort he managed to remove his shirt. With his one good hand he wrapped it about the wound on his arm. "For now, anyway."

Joyce had removed her phone from her pocketbook. After

several seconds of aiming it in every direction, she announced, "*Nada*. No reception out here."

"I could have told you that. We have to get back to the road," David said. "Come on. This way." He helped LaMontagne navigate the woods, following the path carved by their uncontrolled joyride. The cameraman grunted every time he put weight on his right leg; it threw David off-balance but somehow he managed to keep them both upright. It took several minutes but at last they reached the blacktop. David's eyes scanned their surroundings. As he had guessed the old man was nowhere to be seen.

They started in the direction of the Andrews residence. LaMontagne struggled with every step. Joyce walked a few paces behind them and smoked.

After they had covered perhaps a quarter mile LaMontagne said, "Stop. Just stop. Hang on a minute."

David stopped, as did Joyce.

"I'm slowing you down. You said Di is in trouble. You need to get there as fast as you can. Leave me here. I'll be fine."

"We're not leaving you," Joyce replied. "Stop talking stupid."

"She's right," David agreed. "We can make it." But could they? David felt some guilt for agreeing with LaMontagne. The fact was he could travel much faster if he left the cameraman behind. And Joyce, too, for that matter. He thought of his sister and what might be happening while they were stopped on the road. He started to move again.

"Goddammit, *stop*!"

David stopped again.

"Look, man, don't be dumb," LaMontagne said, his teeth gritted against the pain. "She needs you a lot more than I do. I'll be fine. Just fucking go."

David looked at Joyce.

She required no psychic ability to read his eyes. She swallowed and shrugged. "Down to Gehenna or up to the Throne, he travels the fastest who travels alone." When both men looked at her, she shrugged. "Kipling. The point is, he's right. Di needs you. I'll stay with Jim. Worst case scenario, no cars come along so we'll keep going and meet you there. But you should go to her, David."

"Are you sure?"

"Yes," Joyce and LaMontagne said in unison.

David moved aside so Joyce could take his place. She grunted under LaMontagne's weight but otherwise said nothing. He walked a few steps from them before he stopped and turned. "A car will be along, I'm sure."

"Me, too," Joyce replied. "Now go."

David nodded and said nothing. He took off for the Andrews house.

CHAPTER NINETEEN

A CHOREOGRAPHY OF MURDER

Diane watched the minivan swerve from the road and crash into the woods. As it passed her she caught a quick image of her brother in the backseat. Then the vehicle was gone. She could hear it smashing its way deeper into the wooded area that bordered the side of the road. She tried to scream her brother's name, but she could produce no sound. She raised her fists as if to strike the window. It was at that moment she realized the window wasn't there.

Diane was no longer in the mist. She stood on a dark, deserted stretch of road bordered on both sides by woods. She held her hands before her as if to confirm the rest of her had made the trip from the mist.

Her hands were old. The skin was wrinkled, ancient. Her emaciated arms disappeared into the blackness of the robes that clung to her frail body. Diane had just enough time to gasp before her surroundings blurred. She closed her eyes against the assault until she felt the world swim back into focus.

Diane had returned to the mist. It swirled around her arms and puffed up from the ground. The window opened in its proper place. Diane turned from it.

(*David, are you there? Are you okay?*) She expected no reply and wasn't disappointed. *He's not dead*, she thought. *I'd know it if he was. I'd feel it.*

"That's good to know," her voice replied. Diane turned back to the window. She watched her hands resume their task of removing the rest of the skeleton from the duffel bag. "But even if he survived the destruction of that machine, he shan't be along anytime soon. I am afraid it is just us again, my dear."

Diane chided herself for giving Calder any kind of information. She especially wanted to keep him in the dark about her brother. David *did* survive the crash, she knew. And that meant he was on his way here. He was close, too, or she would never have been able to contact him before. She just had to keep Calder busy for a bit longer.

The sight of the minivan careening into the woods filled her head. Who else would be inside? Joyce, no doubt. Probably Jim, too. And Calder had done his best to kill them in front of her. Diane's hands balled into fists. *When I get out of here you're not going to like what I do to you. You won't like it one fucking bit.*

"Idle threats do not concern me," Calder replied. "Now, please, remain silent. I need all my faculties for what lies ahead."

Diane wished for a drum set so she could beat the daylights out of it. Anything that could distract the evil bastard from whatever it was he was trying to accomplish. She tried to create just such a set, big timpani sons of bitches that would shake the ground. Her outstretched arm quivered, her brow furrowed. The fog undulated but nothing formed. Her second attempt failed as well. It seemed she no longer had the strength to create objects from the mist. She watched as her hands assembled the last of the bones from the duffel bag on the rug next to Brian Andrews.

Diane got her first real look at the bones. They were worn with age. She could see several cracks in them. Black dirt clung to most of them; she could see it caked inside both eye sockets of the skull. It seemed some of the bones were simply gone. She counted three ribs among the missing as well as the entire left foot.

She had to do something to slow Calder's progress. David was close. She needed to buy time for him to get here. Diane looked through the window. Nothing within her sight suggested a course of action. "Just get him back in the kitchen. I'm sure there's something under the kitchen sink I could get him to drink." Diane shook her head. It was unlikely Calder could be guided to do something like that. Aiming him at a drug dealer or a telephone was one thing, suicide, another. To go out that way after holding on this long? With her brother so close? No.

She watched Calder roll the big man onto his back so he mimicked the position of the bones. "What the hell are you doing?" she asked the window. "Why—"

Her mind filled with an image of David running along the side of a road. It was dark and the woods seemed to be one large, black mass on either side of her twin. She could hear his breathing, fast and loud, and feel his heart slamming the inside of his chest. His eyes were a mix of deep concern and rage.

(David?)

He stopped running and bent forward, hands on his knees, sucking air in great gulps.

(Di! I'm almost there!)

Diane permitted herself a smile. She just as quickly shook her head. *(David, this spirit, Calder, he can hear our Inside Voices. I don't know how that's possible but he can. You have to stop.)*

Diane sensed her brother straighten. He nodded his head and started running again.

"He's too late to be of any service to you," Calder stated in Diane's voice. "Now, please, remain silent."

Fuck you, I will. Maybe you should come in here and try to make me.

She heard herself sigh. "I shall be glad to be rid of you," Calder said in Diane's voice. "Soon, my dear. Very soon indeed."

Diane had a response ready to go but she stopped short. A sudden wave of nausea washed over her. Her head began to throb. The mist rippled as did the image in the window. No, it was more than the image. The window itself undulated as if it were silk caught in a summer breeze. Diane dropped to one knee. The throbbing in her head graduated to full-on pounding. Her arms gave and she landed on whatever passed for solid ground in this place.

"What the hell are you doing?" She might have whispered, she might have screamed.

The mist exploded around her.

David reached the bottom of the Andrews driveway. He paused, sucked in deep lungfuls of air. The canopy of branches above parted and David could see sky for the first time in what felt like hours. It wasn't quite full dark yet but it was getting there. He could just make out the top of the Andrews house high on the hill. David took another long, deep breath, and ran as fast as he could up the driveway.

Brian Andrews's old Cadillac sat parked in front of the house. David paused there and leaned against it to catch his breath. He remained for only a moment before he mounted the front steps. The front door was open a few inches. He crept to it and peeked inside.

The foyer was deserted. Beyond it he could see someone's legs lying on the living room rug. David pushed the door open as gently and silently as it would allow and stepped inside the foyer.

He could hear the television in the living room. His eyes remained glued to the pair of legs on the rug. He knew right away they didn't belong to his sister. David peeked up the stairs and saw nothing. He wanted to sprint into the living room, through the whole house, if that's what it took to find Di. Something kept him from doing just that. Maybe it was his twin's final message. If Calder had access to their unique form of communication then the rules had gone out the window. *I think that happened quite a while ago,* David corrected himself. *Right around the time we first saw the old fucker.* True enough. This thought alone stopped him from simply charging into the living room to help his sister.

He could see more of the living room now. It was indeed Brian Andrews who lay on the rug. He was bloody but David could see his chest rising and falling. Di knelt between Andrews and an old skeleton that occupied the rug. David knew who the bones belonged to.

Di looked remarkably different from the last time he saw her. Her clothes were torn to shreds and covered with half-dried blood. Her hands and face were stained crimson .

He whispered, "Di," before he knew he was going to speak. David cringed. He expected his twin to leap to her feet, although it wouldn't really be her. He held his breath, his feet rooted to the spot. His sister didn't react in the slightest. David crept closer. His right arm reached for her. Still, she gave no indication she knew he was there. David's fingers touched his sister's hand.

He felt a *whoosh* and was suddenly in the fog. No, not the fog. This was different. Instead of the normal environment of a cemetery, he found himself in a void. He could see nothing but black and mist in every direction.

(Di? Di, I'm here. Where are you?)

He waited but heard nothing. There was no right or left, up or down within this void. David chose a direction at random and began walking. He called to his sister every few moments. Wherever he was he seemed to have the place to himself. He was about to exit this mist when he saw something ahead. It appeared to be a large window frame hanging in space. David headed for it.

As he neared the object, he caught the sound of someone whimpering. David looked around. The mist undulated near the base of the frame and he ran the rest of the way.

Di lay in a fetal position on the floor. David knelt beside her and cradled her into his arms.

(Di, it's me. It's okay. You're gonna be okay.)

His sister whimpered again. Her muscles trembled.

David held her close. He glanced about the area. The window frame seemed to be the sole object in the universe. He looked at it, wondered why it should be here. If it served a purpose it wasn't doing so at the moment.

(David.)

He turned to his sister. Di looked at him through slitted eyes. Her Inside Voice was weak. Even holding her body against his he could barely hear her. He offered her a smile.

(It's okay, Di. I have you now. We're getting out of here.)

She shook her head almost imperceptibly. *(You did exactly what he wanted you to do.)*

David started. His sister's eyes were full of dread. They moved to the window frame hanging in space before them. David followed her gaze.

The frame came to life. It took David a moment to realize what he was looking at. He saw himself kneeling on the floor of Brian Andrews's living room. Someone knelt next to him and held his hand. The hand grasping his was covered with mostly dried blood.

(Is that you? Is this your perspective?)

The other hand clutched a long, thin bone that could only be one of Silas Calder's ribs. The image followed the arm as it raised the bone high in the air above David's head.

(Di, what am I looking at here?)

(I'm so sorry,) she said, her Inside Voice barely a whisper.

David returned his eyes to the image within the window. *Oh, Jesus,* he thought.

Diane looked into her brother's eyes. She saw the awful realization settle there. Beyond him hung the window. She watched her arm raise the jagged bone high in the air.

She couldn't move, and was unable to speak. Whatever Calder had hit her with just before her brother's arrival had done its job. She was nauseated, and weak as a kitten. It took most of her remaining strength to keep her eyes open. She wanted to hold her twin one last time even as he held her.

Get out, David! Get out now, she thought.

Diane closed her eyes.

David catapulted himself out of the mist. One moment he knelt in the dark place, cradling his sister. The next he was back in the real world. His eyes snapped open in time to see his sister's hand bring down the bone. He willed himself to move but his muscles were clumsy and slow to obey. He managed to get to his feet and just as quickly lost his balance.

The bone sliced through the air. It embedded itself in David's left calf. He felt the old, vile thing punch through his skin and sink deep into the muscles. David howled and clutched his wounded leg.

Di rose to her feet and regarded him. "A worthy effort," she told him. "Ultimately for naught." She reached down and wrapped her fingers around the bone protruding from David's calf. "The condemned will be punished." She twisted it.

David screamed. Bolts of lightning shot up his leg. The entire world turned white. His hand grabbed for the bone, but his sister slapped him away. He tried to crawl, but he gained only inches.

"Di, please!" Then, "Calder!"

His sister's lips pulled back from her teeth in what might have constituted a smile in a different setting. The blood which coated most of her face and body cast the expression into hellish delight.

David drew back his other leg. "I'm sorry," he announced. His foot shot forward and caught Diane in the hip. She tumbled backward with a grunt. David's hands wrapped themselves around the bone and pulled. He grunted and then screamed with the effort. The bone emerged from his calf but too slowly. He could feel it tear at his muscles on the way out. For every quarter inch of movement David screamed again. Blood seeped from the wound and stained his pant leg dark red. He had it nearly free when his sister pounced on him. She covered his hands with hers and threw her weight onto the bone.

Stars filled David's vision and were overwhelmed by white light that seemed to permeate all of existence. He might have screamed, was certain he had, but he could hear nothing. His leg felt as if it had been placed into a furnace. His hands moved to the wound and he felt the bone now sunk all the way through his leg.

"Di," he gasped through clenched teeth.

"Yes, you will," his sister replied from somewhere far away.

David blinked several times. The white light remained but he could see some detail through the haze. His sister staggered drunkenly across the living room. She scooped up a small, solid-looking statuette from the fireplace mantle.

David's eyes went to the bone protruding from his leg. Only

the tip was still visible. His fingers flailed for it, but the bone was slick with blood and he couldn't grasp it. He tried to move his leg and he was rewarded with fresh bolts of agony that lanced from the wound. It went through the floor, he realized quite matter-of-factly. *Pinned like a fucking butterfly in a high school science lab.*

Di approached him slowly. She loomed over him again and raised the statuette above her head. Di seemed to struggle with its weight. *It's heavy enough to kill,* he realized. David held up both hands.

I'm gonna die, Joyce concluded as the Andrews house came into view. She and LaMontagne were nearly to the top of the driveway and she was unsure how much longer she could keep them both upright. Her clothes were soaked through with sweat. Her breathing was labored and getting worse by the minute. She could feel her heart trying to pound its way through her chest as if it were trying to escape her body. Her legs shook and her back was on fire.

It had been her intention to wait by the crashed minivan until someone came along. It was less than ten minutes before LaMontagne talked her into following after David. "He might need our help," he implored her. Joyce could not argue with his logic. Still, she had not expected she would have to support him the whole way to the Andrews residence. Now she was paying the price.

Blood had soaked through the fabric of LaMontagne's makeshift bandage. Some of it stained Joyce's blouse. In a different setting she would be angry about her ruined clothing; now she paid it no mind at all.

"Almost there," LaMontagne offered helpfully.

Joyce didn't look at him. She was going to need a few months of R&R after this insanity. Lucky for her she had the perfect resort in mind. Her head filled with images of the beach, the sun, a very large cocktail, and young shirtless men waiting on her hand and foot. She just needed to survive the next few minutes and it was all hers.

They made it to the parked Cadillac out front. Joyce propped her cameraman against the car and sank to one knee. Her chest heaved with each long intake of air.

"Maybe you should quit smoking," LaMontagne told her.

Joyce paused her heavy breathing long enough to shoot him a look that could melt iron. "Maybe you should shut the fuck up," she gasped.

Her head snapped in the direction of the house. Someone had shouted something Joyce could not make out. She looked at LaMontagne, saw her own startled expression staring back at her.

"Go," he shouted and pointed to the open front door. "I'll be right behind you."

Joyce doubted that but she ran as fast as her quivering legs would allow anyway. She surprised herself by taking the front steps two at a time. She was through the front door no more than three seconds after she left LaMontagne's side.

The shouting came from the living room and Joyce ran through the foyer. She stopped dead in her tracks at the threshold between the two rooms.

Diane, looking like the last survivor in every horror movie, was struggling with someone on the living room floor. Their movements were violent, a choreography of murder. Joyce tried to see who the young woman struggled with, but Diane's wild thrashing blocked Joyce's view of her attacker. They seemed to be wrestling over a sculpture. "Di!" she yelled and ran to her.

Joyce got her arms around Diane's midsection and heaved with everything she had. The two women rocketed backward. Joyce's feet became tangled, and they crashed to the floor. Diane landed on top of her and her breath exploded out of her lungs. Joyce gasped for air.

"Joyce! That's not Diane! Get away from her!" David shouted from the living room.

Joyce turned her head and saw David on the floor. A small pool of blood surrounded his legs and he seemed unable to move. What had he said?

Joyce's heart nearly stopped when the realization hit her. Her hands, suddenly clumsy and numb, pushed at the woman still lying on top of her. "Get off! Get off!"

Di scrambled on top of Joyce. Her nose was inches from Joyce's. Di smiled at her. Blood dripped from the corners of her mouth and pattered on Joyce's cheeks. "Guilty," the younger woman told her.

The sculpture was still in her hand. Joyce could see now it was a frontiersman on horseback. One hand held the reins and the other his trusty rifle. Di raised it above her head.

"No!" David shouted.

Joyce's hands still struggled for purchase on what remained of Diane's outfit. She succeeded in tearing the blouse even more, but it did nothing to move the woman off her. Joyce's eyes grew wide as the sculpture started its downward arc.

David watched his sister bring the statuette down directly on Joyce's head. It produced a thick, wet sound that seemed to echo throughout the house. David screamed, *"No!"* again when Diane raised the heavy object above her head a second time. Fresh blood dripped from it.

Joyce's hands covered her face. Blood poured freely from her forehead. Even from ten feet away David could see the large gash on her scalp. She whimpered something unintelligible.

"Calder! Leave her alone!"

The thing in control of his sister's body turned its head and regarded David. It smiled.

The statuette descended again. It glanced off Joyce's fingers and her arm flopped to her side. The frontiersman struck the floor. Slivers of wood erupted from the point of impact. Calder raised it again, swearing incoherently at the deflection. Joyce's unbroken hand grabbed for it and missed. Calder brought it down again. This time he connected solidly. Blood poured from the wound and began to form a small pond around Joyce's head.

"You fucker!" David screamed. He'd managed to roll onto his side despite the agony in his left leg. He tried to pull himself along the floor but he remained pinned in place. "She didn't do anything! She was innocent!"

Calder smiled at him and raised the statuette. He took a deep breath and surveyed his work. "She lied for a living," he informed David in Diane's voice. "She protected the guilty from justice. Her debt to society will now—"

Diane's head snapped in the direction of the front door. David's eyes followed hers. LaMontagne stood braced against the doorframe. His mouth hung agape as his eyes travelled from Di to the body on the floor.

"Jim, look out!" David shouted.

Calder hurled the statuette like a Justin Verlander fastball. LaMontagne had no time to react. The heavy object struck him squarely in the center of his forehead. He stumbled back, one hand moving slowly to the area of impact. Blood trickled from the wound and formed a thin stream down the center of his face. LaMontagne's good leg buckled and he fell back somewhere on the front deck. David heard the sound of splintering wood and imagined that was the cameraman crashing through the railing that bordered the deck.

David's eyes returned to Joyce. Blood covered her face, her neck. He couldn't tell if she was alive.

Calder regained his feet. Fresh blood dripped from his hands and arms, and from his face and hair. He walked on unsteady legs to the front door and looked outside. Apparently satisfied by what he saw he crossed the foyer and stepped over Joyce's body. He stopped in front of David and regarded him.

David looked into the thing's eyes. "I'm going to kill you."

Calder smirked and walked past. David tried to grab for him but missed.

"You should be happy," his sister's voice informed him. "I have elected to execute sentence on you with my own hands. It will be but a few moments. You lie there and be still. I shall be ready for you directly."

Calder knelt once again between the skeleton and Brian Andrews.

CHAPTER TWENTY

UTTERLY CONTEMPTABLE

Diane had managed to rise to her hands and knees. The past few minutes she felt the strength returning to her. The nausea was gone. Whatever Calder was up to must have been interrupted. She took her first look at the window and saw her brother lying on the floor, glaring at her. She'd never seen so much hatred in his eyes, not even when everything went to shit in Mike Higgins's living room , but it blazed there now.

"I'm going to kill you," he vowed through clenched teeth.

She watched herself move away from him and kneel between the skeleton and their unconscious and very reluctant host. She heard, too, Calder's reply to her brother's boast.

Whatever he's gonna do it's gonna happen now, she realized. She remembered at once that he could hear her thoughts but Diane doubted it mattered any longer.

(David, can you hear me?)

Diane waited. Was Calder blocking her again? Even with her brother no more than a few feet from her?

(I'm here, Di,) he said at last.

Diane released a long breath and smiled. *(Thank God. Are you okay?)*

(Not even close. I think Joyce is dead. Jim, too, maybe.)

Diane's eyes moved to the window. It was difficult to make out, but she thought she saw fresh blood on her hands and arms. Calder returned his hands to the skull and Brian Andrews's head.

(Oh, God, no. It was me, wasn't it? I did it.)

Her brother's reply was immediate and forceful. *(It wasn't you, Di. This was Calder from start to finish. Son of a bitch thinks he's still a judge. He's pronouncing sentence on people and executing them. I don't know what the fuck he's doing now but I know it's not good. We need to get you back into the real world fast.)*

Diane's eyes remained fixed on the window. She watched her fingers smear blood on the skull and Brian Andrews's forehead in odd patterns.

It hit her quite suddenly. She gasped with the realization. It was so obvious she couldn't believe it had taken her this long to figure it out. *(David, he's—)*

The wave of nausea crashed over her again. Diane gulped and almost collapsed. She steadied herself but it wouldn't last long. Already her knees threatened to buckle and send her to the ground again.

(Di, what?)

(He's trying to move himself into Andrews,) Diane gasped. *(David, we need to play the game. You pull from that side and I'll try from here. Get Calder into the fog before he finishes—)*

(I'm stuck, Di. Literally. My leg is pinned to the floor. I can't reach you from here.)

Diane's knees gave in and fell to the ground. Her outstretched arms prevented her from face-planting, but she struggled to get her knees under her as more nausea surged throughout her body.

(Just do it,) she told her twin. *(And hurry!)*

David reached again for the top of the bone protruding from his calf. His fingers brushed it but there simply was not enough of it exposed to allow him a good grip. He pushed himself into a seated position as best he could. Fresh bolts of pain upped the wattage with every movement. It was all he could do to stop himself from screaming. He wiped his hands on his jeans and left streaks of crimson. Then he reached for it again. It was no good.

He instead reached for his sister. All he needed was to touch her and he would be in the fog. Assuming Diane was right about this, Calder would find himself there as well. It made no difference. His sister's body was five or six feet from his outstretched fingers. It may as well have been on Saturn.

(David, it has to be now!)

David regarded the bone dug deep into his calf. He steadied himself, took a long, deep breath and he pushed down on his leg with both hands. It felt as if every nerve ending in his body came to life and screamed their protest. His vision exploded into a landscape of stars. He very nearly passed out. The limb dropped three inches and pressed against the floor. The bone popped up by those same three inches. David's right hand grasped it. He pulled with everything he had. It moved a few centimeters, no more. He stifled a scream and grasped the bone more firmly. He felt it free itself from the hardwood at the same moment he fell back.

His hands grasped either side of the wound. Blood flowed between his fingers and saturated his pant leg and the floorboards. He managed to keep himself from screaming but every inch of his body was coated with sweat from the effort. He closed his eyes and took several deep breaths to stop himself from passing out. He opened his eyes and looked at Calder.

David crawled across the floor toward his sister's body and the monster that dwelt therein. He reached Calder's incomplete skeleton and scattered some of the bones with an angry sweep of his arm.

(Di, get ready!)

He didn't wait for a reply. David placed his right hand on his sister's arm and squeezed.

For the first time since the field by the highway Diane found herself someplace other than the mist. Her window onto the real world was gone. The fog swirled about her legs in thick tendrils. Even the ground beneath her feet felt different as it had become the hardwood floor of the Andrews home. The nausea and weakness left her all at once. She felt better, in fact, than she had since her and David's last trip into the fog together at Mount Olive.

Diane looked about. *(David?)*

(Here,) came the immediate reply.

Diane turned, saw her brother emerge from the fog in the direction of the front door. She wished she could hug him in the real world, feel his arms around her. It wouldn't be the same here but it would have to do. Diane flung herself into David's arms. She felt him hug her back, felt the warmth of the embrace. As much as she didn't want it to end she pulled back.

(We have to stop him now, before this goes any further.)

(Agreed,) David replied with a nod. He looked about the fog. *(Any idea where he is?)*

Diane shook her head. *(No. But he's here. I know that much. I can feel him.)*

(Then let's go find him.) David offered his hand and Diane took it. Together they left the foyer behind and entered the living room.

There was no sign of Calder. Diane knelt by the spot where the old judge's bones should have been. The space was empty. Next to it, however, was a zone of warmth. Diane felt the heat radiating from the air near the floor. The area was mostly devoid of fog. *(I think this is where Brian Andrews is. I can feel it. He's still alive, at least.)*

(I'm a lot less concerned about him right now than I am about Calder.)

(Me, too.) Diane stood again and looked about. She indicated the kitchen with a nod of her head. *(Could be in there. That's where we ... um, I mean, he fought with Andrews.)*

David nodded his agreement. *(Worth a shot.)*

They covered half the distance to the kitchen when Diane stopped. *(David?)*

He looked in her direction. *(What is it?)*

(Thank you for coming for me.) Despite the knowledge it wouldn't feel the same, she planted a kiss on his cheek.

Had they been in the real world he would have blushed, she

knew. As it was, he smiled and resumed walking to the kitchen. *(Don't mention it.)*

The signs of the struggle were still very much in evidence. Despite the color wash to cooler tones of gray and blue, and the presence of the fog, the kitchen looked the same as it had the last time she saw it. Diane could see quite plainly the overturned chair, the phone hanging from its cradle on the wall. Even the plate where Brian Andrews had prepared his afternoon snack remained where she left it. The fog obscured the streaks of blood on the linoleum floor and Diane was grateful for that. Calder was nowhere in evidence.

(He's here, I know he is. Maybe he's hiding.)

David's lips turned up in a wry smile. *(I don't think he's afraid of us, Di.)*

(Well, he should be. Let's keep looking.)

She led the way back into the living room.

The twins halted in their tracks. Judge Calder stood in front of the far wall by the fireplace. His head was down but his eyes were fixed on them. The corners of his mouth were turned up in a mad mockery of a smile. "Guilty," he told them.

Diane took an angry step in his direction. Before she could do more than that David shoved her aside and charged the old spirit. She watched her brother swing a haymaker at Calder's head. Something stopped his fist before it could connect. It appeared to be a tendril of darkness, as if the fog had suddenly turned black and come to the old spirit's defense. David braced himself and tried to pull his hand free.

(What the hell is this?) he shouted.

Diane ran to him. It was difficult to see, but it appeared the tendril was part of Calder's robes. Diane grabbed at it and joined her brother in trying to pull his wrist from its grasp.

(It's not coming loose,) she grunted.

A second tendril snaked up from the fog and wrapped itself around Diane's wrist. It pulled her hand away easily. Diane felt her feet leave the ground and she was suddenly suspended above the fog. Her free hand beat and tore at the tendril.

"So utterly contemptable," Calder told them.

(Let her go!) David commanded. *(Don't you fucking hurt her!)* He continued to struggle with the tendril wrapped about his wrist. When that produced no results, he threw a punch with his free hand. It landed feebly on Calder's shoulder. The old spirit looked at him, rage and amusement vied for top billing in his eyes.

Diane had had enough. She gave up trying to free herself. Instead, she slugged the old spirit across his jaw. To her surprise the tendril attached to her wrist let go. Calder himself appeared stunned, more by the result, perhaps, than by any actual pain or damage the punch may have caused. Diane hit him again. The time Calder backpedaled into the wall. The robes released their hold on David and he backed up several steps and massaged his wrist.

Calder looked at Diane with utter astonishment. Diane smiled at him. *(Oh, yeah. I've been waiting for this.)*

Diane rained blows on the old spirit. The rage and helplessness of the last few days lent strength to her arms and legs.

(You murderous son of a bitch! How many people did you kill? How many did you make me kill? Fuck you!)

Calder began to sink to his knees, but Diane grabbed his robes and hauled him to his feet. She punched him again and again until her hands began to throb.

(Go back to hell!) she spat and hit him again.

Strong hands grasped her arms and pulled her back. Diane spun, ready to continue her attack. David struggled to hold her and avoid being hit himself.

(Di, it's me. It's me! Slow down. It's okay. He's down, Di.)

Diane's eyes focused on David. The strength left her and she sagged into his arms.

David stroked her hair. *(It's okay. He's down. You did it.)* He regarded the old spirit. *(You fucked with the wrong Walsh, Your Honor. Di's way stronger than I am. And you really pissed her off. That was so not a good idea.)*

Diane felt her brother's arms around her. Her body shook. She wanted nothing more than to sink into him and let him take her away. But no. Not yet.

(It's not over,) she told him. She turned back to Calder. Everything went black.

LaMontagne came to at the edge of the gravel driveway, between the house and Brian Andrews's Cadillac. The pain in his arm and his leg had been joined by a new arrival. His head pounded and caused a strobe light behind his eyes. LaMontagne groaned and pushed himself onto his elbows. His hand instinctively went to his forehead. It was wet and he could feel torn skin. What the hell happened?

He remembered shouts from within the house. Joyce went inside first and he did his best to keep up. He remembered getting to the door and seeing—

Joyce. Diane was on top of her, about to strike her with something. There was a lot of blood. Diane was covered with it, in fact. He thought he caught a glimpse of David lying on the floor. Had she attacked him, too? He remembered nothing after that.

The Caddy was close and he used it to pull himself to his feet. The throbbing in his head pounded so hard LaMontagne could barely see. He steadied himself against the car and tried to slow his breathing.

When his heartbeat slowed he looked at the house. He could hear nothing from within, nor could he see any sign of movement. *Get the hell out of he*re, he thought. *Get back to the road and flag down a car and call the cops.* The urge was ridiculous on the face of it. He was in no condition to go anywhere. He doubted he could even make it back down the driveway. He considered the guest house. It had a phone and it was far enough away from the main house that he could probably hide from Diane until someone showed up to deal with her. He rejected that idea as well. He wouldn't be able to negotiate the steep decline to get there. He wasn't likely able to break into the place either, not in his present condition. That left him a single destination.

LaMontagne pushed himself away from the Cadillac and limped toward the front deck. The steps were a problem, and he took them even more slowly than he had the last time. He looked for something he could use as a weapon. The small table and chairs to the right of the front door were too flimsy, and he might not be able to use them effectively, anyway. *Just be quiet, asshole. Sneak in, find a phone, dial 911. You don't even have to say anything. They'll trace the call and send the cavalry. All you have to do is avoid being seen and heard.*

He whispered, "Shit, and here I thought this was going to be difficult."

He peeked inside the foyer. Joyce was on the floor, her head and most of her upper body surrounded by a pond of blood. LaMontagne swallowed.

His eyes moved up, scanned the immediate area. The foyer and the stairs leading to the second floor were clear. He held his breath when he saw the living room. Someone was lying on the floor but he couldn't see the rest of the body. What looked like bones were scattered around the hardwood. Nothing moved inside the living room. He heard nothing but the television.

To his right stood a coatrack. Two windbreakers hung there. The smaller of the two was white with a pink lining. LaMontagne thought of Emily Andrews sitting in her wheelchair by the grave of her husband while the twins did their thing. Teddy stood next to him, earphones on his head and boom mic in his hands. *At least two of the people there that day are dead.* The thought struck him harder than whatever Diane had hurled at him.

As quietly as he could LaMontagne took both jackets from the coatrack and lowered them to the floor. The coatrack was tall and unwieldly but he saw nothing else he could use if Diane suddenly charged at him from around a corner.

He used it as a crutch. Every soft *thud* it made on the hardwood caused LaMontagne to cringe. He craned his neck as he got closer to the living room. Brian Andrews was lying on the rug. His eyes fluttered weakly, the only sign he was still alive. David was on one knee. The wound on his leg bled profusely; most of his left pant leg and the surrounding hardwood were dark crimson. He had one hand on Diane's arm.

Diane knelt on the rug, between an odd collection of bones and Brian Andrews. He'd seen them do their act enough times to recognize what they were doing now. Were they in this together? *Diane attacked Joyce and me. Did she do the same to Teddy?* David's story of her being possessed by some dead judge suddenly felt ridiculous. Maybe the old lady's husband told them where he kept the money, after all. Everything since then was smoke and mirrors so the twins could get the cash. If their plan required a few bodies along the way, so what?

Stop being insane, he chided himself. Di might be off the deep end, but David had been in that car, too. If that branch penetrated another few inches to the left it would have skewered him. And LaMontagne *had* seen the old judge standing in the middle of the road. While Di might be in this up to her tits, LaMontagne doubted David had anything to do with it.

He stepped into the living room. His foot sent a piece of bone skittering along the hardwood. The sound filled the world. LaMontagne brought up the coatrack, ready to smash Diane when she jumped to her feet. No one moved. He limped closer, no longer caring if he made any noise. He was within range now.

He squared himself like a Major League hitter in the batter's box. He adjusted his grip on the coatrack and swung it as hard as his wounded arm would allow. It connected solidly with the side of Diane's head. Droplets of blood sprayed from the wound. She sprawled onto the floor and rolled right up to the fireplace.

LaMontagne readied himself for another swing but it seemed unnecessary. Diane didn't move.

CHAPTER TWENTY-ONE

THE ARCHITECT

David stood in absolute shock as his sister vanished from the fog. He had enough time to look at Calder before the fog itself vanished and he was back in Brian Andrews's living room—back in the real world. The agony in his leg returned immediately and David gasped. His head snapped left and right. The first thing he noticed was his sister lying on the floor in front of the fireplace. The hair on the side of her head was stained red and blood flowed freely from the new wound. *Oh, Jesus, she's been shot.* He started to crawl toward her. He imagined Andrews coming to and finding them in his living room. If he had a gun …

"David!"

David didn't stop at the sound of his name. He reached Diane. His fingers probed the side of her head. He could find nothing to indicate a bullet wound. One hand went to her neck and he felt for a pulse. He found one, strong and regular.

"David!"

He turned his head. LaMontagne stood a few feet away. Blood dripped from the coatrack in his hands. David's eyes narrowed. "What the hell did you do?"

LaMontagne limped back a step. "If you're in this with her you'd better stay away. I'll dent your fucking skull, too."

David lunged for him. LaMontagne staggered back out of his reach. David tried to stand and failed. "No one's in on anything, you asshole! We had him beat! *Di* had him beat!"

LaMontagne got the coatrack back under his arm and

retreated another step. David saw the confusion play across his features. The cameraman pointed to Diane. "She killed Joyce. She probably killed Teddy, too."

David used the recliner to pull himself up. He braced himself against it. "She didn't kill anybody! That was Calder. And she had him down. And then you hit her."

David didn't wait for LaMontagne to respond. He limped to his sister's side and knelt there. His hand stroked her hair. "Come on, Di, come back to me. I know you're in there somewhere."

She moaned so softly David almost didn't hear her. His heart leaped into his chest. He leaned in a little closer. "That's it, kid. Come on back."

"Um, David?"

David ignored LaMontagne. He continued to whisper into his sister's ear. Blood continued to seep from beneath her hair but it had slowed to a trickle. David took that as a good sign.

"Call 911," he told LaMontagne without taking his eyes from his twin. "Get an ambulance here right now."

"David, you need to see this."

Something in the man's voice penetrated David's concern for his sister. There was another sound, a new sound, in the living room. It might have been the chittering of a wild animal.

The bones of Silas Calder rolled across the hardwood from every direction. At first David's mind refused to quantify the sight. He could see nothing moving them, certainly not from every direction at once. They converged on a single spot on the rug. If Calder had enough control of his mortal remains to do that, it would mean...

Di was wrong, he thought. *Calder wasn't trying to transfer himself into Andrews. He was trying to ... what? Take the man's flesh?* There could be no proper term for what Calder planned to do with Brian Andrews. David knew, beyond any doubt, he was right about the old judge's plan.

At the same time David experienced his epiphany the living room was plunged into near darkness. The light from the lamps, from the television, seemed to have bled in the direction of the bones. The darkness became a shadow. The shadow began to move.

"David, what the fuck is this?" LaMontagne had backed himself into the foyer. He held the coatrack in front of him as if it were a sword.

David saw too late that LaMontagne had reached Joyce. Before he could shout a warning, the cameraman tripped and fell backward. LaMontagne yelped with the impact and tried to scramble to his feet. He did little more than entangle his legs with Joyce's.

David's eyes returned to the shadow that blotted out the skeletal remains of the old judge. The darkness climbed the wall next to the fireplace and David dove for his sister. He grasped her hands and started to pull her away from the shadow. Diane groaned again, a bit more loudly this time.

"Now would be a very good time to wake up, Di," David told her through gritted teeth. He pulled her all the way back to the threshold with the kitchen hallway before he allowed himself to stop. David's eyes rose to the shadow again.

It remained in front of the wall. Tentacles of darkness writhed within the shadow without rhyme or reason. David patted his sister's cheeks. "Come on, Di. Come on back. We're in trouble."

His eyes were drawn to Brian Andrews. The big man rolled onto his side, coughed. One hand went to the side of his head. His movements were slow, confused. He seemed oblivious to everything around him.

"Andrews," David called to him. "Get out of there! *Move*, man!"

Brian Andrews looked at him. His eyes were unfocused. His hand came away from the side of his head. He turned it over in front of his eyes as if he had never seen such a thing before.

A few feet behind and to Andrews's left the shadows coalesced. Arms separated themselves from the central mass. The skull rose from within the darkness and parked itself atop its shoulders. The whole thing moved a few feet from the wall. It didn't walk; it glided a few inches above the hardwood.

Brian Andrews at last took note of his surroundings. His jaw dropped, his eyes narrowed in confusion. He sat still on the rug, unable to take his eyes from the thing.

"Andrews, run!" David shouted.

Calder's skull turned in David's direction. The hollow eye sockets focused on him.

David froze.

LaMontagne shouted something from the foyer.

Calder moved across the living room, the shadows undulating like the fabric of a judge's robes with the movement. It reached the twins and paused, hanging in space before them. Its skeletal hand reached for them.

Arctic air radiated from the thing. Frost coated David's exposed skin.

(Di, it's now or never.)

Diane woke with a start.

David held her more tightly.

Diane, seeming to recognize instantly what was happening, grabbed Calder's wrist. Without a word she hurled all three of them into the fog.

LaMontagne stumbled to his feet in time to see the shadow become Silas Calder. He leaned against the wall beside the front door. He couldn't see David or Diane from his vantage point. Brian Andrews, on the other hand, picked the worst possible moment to regain consciousness. LaMontagne watched the portly man struggle onto his hands and knees, mere feet away from the architect of all the death and misery they had experienced since the first round of the Cemetery Game.

"Jesus," LaMontagne whispered, and then with far greater volume he yelled, "Andrews, get outta there!"

Andrews saw the shadow-thing and froze.

LaMontagne would have to run for help after all, wounded leg be damned. He felt along the wall until he found the open front door.

Joyce groaned. LaMontagne froze. He took a single step toward her before his knees gave and he collapsed nearly on top of the woman. "Joyce! Joyce, are you alive?"

Her head lolled to one side. Her lips parted and another groan escaped.

"Jesus, you are!" LaMontagne leaned in close. Joyce's eyes remained closed. Blood continued to seep from the gashes on her face and scalp. LaMontagne's head snapped up. "David! She's alive! Joyce is alive!"

He couldn't see David or Diane. Calder left Andrews behind and glided across the living room and out of LaMontagne's line of sight.

Andrews regained the power of movement. He climbed to his feet and stumbled into the foyer. He sidestepped the two people on the floor without a pause. He took the stairs to the second floor two at a time and he, too, was gone from LaMontagne's sight.

LaMontagne eyed the door. He paused when he heard a racket from upstairs. It sounded as if Brian Andrews was tearing the house apart. LaMontagne cast a final look at the living room. He saw nothing, heard nothing. *You know what it's doing. It's after David and Diane.* "Yeah, well, there ain't much I can do about that, is there?" He tapped Joyce's cheek. "Joyce, come on. Wake up. We can't stay here."

Andrews chugged down the stairs. He gripped a rifle with both hands.

LaMontagne knew he had no chance of wresting the firearm away from him. He closed his eyes and wished he could have seen his family one last time. When nothing happened after several seconds LaMontagne opened one eye.

Andrews stood with his back to LaMontagne at the threshold between the foyer and the living room. He'd brought the rifle up to his shoulder and was taking aim at something.

Calder ... or the twins? Or all three?

LaMontagne yelled, "No!" and threw himself at Andrews.

His momentum carried them into the living room. LaMontagne caught his first look at Andrews's intended targets. The shadow-thing hovered inches above the floor and directly in front of the twins. Even from here LaMontagne could see Di's hand wrapped around the thing's wrist. Both she and David appeared calm; they were certainly not struggling with it. LaMontagne recognized what was happening.

"Don't shoot them," he gasped, struggling to get a grip on the rifle.

"Get off," Andrews grunted. He twisted and turned, tried to pull the rifle away from the man clinging to his back.

"They're all that's standing between us and that thing," LaMontagne told him. He had a solid grip on the rifle barrel. Not enough to wrest it from Andrews but enough to keep him from aiming it. "You kill them, we die!"

"Get off me, you fuck!" Andrews roared. He spun around as fast as his feet would allow.

LaMontagne hung on for all he was worth. They moved about the living room, crashing into the walls, the furniture. LaMontagne lost his grip on the rifle more than once but each time he was able to grab it again before Andrews could take aim. Every time Andrews turned LaMontagne caught sight of the twins. Neither they nor the shadow-thing had moved an inch since he first spotted them. *You two better hurry it up. I can't hold on like this much longer.*

Andrews tripped over the coffee table and went down in a heap. He took one hand off the rifle to break his fall. LaMontagne tore it from his other hand and rolled away from him.

LaMontagne found himself sitting against the wall. He surprised himself when he realized he had the rifle. He aimed it at Andrews.

Andrews got his arms under him and saw LaMontagne. His eyes shot fire but he said nothing. Slowly, like the bad guy in every Clint Eastwood movie, he raised his hands above his head.

I've never even held one of these things, much less fired one. But there's no reason to tell you that, is there? He regarded Andrews, on his knees with his arms high in the air. "Just don't move. You don't know it yet, but I just saved your life."

Diane felt her brother's arms around her. She also felt the cold radiating from Calder. It infected her hand and was climbing steadily up her arm. She released the old monster's wrist and he backed away.

They'd returned to the fog and stood against the wall in the Andrews living room. David let go of her and together the twins rose to their feet. Diane took a single step back to stand directly beside her brother. She felt the numbness leave her arm and, a moment later, her hand.

(You cut it pretty close,) David told her.

(I like being dramatic,) she replied. *(What happened?)*

(I'm pretty sure Jim clobbered you. Don't be mad. He thought you were on a murder spree.)

Calder stood a few feet in front of them. His skin hung in tatters from his skull. His eyes were gone. A few wisps of long white hair still clung stubbornly to what was left of his scalp.

"You erred bringing me here," he told them.

Diane smirked. *(I erred, all right, but it wasn't that.)* She turned to her twin. *(As good as it felt to pummel the shit out of him, it was the wrong approach. I know that now. We don't beat him by beating him.)*

She searched her twin's eyes. When they lit up with realization, Diane smiled.

(Because this place isn't physical,) David said. His tone was soft and full of awe, that of a student who had just worked out the answer to a difficult philosophical question.

Diane looked again at Calder. *(He sees,)* she told him. *(And so do I.)*

She grasped David's hand. The warmth of the contact filled her. She felt stronger immediately. Diane sensed the same feeling of strength in her brother. She smiled.

Calder surged forward. He grasped both of them, his skeletal fingers wrapping themselves around their throats.

It was as if her neck were encased within a block of ice. The glacial numbness was so sudden and pronounced that she nearly lost all concentration. It spread its way into her shoulders and chest.

Diane tried to take a step back. Calder drew her closer until her eyes were inches from his empty sockets. *(David!)*

She felt her brother try to pull her away. His grip remained strong, as did hers, but they were unable to move.

"You are both hereby sentenced to death," Calder informed them. "Pronounced sentence to be carried out immediately."

Diane squashed down her surprise at the sudden attack. She reached down and found the warmth of her connection to her twin. She allowed it to fill her, felt it flow from that hidden well to all parts of her body. The sheer cold radiating from the judge retreated, replaced by that warmth.

Diane stared into the hollow eye sockets mere inches in front of her. (*Go to hell, Your Honor.*)

The heat flowed from her and from her twin. Calder tried to back up. He tried to pull his hands from their throats but couldn't. It tugged at their throats, although Diane felt no pain from its attempts. Her smile remained in place.

The judge's robes sloughed from his body and became part of the mist—streaks of black within the gray. They were quickly overwhelmed and absorbed by the fog. The skeleton remained but Diane could see flakes of bone shake loose and disappear in the fog.

(*I love you, Di,*) David told her.

Diane cast a sideways glance at her twin. (*I know you do. And I love you, too.*)

Most of the skeleton was gone, now, absorbed or scattered by the fog. The hands dropped first from David's neck and then from hers. The skull and part of the spine hung in the air before them and the jaw worked but nothing more than a gasp escaped from the thing's mouth. After another moment the spiritual remains of Judge Silas Calder were gone from their sight.

Diane looked about the fog. She half-expected the old spirit to reconstitute itself and attack again. *Not this time.* She reached out and no longer felt its presence. The fog swirled about them gently, slowly, as if it, too, rejoiced at the old monster's absence.

(*Is that it?*) David asked.

(*I think so,*) Diane answered. She sniffled. Had this place allowed tears they would have poured from her eyes.

David looked alarmed. (*What is it? What's wrong?*)

She turned to her brother. (*David, I remember everything. I saw it all play out through my own eyes. Everything he did. He murdered five people and I couldn't do a thing to stop him.*)

David pulled her close. The warmth radiated from him.

Diane took as much of it as her spirit would allow. *(That wasn't you, Di. You didn't kill anyone. It was all him. He's gone, now. He can't hurt you or anyone else ever again.)*

(I know.) She held him close for another few moments. *(But I couldn't stop him. I wasn't strong enough. Teddy, Joyce, all those innocent people. They paid for that.)*

(We'll deal with it, Di. We will. Are you ready?)

She pulled away and offered him a weak smile. *(Let's get out of here.)*

David came back from the fog. Diane was still in his arms. He looked immediately for LaMontagne. The cameraman sat against the wall, a rifle aimed at Brian Andrews. LaMontagne saw David and the rifle dropped a bit.

"David?"

David nodded. "It's okay, Jim. We're okay."

Diane stirred. She sat back, rubbed the side of her head.

LaMontagne's eyes asked the question.

David held up his hand. "She's okay. Calder's gone."

"I know," LaMontagne replied. He indicated the floor in front of the twins.

The bones of Silas Calder were mostly dust now. The skull remained but as David watched it started to collapse into itself. Before he could take another breath it, too, was gone. The dust formed a rough outline of a human body. Diane gasped when she saw it.

"Is that what killed my mom?" Brian Andrews asked. "I would never have believed it if I didn't see it myself."

Fresh tears welled up in Diane's eyes now that she was capable of crying. "I'm so sorry."

"Jim, put down the rifle," David instructed. "We've had enough fighting for today." He looked at Andrews. "Right?"

Andrews nodded wordlessly, his eyes were still glued to the gray dust that used to be Silas Calder.

David pushed himself up the wall until he got his feet under him. "Phone's in the kitchen?" When Andrews nodded David limped toward the hallway. "I'll get an ambulance. Everybody stay put."

"David, wait," LaMontagne called to him.

David paused in the doorway.

LaMontagne nodded in the direction of the foyer. "Joyce is alive. At least, I think she is. You have to check on her. Please."

David looked at his sister and saw the same faint hope reflected in her eyes. He limped into the foyer as quickly as his wounded leg would allow.

Diane beat him to it and placed her hand on Joyce's neck. "There's a pulse. You stay with her. I'll make the call."

Diane headed for the kitchen.

"Stay with us, Joyce," David whispered to her. "Help is on the way. We'll take care of you. Just hang on."

The next morning David lay in his bed in a private room in Robinwood Hospital. The nurse, an old crone whose nametag read IRENE, left after securing his new IV drip. They had given him the good stuff; he felt almost no pain at all. He craned his neck to examine the area for the fiftieth time since he awoke in the recovery room. There were four staples on his shin and eight more on his calf, all covered by a thick bandage. The doctor had already been in to advise him of the care he'd require once he was back in Los Angeles. David listened politely and nodded a lot. He barely heard a word the man said.

When Irene left, Detective Ahmad entered the room. His eyes were glued to his notebook. He dragged a chair across the tiled floor, oblivious to the obnoxious sound it produced, and placed it next to the bed. He sat, flipped the page, and took a pen from his shirt pocket.

"Like I said before we were interrupted, you and your friends have had one hell of a time since you got here."

David made no reply.

"But since no one wants to come clean about last night, and no one wants to press charges,"—he scowled at this last—"I have to take your bullshit statement and assume it's accurate."

David shrugged. "It's like we said, Detective."

"Uh huh." He flipped back to the previous page and reread his notes. "You had a pretty serious injury. So did your sister. And your agent is only just getting out of surgery now. That's a hell of a party."

David pushed himself up a bit more. "How is she?"

"Ms. Clark? From what I understand she'll be fine. Your other friend, too. And Mr. Andrews." He closed the notebook and leaned forward in the chair. "Are you absolutely positive you want to stick with this story? We both know you're full of shit."

David smiled as he did so often for the camera. The gesture was so second nature he almost didn't realize he was making it. "Did my story contradict any of the others, Detective?" David knew the answer already. That was one reason for the smile.

Ahmad almost managed to hide the frustration in his eyes. "No."

David shrugged again. "Then there you have it."

Ahmad stared him down for another moment before he slid the chair back and stood. The notebook and pen went into his pocket. He started for the door, but stopped and turned. "There's still the matter of the investigation into the murders of Theodore Jung, Scott Alexander, and Megan O'Leary. Don't make yourself too difficult to find."

David gave him a thumbs up.

Ahmad's scowl returned. He left the room without another word.

David sat back in the bed and released a long, steady breath. A few minutes after Ahmad vacated the room Di entered.

(It's okay?)

David nodded. *(He doesn't believe any of us. But he can't disprove our statements, so there's that.)*

Di indicated the hallway outside the room with a nod. *(Jim's okay. Got out of surgery an hour ago. He's asleep in the recovery room. And I heard Joyce will be okay, too.)*

(And you?)

Di shrugged. *(Hell of a headache, but they gave me some badass painkillers to deal with that. I'm okay, all things considered.)*

David nodded. "Good. I'm very happy to hear that." He licked his lips. "Di, I'm so sorry I wasn't there for you. What that bastard did … I don't know how you got through it."

She shook her head and smiled sadly. "Teddy. That poor man at the cemetery. The woman in the alley. He almost killed all of us. David, I'm so sorry." Tears filled her eyes suddenly.

David grasped her arms and pulled her close. When her tears came, his did, as well.

Four months after she watched Calder's earthly remains disintegrate, Diane sat in the front seat of Joyce's Lexus and held on for dear life. The stores along Franklin Avenue zipped by in a blur as Joyce tried to beat the traffic lights. Diane's stomach, in knots since her flight began its descent into LAX, threatened revolt. The three small drinks she'd consumed during the flight sat in her stomach like a lead weight. The air whipping into the car through her open window did little to help.

"Joyce, I swear to God, if you don't slow down, I'm gonna decorate the inside of your car with the contents of my stomach."

"Just let me get through this last intersection, dear," Joyce replied. "Then we'll be home free." As if to prove her point Joyce pointed out the windshield.

Diane could see North Beachwood coming up. The light turned yellow and Joyce stepped even harder on the gas pedal. Diane braced herself.

The Lexus's tires squealed as Joyce made the turn. North Beachwood Drive straitened ahead of them and Joyce, as promised, backed off the accelerator. Diane released a long, deep breath.

Joyce lit a cigarette. "Can you talk to him yet?"

Diane relaxed a bit in her seat now that the prospect of dying had diminished. The air stream coming through her window had diminished, as well; it felt cool on her arms and face. "I *can.* I haven't, yet."

"Why not? We're almost there. It's not like he doesn't know we're coming. It won't be a surprise."

"I know. I'll give it another minute or two."

"Suit yourself."

If Diane was being honest with herself, she was nervous about seeing her twin. David was only two weeks out of rehab. They'd spoken by phone and text at every opportunity during the two months he spent in Galveston getting sober.

"Fucking Texas," he told her before he hopped on the plane. "That's where my therapist is sending me. Isn't that where people go to *start* drinking?"

She had done the polite thing and laughed at the joke. The fact was, she was nervous for him. David had gone back to his old ways seemingly the minute he returned from Lansing. Not that Diane could blame him; after what occurred in Brian Andrews's home she'd gotten drunk a few times herself. David, however, had gotten so bad that he signed himself up for therapy. That led to rehab. Now, here he was. Seventy-four-days clean, or so he claimed. Diane hoped he wasn't trying to deceive her. If that was the case she'd know right away.

"Earth to Diane."

Diane turned to Joyce. "What?"

"Don't zone out on me, honey. Not now. We're almost there. I asked if you thought he was really clean."

Diane shrugged. "I think so. I hope so. I guess we'll know for sure when we get there."

Joyce nodded. "Want to hear something funny? I asked that same question about you when I went to see him about the Lansing job."

"Uh huh." *Really funny, Joyce.* But Diane had to admit, it was a legitimate question, both then and now. "I'm sure he's fine."

Out the window North Beachwood Drive was almost a perfect straightaway. Two or three more blocks and they would reach the turnoff for her brother's street. Her anxiety should have ratcheted up another few notches but Diane felt the opposite. The dread seemed to be transitioning to excitement with no conscious effort on her part. Maybe that was a good sign.

(Almost here? You feel pretty close.)

Diane started but only for a moment. The unexpected contact

was familiar and reassuring. The rest of her anxiety vanished. For the first time since she left her house for JFK Diane smiled.

(About ten minutes, maybe less if Joyce starts driving like Joyce again.)

She could sense her brother's laughter. It felt honest. Diane smiled again. Now she wished Joyce would hit the gas a little harder. *He's sober,* she thought. *Not just right now. He has been for some time.* Diane's fingers drummed an impatient beat on her armrest.

(See you in a few,) came David's excited reply.

Diane couldn't wait to get there.

THE AUTHOR WISHES TO THANK:

Miki MacKennedy, who should be a literary agent.

My go-to source for all things related to law-enforcement,
Detective Kevin Macharelli, Milford (CT) P.D.

Michele Cheney, for her eyes.

Karen Mueller, R.N., for answering absurd medical questions.

Mostly, the Author wishes to thank you for walking beside me
into the Fog. Hope you enjoyed the Game.

ABOUT THE AUTHOR

Joseph J. Christiano was born in the U.K. and raised in New England, where he resides today. His published works include:

The Last Battleship
Moon Dust
Dark Annie
Old Ghosts
The Shadow Man

The Raven Queen
(As J.C. Logan, Young Adult)

Curious about other Crossroad Press books?
Stop by our site:
http://store.crossroadpress.com
We offer quality writing
in digital, audio, and print formats.